Guardians Of The Round Table 5
Crystal Mine

Guardians Of The Round Table 5 Crystal Mine

Avril Sabine, Storm Petersen
and Rhys Petersen

Cracked Acorn Productions
Australia

Guardians Of The Round Table 5: Crystal Mine

Published by

 Cracked Acorn Productions

PO Box 1365

Gympie, Queensland 4570

Australia

978-1-925617-93-1 (Kindle)

978-1-925617-94-8 (EPUB)

978-1-925617-95-5 (Print)

Genre: Young Adult Fantasy LitRPG

*For all those who know and love the joy of
tabletop gaming.*

Mallory is beginning to wonder how far the dark forces have spread on Ruby Isle. It is beginning to seem like everywhere they turn, they face another challenge. But some things they can't turn their back on, no matter how great the danger. Even if it's something that might be beyond their abilities.

*

This story was written by Australian authors using Australian spelling.

Name Pronunciation

Like many names there is more than one way to pronounce the following ones. These are the pronunciations used in this story.

Characters

Barle (barl)

Danae (da-nay)

Deneg (den-eg)

Emica (em-e-cah)

Esben (es-ben)

Herena (her-en-ahh)

Hisoki (hiss-oh-key)

Jorgen (jaw-gen)

Kruth (kr-uth)

Melsed (mel-said)

Ninette (nin-et)

Pelga (pel-guh)

Rodina (row-dean-uh)

Sarisa (sa-risa)

Welby (well-bee)

Places

Buckneth (buck-neth)

Cachen (car-chen)

Delten (del-ten)

Eridell (air-a-dell)

Eswen (es-when)

Inadon (in-ah-don)

Maregan (mare-eh-gan)

Merrow (mare-row)

Shadhurst (shad-hurst)

Simria (sim-re-ah)

Velkden (velk-den)

Wrentville (rent-vil)

Foreword

Opening stats, Mallory's notebook entries recapping the previous adventures and other details can be found at:

www.avrilsabine.com/series/gotrt

The notebook entries will contain spoilers if you haven't read the book they refer to.

Chapter One

Mallory picked a cluster of herbs, straightening and putting them in the cloth sack Ryan held out. They weren't far from the road, the wagon several metres ahead of them, Ninette nearby keeping guard. The countryside around them was sparsely treed and the dirt track was rough, large ruts in some places.

Wiping her hands against her trousers, Mallory sighed. "I was so certain that would be enough." She brushed several strands of her brown hair back from her face. It had come loose from her plait, the natural copper highlights glinting in the late afternoon sunlight.

"One XP to go." Ryan gestured to some herbs further along the edge of the road, the faint glimmer to the plants that could be harvested, making it easier to spot them. "That should do it and then you'll have your ten CAS points to put in apothecary." He'd left his backpack in the wagon, but carried his bow on his back and his swords at his sides, along with his quiver. His black hair was tied at the nape of his neck and his dark eyes were filled with humour. "Brodie will be glad you can do average rapid mend." He paused a moment. "For all of two seconds."

Mallory laughed softly as she strode towards the herbs. "We'll be sick of hearing him tell us how unfair everything is by the time he catches up with my level." Her hand rested on the wand in the canvas hoop at her side. "I wonder if there's some sort of gag spell." Her hand lightly brushed the short sword that hung at her other side. Threatening him with it wouldn't work since he'd know she wouldn't use it on him.

Ninette, who continued to follow them, laughed. "Silent tongue. Ma used to threaten us with it." Her laughter faded. "Back when she was alive." Her hand rested on the hilt of her short sword and she regularly scanned the area.

Reaching the herbs, Mallory picked them, shoving them in the cloth sack. She was now one CAS point off character level five. "Finally." She glanced at the wagon that was leaving them behind, a canvas stretched over arched saplings so that it reminded her of an Old West wagon. "That was the worst plan ever. There has to be a better way to power level." Breathing out heavily, she trudged after the wagon wishing it were closer. She was exhausted after how many resources she'd gathered over the past three days. And in particular the resources everyone had helped her gather during the journey today. So much for being able to relax in the wagon after dealing with the crypt. Not much of that had happened. At least the clothes she'd washed hadn't taken too long to dry and she'd been able to change out of the dress and into the more practical shirt and trousers she preferred to wear. "What are we going to do with all the herbs if we can't sell them in Velkden?" The vegetables she'd gathered could be eaten, but there were too many herbs for them to use all of them. Although there were also probably too many vegetables to use before they started going bad.

Ryan shrugged. "Maybe Danni will have a suggestion."

Mallory smiled as they approached the wagon. Brodie and Kruth were still teaching each other insults that were common in each other's world. Most of the ones Brodie had tried to teach Kruth hadn't made sense to him.

Kruth shook his head, the canvas brushing against it. At six and a half feet tall and with a muscular build, the space in the back of the wagon was cramped for him. He grinned showing protruding lower canines. "I have a better one. As bright as a swamp rat." He had greenish grey skin and wore heavy cotton trousers, a hide vest, leather boots and had a wide copper bracelet on each wrist.

"What's a swamp rat?" Brodie was sprawled out next to Fang, absently patting the wolf's head. He had the same coloured green eyes as Mallory and his short brown hair was in need of a trim. Fang made a noise in her sleep and he smiled down at her before returning his attention to Kruth. The wolf cub was a mixture of colours. Her legs were mostly white while the rest of her was grey with some red amongst it along with a few white sections.

Kruth stared at Brodie. "You've never heard of a swamp rat? They're the dumbest creatures imaginable. Chew off their own leg if they were hungry enough and then wonder what happened to it."

Emica glanced at Kruth and Brodie. "I'll be glad when we reach the farmhouse out from Velkden." She sat on one end of the vampire Deneg's travel coffin, using the whetstone she'd borrowed from Ryan, on her two short swords. The twenty-year-old kitsune currently had only her ears shapeshifted into her fox form, wanting to hear anything well before it reached them. Her hair was the same russet colour as her fox pelt and her dark brown eyes continually scanned the area.

Callum chuckled, also glancing towards Kruth and Brodie. "I'm not surprised." He had the same dark coloured eyes and hair as his brother, but where Ryan's hair was long, his was kept short. He sat on one of the chests at the front of the wagon, Smudge curled up on his lap, the river otter chattering softly as if in agreement with him. Callum chuckled again, running his finger across Smudge's nose. There was a paler section of fur near the tip of his nose, the same pale colour as his under body, bright against the darker fur of his upper body. Behind them, the wagoner, Welby and Roast sat on the wagon seat, talking quietly amongst themselves.

Jorgen, who sat on the opposite end of Deneg's coffin to Emica, plaited his pale blond hair back from his face, including the eight thinner plaits with the glass beads scattered along them. "The greatest insult amongst my people is to tell someone they're clanless."

Brodie frowned. "That doesn't make sense."

"If you're clanless, it's because no clan has been

willing to accept you." Jorgen pulled his hair over his shoulder to continue plaiting it.

"Aren't you without a clan?" Brodie asked.

"Even if I find none of them have survived, there are other clans that would accept me." Jorgen's tone was cool and his blue eyes narrowed as he looked at Brodie.

Mallory tried not to wince as she thought of and discarded several comments and questions to change the subject. She felt like throwing something at her brother for his comment. "Why only eight plaits?" She gestured to his hair that he was tying off.

"They signify the eight main compass points," Jorgen said.

"Eight?" Brodie asked. "Aren't there only four? North, south, east and west."

"There are also the compass points between each of those," Jorgen said.

Danae, who sat on one of the chests at the front of the wagon next to Callum, said, "Most people only count the four as major compass points. Travellers are different. But then they spend a lot of time going from place to place when many people remain in the town or village they were born in." Her blond hair was drawn back into a plait to show her pointed ears and her pale green eyes were filled with excitement, her gaze continually scanning the area as she soaked in her surroundings. "You're so lucky you've seen so much of Eridell."

Jorgen nodded. "I went to Trinity Crossing once."

Mallory recognised the town name from having read 'Legend Of The Ancestral King'. It was on the border of where the three countries of Eridell, Maregan and Cachen met. It also reminded her of all that could go wrong if they didn't prevent Emica's father, Hisoki, from waking the ancestral king. Once again, she found herself looking for a way to change the topic. "Are any of you going to pick herbs and do some levelling up now I can level apothecary up to forty-five?" She supposed she should probably put her points in the crafting ability. Before she needed to mend Brodie's knee again at six o'clock.

The wagoner glanced over his shoulder. "We're nearly there. The river is ahead of us. From here you can see the demonic shrine that's along the banks of the river."

Brodie, who was sitting on the floor of the wagon, on the bedrolls that had been laid out, tried to sit up straighter so he could peer between the chests and the arch of the canvas. "I can't see anything from here." He glared at his knee. "I can't wait until my knee is fixed." He looked at his sister. "Have you put those points in apothecary yet?"

"I can't heal you until six. There's no rush." Mallory added the points in, barely managing not to smile at Brodie's muttered comments. She read over only the notifications that mentioned something new, glancing past the rest of them. *You have reached level thirty-seven apothecary. You now have the ability to treat rare diseases. You have reached level forty apothecary. You now have the ability to do average surgery. You have reached level forty-five apothecary. You now have the ability to use average rapid mend on broken bones.*

Ryan checked the pocket watch, returning it to his belt pouch. "It's only fifteen minutes till six. Those bandits we ran into earlier slowed us down."

Mallory's gaze was drawn to the chest Danae sat on. They'd put the bow they'd gained from the motley crew of bandits that had attacked them earlier, inside it. The five bandits hadn't lasted long. Nor had they gained many drops. The short bow, enough arrows to replace those they'd used and twelve copper pieces. Gaining XP from a fight rather than picking herbs had been a nice change.

Callum glanced over his shoulder. "I wouldn't mind stopping and having a closer look at the shrine."

"So would I." Mallory didn't bother trying to see

out the front of the wagon. She already knew she wouldn't be able to. At least not clearly with everyone sitting at the front. They'd passed a shrine earlier, on the banks of a lake, and she and Callum had been outvoted when they'd wanted to stop and look at it. Everyone had said they'd wanted to reach Velkden before dark. But she was sure it was more likely that most of them wanted to be closer to reaching Cutthroat Harbour and rescuing those held there.

Chapter Two

Mallory glanced around the wagon, already cramped. Eventually, the majority of them were going to have to walk. She doubted the ones they rescued would be capable of doing so and the wagon was already crowded. Although they'd be dropping Deneg, his travel coffin and chest off soon. Brodie had tried to lift the lid earlier and learned it had been locked from the inside. He and Callum had argued over Brodie risking Deneg's life. Brodie had protested that he hadn't planned to open it fully, just peek inside. He'd wanted to see how a vampire slept. She almost shook her head at the memory.

Brodie looked at Mallory. "About time you sorted out your apothecary."

Ignoring her brother, Mallory looked around the wagon at each of her companions. "Can we stop at the shrine?"

The wagoner glanced over his shoulder again. "The shrine isn't far from the farmhouse Deneg wishes to visit. You could ride back and have a look while we set up camp. We'll be struggling to get that done before dark as it is."

"We could all have a look once we set up camp," Ryan suggested.

"In the dark." Emica looked at each of them. "You do realise most people avoid wandering around in the dark for a reason."

"I can go with you," Ninette offered. "The more of us the less likely we are to be attacked." When no one immediately answered, she added, "Or I can stay with the wagon and help set up if you want to visit the shrine while the rest of us travel on to the farmhouse."

"Better make up your mind," the wagoner said. "I'm about to cross the bridge."

"You're not leaving me behind," Brodie said.

"We're doing this?" Mallory asked.

Ryan grinned. "Pull up and let us off." He glanced at Brodie. "Some of us aren't capable of jumping off a moving wagon these days."

"Like I asked to be shot in the knee," Brodie muttered.

"Did you want me to stay with the wagon or come with you?" Ninette asked.

Mallory hated to say no with the hopeful look in Ninette's eyes. "Someone needs to guard the wagon." She jumped off it, turning to Kruth. "Can you stay and help Ninette?"

Kruth nodded, his hand resting on the hilt of his longsword. "I'll protect the wagon with my life."

"Ah, thanks," Mallory said.

Callum put Smudge in the makeshift sling, chuckling. "We'd rather you didn't actually lose your life protecting the wagon."

"Do we have to stay with the wagon or can we come with you?" Emica looked at Mallory, glancing once at Jorgen as she spoke.

"You can come with us." Ryan helped Brodie onto Bug. The mixed draft horse stood patiently.

Emica and Jorgen jumped down off the wagon, walking alongside them. They left Augusta and Bobbi behind, after a brief discussion, deciding the rest of them would walk and Ryan would take his backpack in case they came across anything worth gathering.

Mallory waved to those left on the wagon as it crossed the bridge. "Not that we really need to collect anything else. I doubt we could fit anything more in the chests with everything I've gathered today."

Ryan shrugged. "You never know what we might find."

Mallory fell silent as they strode towards the shrine. It reminded her of a cross between a garden gazebo and a miniature temple. The octagonal structure was made from black rock, three stone steps leading into the open space, railings around all sides except one. She slowed as they entered the shrine. In the middle was a stone plinth, the imprint of a hand on it. Demonic runes were written above and below the handprint. "We should have brought the book with us." She checked the journal icon in the corner of her vision. It was fifteen experience points for a location.

Brodie entered the shrine. "Finally. I gained a CAS point." He paused. "So did Ryan and Danni."

Mallory tried not to smile at the disappointment she could hear in her brother's voice. It was impossible not to. She supposed she should be glad he hadn't yet complained again about how unfair it was that everyone was ahead of him in experience points.

Callum ran a finger over the runes. "We really need to learn them so we don't have to keep consulting the book."

"The word across the top is the name of the divine demon the shrine is dedicated to. Melsed. Beneath the hand is their offer. Ten mana in exchange for a plus two charisma buff for an hour," Jorgen said.

"How does that work?" Brodie remained on Bug.

"You place your hand on the imprint and say the demon's name." Emica stepped around Jorgen and placed her hand against the stone. "Melsed."

"Nothing happened," Brodie said.

Emica smiled, removing her hand. "Yes, it did."

"Let me try." Brodie looked to Ryan, who was closest to him. "Help me down?"

"Do you know who this demon is?" Jorgen gestured towards the plinth.

Emica shrugged. "It's not like I follow any particular divine demon like you do."

"What if they're evil?" Mallory asked.

Brodie hesitated, his hand above the plinth, Fang at his side. "Evil divine demons could have shrines on Ruby Isle?"

Emica shrugged again. "It's possible. Not likely, but possible. The Duke wouldn't tolerate it if he learned of one on his island. Soldiers would be sent to deal with it."

Brodie continued to hold his hand above the plinth. "So it's okay?"

Before anyone could answer, Emica shoved him out of the way, an arrow whistling through the air where he'd been. "Take cover." She slipped an arm around Brodie's waist, helping him towards a cluster of trees, one of his crutches left behind, Fang keeping pace with them.

Mallory followed, grabbing Bug's reins as she ran past her. Reaching the cover of the trees, she dropped the reins and turned to face the direction the arrow had come from, drawing her wand. "Where are they? And is it more than one?"

Ryan stopped beside her, hunting bow in hand. "The thicket of trees behind the shrine." He glanced at those with him. "Where's Callum, Danni and Jorgen?"

Emica pointed to berry bushes near the river. "Hiding over there."

"That's where we should have gone. Look at all the berries. I need a pie recipe. We have the blueberry pancake one, but pies would be good too," Brodie said.

Ryan grinned. "Of course they would."

Mallory remained close to a tree. "We can't stay here all day. Not that there's much left of the day." The shadows were lengthening and soon there'd be no light left.

"We've got to get that necklace off Smudge so you

can heal my knee," Brodie said. "I told you that you shouldn't have left it with Smudge."

Ryan checked the pocket watch. "Two minutes."

Emica pointed at the trees past the shrine. "Look. They're aiming at the berry bushes. And I can't use my lightning yet. Not after being near Jorgen for so long."

Chapter Three

Mallory caught sight of the archer at the same time as Emica, throwing a fireball at them. They stepped back out of view. "We need to draw them out."

"Or sneak up on them," Ryan said. "We could wait until dark and use the night vision potions. We still have three left."

"Mal should learn the vanish spell and turn us invisible," Brodie said.

Emica looked Brodie up and down. "They'd hear you coming. No point wasting mana on you."

Mallory took the spell out of her belt pouch, frowning as she tried to read the words in the fading light. The parchment vanished as she reached the last word. "I can use it on two people, but I won't have all my mana back again for just under five minutes. The spell only lasts for a minute."

"We've got invisibility potions," Brodie said. "Four of them."

"I want to keep them for Cutthroat Harbour," Mallory said. "Just in case we need them."

"We have to make a decision quickly." Ryan fired at the archer that came into view again. "Before it's too dark. We have a lantern in Bug's saddlebags, but that will only make it easier for the archers to target us."

"There's a second one." Emica pointed to another archer.

Mallory threw a fireball at them.

"Don't waste all your mana," Brodie muttered. "You won't be able to use vanish if you do."

"Fireball only takes three mana. I've still got enough to use vanish twice." Mallory kept watch on the trees across from them. Nothing moved. "What are we going to do?"

"I can become a fox and you can make me invisible," Emica suggested. "They won't know what hit them. I bet I can take out one, if not two of them, before the minute is up."

Ryan nodded. "Sounds good." He turned to Mallory. "I'll stay with Brodie. You make yourself invisible and go after Callum, Danni and Jorgen. Let them know what's going on."

"Bring the necklace back and heal my knee," Brodie said. "I'm sick of not being able to help."

"Don't risk it." Ryan fired at an archer.

Mallory saw an arrow come from where Callum, Danae and Jorgen hid. "Okay. Let's do this before someone gets hit by one of those arrows." She glanced at Brodie's knee. "We've already spent enough on boneset salve without needing to spend more." Not now that it was beginning to feel like they were starting to earn money again.

"I'm ready." Emica became a fox the moment she finished speaking, remaining in front of Mallory, looking up at her.

She cast the spell on the kitsune who vanished instantly, trying not to think about having used up nearly half her mana. Before she could cast the spell on herself, Ryan drew her to him, his arm around her waist.

"Don't risk returning here until we've taken out the ones attacking us." Ryan's lips met hers, his arm tightening around her. Letting her go, he stepped back.

Nodding, she used vanish I on herself before running towards the berry bushes. Before she could reach them, Jorgen, in crystalline wolf form, burst from them, racing towards the trees where enemies hid.

His snowy white coat, with its crystal blue tinge to it, stood out starkly against the falling darkness. She wanted to tell him to remain in cover, but they couldn't leave Emica to take on enemies on her own. Guilt struck her. Which was exactly what they'd done. Pushing herself to run faster, Mallory reached the cover of the berry bushes. "Callum."

"Where are you?" Callum put a hand out, trying to find her.

"Mallory? You used a potion?" Danae asked.

"Callum, I need the necklace."

Smudge slipped it over his head, making soft sounds as he held it out.

"Thank you." She took it from him, slipping it over her head as she started to turn away. "Ryan said to stay here." She didn't mention he'd also told her to remain there too. "I'm going to help Emica and Jorgen." She raced towards the trees, not waiting to find out what Callum and Danae had been about to say. She needed to get in cover before the spell wore off. Bringing up her journal, she checked her buffs. Along with the double healing, the necklace gave her was twelve seconds of invisibility. She eyed the distance between her and the trees. There was no way she'd make it before she was visible again. What she needed was a spell to make her run faster. If there even was such a thing. She checked her stamina. Luckily she'd had a short break while collecting the necklace or she'd be out of stamina. As it was, she'd be lucky if it lasted long enough to get her to cover. She really needed to get in the habit of taking stamina into account.

Her grip tightened on her wand as the last few seconds counted down, the trees were well out of reach. She had seventeen mana. Enough to cast five fireballs. Or two poison dart I. Not enough at all. She really needed to put more points in wisdom. Glancing around, she saw no enemies and no arrows coming towards her even though she was visible. Ahead, she heard the sounds of fighting. Behind came the sounds of running footsteps. Glancing over her shoulder, she saw Ryan, Callum and Danae running in her direction. She grinned at the look on Ryan's face. She was sure he'd have something to say later. Once they were safe.

Reaching the trees, she slowed her pace to a fast walk, not wanting her stamina to reach zero. She spotted four archers attacking Emica and Jorgen, both still in their animal forms. Two archers attacked from a distance while the other two fought the shapeshifters up close.

Mallory attacked the archers firing on the shapeshifters from a distance, using poison dart I on each of them. She might have been able to attack them more times with fireball, but with its damage over time and the fact the archers weren't wearing armour, she'd do anywhere between twenty-three to twenty-eight damage on each of them. Fireball would only give her eighteen at the most on one and twenty-seven on the other, with how many times she could cast it. That was if she managed to get a crit. Which wasn't a guarantee.

When the archers turned their attention to her, she ducked behind a tree, wishing it was twice the size when an arrow came close to hitting her. She wanted to check if the archers were coming after her, but didn't dare. What if that was what they were waiting for? She didn't know how much health they had. For all she knew, they could be dead. Checking her XP, she saw it was the same. About to close her journal, the XP changed. She'd helped kill one. Although, maybe not one of these ones. There were the two she'd attacked earlier.

She couldn't remain pressed against the tree all night. With how little light was left, everything was shadows and darkness. Which might work to her advantage if the archers weren't using night vision potions. She really needed a spell that created light. Breathing out heavily, she forced herself to move. There were so many things she needed. She peered around the edge of the tree.

A flash of light lit up the sky through the trees and thunder sounded overhead. The scene was momentarily highlighted, the two shapeshifters now joined by Ryan. An arrow came from a nearby tree, striking one of the archers. Mallory threw a fireball at one of the ones still attacking the shapeshifters. The lightning vanished, leaving her blinking as she tried to adjust to the darkness.

"Mal!"

She looked in the direction her brother's call came from. A light came towards them, two figures moving awkwardly towards the trees.

"You need to let her people go or she'll kill me, Mal."

She heard the fear in her brother's voice. He might have a revive left, but that didn't mean he wanted to lose it. A sound drew her attention and she started to reach for her sword.

"Don't attack me," Callum said.

She lowered her hand. "What do we do? Most of them are dead."

"All of them are dead," Callum said.

"Can you use your invisibility spell on me?" Jorgen asked. "I can activate stealth and she won't hear me coming."

"Callum, Danni and I can attack from the treeline." Ryan glanced upwards when lightning again lit the sky, thunder rumbling around them.

"Mal! You need to give an answer now," Brodie said.

Chapter Four

"Don't attack. We're coming out." Mallory cast the spell on Jorgen. "Hurry." She checked Brodie's stats, relieved his health was at twenty-seven. As it should be. Trying to be as quiet as possible, she hurried towards the lantern light, trying not to think about all the terrible jokes about going towards a light. They circled around in her mind anyway.

"Come on, Mal."

Mallory reached the edge of the treeline, peering past a tree at a woman with a knife at her brother's throat. She recognised her as the woman who'd been at the ruins with Rass. A glance around showed no others. "I'm coming out." She hoped Jorgen didn't take much longer. She only had the chance to take a single step before the woman was dragged away from Brodie. Three arrows impaled the woman. Before

Mallory had the chance to attack, the kitsune sped towards the woman, leaping at her.

Another arrow struck the woman and Emica landed on the ground. Emica became human, but still kept her fox ears, as the woman fell and Jorgen became visible, the woman vanishing before she hit the ground.

Emica glanced around the area. "It's clear. Or at least I can't hear anyone nearby."

Ryan stepped out of the treeline, staring at the spot where the woman had been. "She was with Rass."

Jorgen picked up the lantern the woman had dropped. "The hellion you've been hunting?" His words were punctuated by a flash of light and rumbling thunder.

Ryan half shrugged, half nodded. "Not deliberately."

Mallory wanted to point out that it didn't mean Rass wasn't in the area, but the words wouldn't form. What if he was. And what if he'd levelled up even further.

Callum followed Danae into the open. "I wonder if there's another encampment around here."

"We're not going after every encampment between here and Cutthroat Harbour," Emica stated. "We don't have time."

"You need to heal my knee," Brodie said. "I couldn't do anything when she grabbed me."

Mallory came out into the open, scanning the area, feeling like she had a target painted on her. Putting her wand away, she crouched in front of her brother. "We need to check bodies and get out of here. Who knows how many other bandits are in the area."

"One of them was a hellion," Emica said.

Mallory placed her hands on Brodie's knee and, once she saw she had enough mana, activated average rapid mend. "The break is seventy percent of the way through the healing process."

"Use the salve on it. See if that gets double healing too," Brodie urged. "If it does, my knee will be fixed tonight."

Mallory took out the boneset salve from her satchel while Ryan and Callum lowered Brodie to the ground. She glanced up as lightning streaked across the sky, followed by rumbling thunder. "I hope we reach the farmhouse before it rains."

"I'll collect Bug." Danae took a step towards where the horse had been left.

"That woman had a horse with her," Brodie said. "Left it with Bug."

"I'll go with you." Jorgen followed Danae.

"Wait up for Mal to finish and I can help," Brodie called out.

Danae kept walking. "We won't be long."

Mallory grinned when her brother kept looking in the direction Danae had taken. She lowered her voice. "If you don't speak up…" She let her words trail off, certain her brother didn't need her to fill in the blanks.

Brodie glared at her.

Callum chuckled, glancing over his shoulder. "I'll help them. Then we can use the lantern in Bug's saddlebags to check bodies."

Mallory applied the boneset salve to Brodie's knee, putting the salve away before she checked how her brother was going. She sighed. "It doesn't work with the salve. Only my ability."

"My knee will be fixed tomorrow morning though, won't it?" Brodie demanded.

Mallory re-splinted his knee. "Yeah. With the double healing, I'll be able to finish fixing your knee tomorrow morning." She turned to Ryan who'd remained with them, one sword drawn as he scanned the area. "What's the time?"

Ryan checked the pocket watch, tilting it towards the lantern on the ground next to Brodie. "As good as seven."

Mallory nodded, rising to her feet. "I'll finish fixing your knee at seven in the morning." She glanced at the rest of their companions who returned with Bug only to leave with the lantern, heading towards the trees where the archers had hidden. Lightning again filled the sky, thunder rumbling around them.

Danae remained behind. "The other horse was gone. It probably left when we killed its owner."

Ryan helped Brodie to his feet. "How would it know?"

"It might have been a companion." Danae picked up the crutch lying on the ground, handing it to Brodie. "I'll get the other one." She hurried towards the shrine.

"Wait up." Brodie awkwardly followed.

Ryan leaned his head close to Mallory. "Think he's finally going to ask her out on a date?"

Mallory laughed. "I doubt it."

Ryan slid his arms around her waist, tugging her close. "What were you thinking earlier? If you want to play tank, start putting more points in constitution to increase your health."

"I need to increase my mana. Spells cost too much." She slipped her arms around his neck, smiling up at him when lightning split the sky, making it easy to see his expression. Thunder followed close on its heels. She waited until the sound died away before she spoke. "You're not a tank either. So why did you follow?"

Ryan grinned. "Did you really think I'd let you run into danger without me?" His lips met hers before she could answer.

By the time their kiss ended, she was distracted by their returning companions and her answer was forgotten. She half turned in Ryan's arms. "How many hellions?"

"Two." Callum set the lantern down beside the other one, holding out some coins. "They didn't have much on them."

Mallory took the coins, counting them before adding them to her belt pouch. Three silver and fourteen copper pieces. It was going to take them ages to earn the money they'd spent in Wayholt.

"We got leather boots, a black shirt, a leather belt and a small meat pie wrapped in calico."

Brodie joined them in time to hear Emica's words, Danae and Fang with him. "Pie? Who gets the pie?"

"Ninette and Kruth," Ryan said. "They stayed behind so we could check out the shrine."

"Oh." Brodie's gaze followed the pie as Emica put it in Bug's saddlebags, lightning streaking through the darkness of the sky, followed by the sound of thunder.

"We better get back and check on them. Who knows what else is in the area." Mallory took Brodie's crutches when Callum helped him onto Bug.

Callum gathered Bug's reins. "Did the necklace work on the salve?" He nodded towards the pearl necklace that was lying against Mallory's shirt.

"No. Only for my ability." Mallory picked up one of the lanterns. "But his knee will be mended at seven tomorrow morning."

"That's not bad. Three days to heal shattered bones." Callum smiled down at Smudge who poked his head out of the sling to chatter softly.

Mallory nodded. "It'll only be two and a half days now my apothecary is so high and I have the bonus from the necklace." She walked beside Ryan, the lantern in one hand, her wand in the other. "It's hard to believe. It would have taken ages back home." She worked on healing Danae, Callum and Ryan, all who'd lost some health.

Brodie groaned. "I don't even want to think about it. If I ever break anything while we're at home, we're coming back here for you to fix it before Mum finds out I've broken it. Before anyone finds out."

Mallory laughed, her companions echoing her as

they crossed the bridge where the wagon had dropped them earlier. "If it's possible."

Chapter Five

They fell silent as they continued along the road, taking a narrower one that led along the river. Lightning regularly lit the sky, the sound of thunder coming ever closer. They picked up their pace, all of them glancing skywards each time the thunder sounded.

Ahead of them, Mallory saw lights and campfires, not sure if she should slow her pace. "Aren't we meant to be going to a farmhouse? Is it normal to have so many campfires?"

Emica drew her sword. "No. There are too many people there."

"What if it's a party?" Brodie asked.

Emica sent him a look that clearly told everyone how ridiculous she found that comment, lightning making it easy for them to see it. She waited until the rumble of thunder faded away. "Do you want me to go ahead and see what's happening?"

Kruth stepped out from behind two trees growing close together. "Velkden was attacked yesterday. Not everyone in the village survived." He gestured to the farm behind him. "They headed here. Some have already left for other places. Most of these ones plan to stay. They sent a message to the Duke to let him know what happened. They're hoping soldiers will eventually be sent."

"What are the chances of that?" Ryan asked.

Kruth shrugged.

"They'll be sent," Emica said. "Doesn't mean anyone will be alive by the time they arrive."

"With how bad some of them are injured, there's a lot that won't make it through the night," Kruth said. "They've got no healer and no apothecary."

"We could make a fortune healing them," Brodie said.

"Some of them only have the clothes they're wearing," Kruth said.

"I can make healing tea for them," Danae suggested. "But it won't help much." She glanced past Kruth. "Where's the wagon? I can put together more batches of healing tea from the herbs Mallory gathered today."

Kruth gestured towards the farmhouse. "We've set up past the farmhouse, close to the river. It's less crowded over that way." He glanced up when lightning lit the sky, closely followed by the rumble of thunder. "Reckon it's going to rain soon. It's been getting closer and closer." He turned to stare at the closest campfire. "Most of them have no shelter or protection from the night other than what they can get from huddling by a fire."

Mallory's heart sank. They needed to travel to Cutthroat Harbour, but there was no way they could leave so many injured and dying people behind. "Who do we need to talk to about helping?"

"The elder. She's staying in the farmhouse. I'll take you to her." Kruth took a step towards the farmhouse before turning and taking coins out of his belt pouch. "Deneg left about twenty minutes ago. He got a lift on a wagon with a family headed towards Delten. A couple of other families went with them."

Mallory handed the lantern to Ryan before she took the five gold pieces, dropping them into her belt pouch. "Thanks." The journal icon appeared in the corner of her vision and she opened it, finding it was the completion of the quest like she'd assumed. *You escorted Deneg safely to his destination. You were rewarded with five gold pieces for your party. You also earned twenty experience points each.* She'd barely finished reading over the quest details, following Kruth towards the farmhouse, when a location notification arrived.

"We earned fifteen XP for finding a farm," Brodie said. "Why haven't we earned XP for farms before?"

"It isn't for finding a farm," Danae said. "It's for finding a refugee camp. You'll only earn XP for farms that are in the middle of nowhere with no towns or villages nearby."

"And what about earning XP for the quest? We weren't even here when Deneg left," Brodie said.

"He didn't finalise the quest with me," Kruth said. "He asked me to give the gold to Mallory to finalise his obligations for the escort."

Mallory half listened to the discussion as she walked through the refugee camp, smiling at Ryan when he handed the meat pie to Kruth and told him it was for him to share with Ninette. Her smile faded when Callum asked if Deneg had left any messages for him. She scanned the area, her gaze drawn to the nearby villagers. Very few walked around. Most of them lay by campfires, many appearing half dead with their many wounds. A few had scraps of canvas or blankets rigged up over them for shelter, but it wouldn't be enough when the rain broke. Her steps slowed when she saw a campfire with only children around it, two of them hobbling around and attending three lying by the dying campfire.

Danae rested a hand on Mallory's arm. "You talk to the elder. I'll find the wagon and start making health tea."

Mallory nodded, unable to speak. The children had to be easily half her age. "Who attacked?"

"Hellions," Kruth said.

"How many?" Her hand tightened on the wand she continued to hold.

Kruth shrugged. "No one said. But there was once over a hundred people in Velkden. Not even half of them escaped."

"They killed children." Mallory couldn't stop looking at the children by the campfire.

"They tried to kill every single resident."

At the sound of the unfamiliar voice, Mallory turned to face the woman. She was bruised and bandaged, a sheathed sword at her side, mismatched pieces of chain armour over her torn and bloody clothes. Her black hair was close cropped and she looked as if she was barely twenty-years-old.

"I was bringing them to see you," Kruth said.

"You're the elder?" Brodie blurted out.

Ryan clapped his hand on Brodie's shoulder.

"Maybe you should go help Danni sort herbs rather than stay here and risk insulting someone."

The elder smiled briefly, holding her hand out to Mallory. "Call me Rodina. You can't exactly call me elder when I have no village to be elder to."

Mallory returned her wand to the loop of canvas and shook the woman's hand, introducing each of them.

Rodina shook everyone's hand before half turning away and gesturing towards the children. "We've used up all the healing potions we had with us. None of us have any healing skills or abilities. I should have been a mage instead of a warrior. At least then I might have had a healing spell."

"I have one. It only heals two health at a time. Barely useful." Mallory flinched when the sky was lit up, thunder rolling around them. She glanced upwards. "What will they do when it rains?"

"We don't have enough able bodies to organise anything. Two men and three women along with the farmer, his wife and young son. Their two workers were in the village when we were attacked. Most of them are on patrol, keeping a watch for any hellions," Rodina said.

"How can we help?" Ryan asked.

"We can't pay you." Rodina met his gaze. "We managed to take very little with us."

"We didn't ask for payment," Callum said.

Danae took a step away from Mallory. "I'll start the tea." She turned to Brodie. "Did you want to help me?"

Nodding, Brodie followed, Fang at his heel.

Rodina stared at Ryan a moment longer. "The farmer has several large pieces of canvas that we can rig as tents. It won't be enough to get everyone under shelter, but it'll come close." She beckoned an old man over who used a roughly chopped stick as a walking cane. "Show them where to set up the canvas."

When the man started to move away, Mallory stepped forward. "What happened to your leg?"

"Hit by the back of an axe." The man shrugged. "It could be worse. Could have been the sharp end."

Chapter Six

Mallory rested her hands on the man's arm, gaining a sense of his injuries. "I can set the bone and begin the healing process." Sensing his health was low, she healed him for two health points.

"I can't pay you," the man said.

She met his gaze, seeing the pain in his blue eyes. "I know."

"We have to get the canvas set up." The man nodded towards the children by the campfire. "One of them is my granddaughter."

"It won't take long. I need you to sit down," Mallory said.

He shook his head. "You want to heal someone? You heal my granddaughter and the other kids."

"I will. Once I've helped you. They won't be able to help around here. You can." Mallory kept her hands on his arm.

Rodina draped an arm around the man's shoulders. "Come on. Surely you're not scared of an apothecary. Not after all you've faced."

"Last one I went to made me drink a horrid concoction every day for a week," the man grumbled as he let Rodina lead him to a stump.

Mallory followed, setting the bone once he was seated and doing average rapid mend on it. "If you come see me tomorrow morning at this time, I'll do another rapid mend on the bone." She rose to her feet. Why hadn't she kept levelling up? Why had she stopped so often and complained about how much effort it was to gather resources? If she'd only gained another ten CAS points she would have been able to unlock strong rapid mend and have been able to reduce the healing time even further. "I'm sorry I can't do more."

He gripped her shoulder. "You've done more than enough for me. You heal my granddaughter and I'll owe you for life."

She shook her head. "No, you won't." She glanced at his leg, feeling uncomfortable with how intense his gaze was. "Just don't wreck the mending I've done and set your progress back."

With a single nod, he hobbled away with the help

of his makeshift walking cane, beckoning to the rest of Mallory's companions.

She faced the campfire with the children, drawing in a deep breath before she strode towards them, crouching by each one and sensing what was wrong with them. She left the granddaughter until last. Drawing in a sharp breath, she sat back, staring down at the child who looked to be around ten-years-old.

"What's wrong with her?" Rodina asked.

Mallory was relieved to see Danae stride towards her, a waterskin in her hands. She rose to her feet. "It looks like Danni is bringing me health tea." She hurried towards the half-elf, taking the waterskin from her.

"I left Brodie sorting herbs and I've put several batches of tea on. I don't have enough pots though." Danae glanced at the waterskin Mallory now held. "There are only seven doses, but it should get you started while we wait for the next lot to be ready."

Rodina joined them, grabbing Mallory's arm and turning her to face her. "What is wrong with Herena?"

Mallory placed her hand over Rodina's, gaining a sense of the woman's injuries. She drew back, gasping, looking from the child to the elder.

"She has corpse rot too," Rodina stated.

Mallory nodded.

"Too?" Danae asked.

Mallory again nodded, her gaze drawn to Rodina. "Yes. Rodina has a wound that has been left unhealed. A fatal wound."

"We ran out of health potions pretty quickly." Rodina shrugged. "I've lived more than a hundred years. It didn't seem right to have one of the potions when it wouldn't be enough to heal me. I gave it to someone who had a chance."

Mallory kept her hand on Rodina's. "I don't know how to make the poultice. I know the herbs, but have no idea what they look like or how to blend them. I also have no surgical instruments to help those whose wounds are beyond the ability of being healed by potions and teas." She closed her eyes, the many abilities she wasn't a high enough level to do filling her mind. Increased healing. Rapid healing. Healing hands. Improving potions, salves and ointments. She felt powerless. "I'm sorry." Opening her eyes, she met Rodina's gaze. "I don't have the abilities to save everyone. I don't even have the mana to help much."

"I'll gather all the mana potions, mana boosting jewellery and essence crystals. You do what you can." Rodina stepped back from Mallory. "Heal whoever you think will survive first. If you have enough mana left, then heal the rest."

Before Mallory could argue, Rodina strode away. "I can't do that."

Danae glanced in the direction Rodina had taken. "Then don't. We try and save them all. I didn't decide to learn alchemy to stand by and watch people die."

"How? You're not a high enough level to make salves or ointments and I don't know enough about herbs to tell which ones I need to use in a poultice. Not that they're guaranteed to work since they're the most basic form of healing. But that's all I have available to me when it comes to treating illnesses, diseases and wounds."

"I know a lot of different herbs. There might be other people around here who know more than me. Tell me the ingredients and I'll find them for you," Danae said.

"We can do that? I don't have to know the herb to use it?" Mallory asked.

Danae smiled. "You will know the herb once I tell you what it is."

The feeling that had been weighing Mallory down, making her feel powerless and more than a little ill, began to lift. "Okay. Let's give it a go." Anything had to be better than doing nothing.

Danae's smile remained in place. "As Ryan likes to say, we've got this. Now, what are the ingredients?"

"It's weird. I only need three ingredients, but each time I try and figure out which herb I need for each ingredient, I think of several."

Danae laughed softly. "That's exactly how it is. You have options for each ingredient. What are the choices for the first one?" She spoke again almost immediately. "I should be writing them down. Recipes are hard to come by and you will only be able to recite them when you need them if they're not written down."

Mallory took the letter from Deneg out of her belt pouch. "You can write on the back of this." She rummaged in her satchel for the nib pen and ink. "I want to make up batches of herbs for healing different things. I don't want to be unprepared again." She held the ink and handed over the pen.

Danae dipped the pen into the bottle of ink Mallory opened. "What are our options for the first ingredient?"

"Echinacea, comfrey, arnica, goldenrod or nettles." Mallory couldn't help wondering if they were the same plants as what could be found back home. Before she could comment on it, Danae spoke again.

"The second ingredients?"

"Grave weed, ekra, corpsebane, smoke berries or widow's tears." She watched Danae write the words on the back of the letter. "How hard are these to find?"

Danae looked up from the paper with a smile. "We have widow's tears. They're those stems with the cascade of pretty white petals along them."

"And the first ingredients?"

"Nettles. We have plenty of them." Danae dipped the pen in the ink. "What are the last lot of ingredients?"

"Shulken, river moss, night bloom, coral puffball, crimson shelf fungi, vilen root, death tulips." She held her breath as she tried to make herself ask the next logical question. She couldn't bring herself to voice it and let her breath out in a soft sigh.

Danae handed the pen back. "I'll fetch the ingredients."

Chapter Seven

"We have them?" Mallory continued to hold the pen and ink, staring at Danae.

"Yes. Death tulips. Those fragile looking black flowers you picked by the lake."

Mallory's legs nearly gave way at the rush of relief that washed over her. "We can help them?"

Danae smiled. "We're certainly going to try."

Mallory put the lid on the ink and cleaned the nib pen before she put them away. Danae's words echoed over in her mind as her lips curved into a smile. They were going to try and save all of them. She returned to the children, healing each for two health, setting bones for those that had broken ones. She ran out of mana before she finished, sitting on the ground next to one of the children while she waited for enough mana to return to use rapid mend.

Rodina arrived as Mallory's mana returned, placing

a calico bag beside Mallory as she healed the child. She nodded towards the bag. "To help."

Finished healing the child, Mallory looked inside the bag. There were three rings, a bracelet, a dozen potions and a large, sky blue, see-through crystal. It didn't seem like a lot. "What does the crystal do?"

"You've never seen an essence crystal before?"

Mallory shook her head, taking out the jewellery and putting it on. Between all of them, she was regaining a mana every second. She needed to get some of her own jewellery to increase the rate at which her mana regened. She took the crystal out of the bag. It was about the length of her hand.

"A crystal that size contains two hundred and seventy mana that you can draw on as you need it."

Mallory stared up at Rodina. "Are you serious?"

Rodina chuckled, a deep sound that seemed surprised from her. "Yes, so use up the potions first and keep that for when there are no other options."

Mallory returned it to the bag. "Okay." Before she could rise to her feet and find her next patient, Danae ran towards her, carrying a wooden bowl and a waterskin.

Danae held out the bowl as soon as she reached Mallory. "I left Brodie chopping up more of these herbs so we can create poultices if we need to."

"I need bandages." Mallory set the bowl beside her. It contained a mess of finely chopped herbs that had been dampened enough to make them clump together.

"I'll bring you some." Rodina hurried away.

Danae held up the waterskin. "I'll give everyone a drink. Or at least everyone that's conscious." She took the second waterskin she'd left with Mallory. "I'll probably need this one too."

Mallory nodded, too busy drawing up the leg of Herena's trousers. The girl stirred and she paused, watching her face. When her eyes remained closed, she continued to draw the trouser leg up until she could see all of the bandaged area. It went from ankle to knee. Letting out a slow breath, she began to unwrap the wound, hoping it didn't cover all the leg. There weren't enough herbs in the bowl for a wound that large.

Finished unwrapping the wound, Mallory discovered it wasn't as large as she feared. But it wasn't small either. She needed to use half the poultice. When Rodina returned, she took a bandage from the elder and wrapped it around the wound. She rose to her feet, taking the bowl and calico bag that Rodina had put the rest of the bandages in.

Rodina nodded towards Herena. "Will that cure her?"

Mallory shrugged. "I don't know. I haven't been an apothecary for long. But everything tells me that's the correct treatment." Lightning forked across the sky, highlighting Rodina's expression. She was half tempted to ask the woman what she was thinking. The crack of thunder was so close it made her flinch. She'd been so focused on healing she'd barely noticed the regular flashes of light and crack of thunder.

Rodina inclined her head. "I'll go help set up the shelter. I'd like to get everyone moved before the rain begins."

"Not so fast." Mallory took a step towards Rodina. "It's your turn."

Rodina shook her head. "There are others who need to be attended to before me."

"No. You're next. What are you afraid of?"

She stepped close to Mallory, lowering her voice. "Not out here where anyone can see." She glanced around. "I don't want them to worry more than they already do. People need a strong leader."

"Then why didn't you heal yourself first?" Mallory asked.

Rodina's lips twisted into a wry smile. "A leader needs people to lead."

"The farmhouse then?"

Rodina nodded, leading the way.

Mallory stepped inside the farmhouse. The room was warm, a fire beneath a pot on a tripod in the middle of the room, the floor uneven stone pavers. At one end of the room was a closed door. She followed Rodina into what was a bedroom. A timber bed took up most of the space in the room and a mattress was set on the floor along the far wall.

Rodina faced Mallory, removing her armour. "You're probably wasting your time." She turned around, raising the back of her tunic.

Mallory managed to contain her exclamation that nearly escaped at the sight of the wound. "What happened?"

"I was protecting one of my people from a hellion."

"I need to clean this up before I can put a poultice on it."

"Do what you have to." Rodina remained where she was, the back of her tunic still drawn up.

"Okay. I won't be long." Mallory returned to the other room, looking for a bucket. She found one by the fire, water in it. Checking, she discovered it was clean water. Returning to the bedroom, she set the bucket beside Rodina. "Do you know what the bucket of water beside the fire is for?"

"Putting out any sparks that might escape." Rodina, who'd lowered her tunic, raised the back of it again, hissing when Mallory began to clean the wound.

"Sorry." She used one of the smaller bandages she'd taken from the bag. "It needs to be cleaned."

"I know." Rodina drew her breath in sharply. "You'd think I'd be used to this by now."

"Why?"

"I've spent a lot of years wandering the world looking for the next challenge."

"How did you end up here?"

Rodina chuckled, the sound broken off. "What greater challenge is there than living near an essence crystal mine when the dark forces are almost on your doorstep?"

"Why is that a challenge?" Finished cleaning the wound, Mallory dropped the wet bandage in the bucket and picked up the bowl.

"Every mage wants the crystals. Even those of the dark forces. Especially those of the dark forces. They are also used for travelling long distances through demonic portal gateways. A good way to shift armies quickly."

Mallory used up the last of the poultice on Rodina's back, setting the bowl on the floor and taking a bandage out of the bag. "They're moving an army?"

"I don't know. But it makes sense. Why else would they target a mine other than for portals?"

Mallory dreaded to think of what the dark forces might be planning. She doubted it'd be good. Taking a step back from Rodina she surveyed her work. "I'm done."

Rodina lowered her tunic before facing Mallory. "Thanks. It feels a lot better."

Mallory nodded, healing Rodina a few times to help.

Rodina chuckled. "My health is high enough it'd take you a while to get it to full at that small an amount. It also means it'll take a while for me to die of a wound like this."

She met the elder's gaze. "I'd rather you didn't die. I've got a feeling your people are going to need you."

Rodina inclined her head before picking up the bucket. "I'll get rid of this and refill it."

Before either of them could move, a scream rang out in the next room. Both broke into a run, Rodina leaving the bucket behind, coming to a stop to stare at a woman standing by a set of shelves at the far end of the room. Her hands were clasped tightly together and she slowly shook her head.

"What happened, Kyla?" Rodina demanded.

Kyla faced them. "Someone kidnapped my great-grandmother. I left her right here." She gestured towards the shelf she stood near.

"Why would anyone kidnap an old woman?"

Mallory turned to find her brother in the doorway, Fang and Danae behind him. She gave him a look to tell him to be quiet, that he wasn't helping.

Kyla gestured towards the shelf again. "She was right there. In her travelling case."

Chapter Eight

Mallory stared at the woman for a moment. "In her travelling case. Your great-grandmother." The words made no sense.

Rodina chuckled. "She was cursed by a demon and turned into a harp. Kyla wouldn't stuff a relative into a travelling case if they were in human form."

"Oh." Mallory slowly shook her head. It made a little more sense, but not much. "How does that work? Is she still alive?"

"She'll live forever. Unless damaged beyond repair," Rodina said.

"I ask every traveller if they'll take her to have the curse removed, but none are willing to risk the dangers. I have money to pay them, but still, no one is willing to accept."

"You have got to be kidding," Brodie exclaimed.

"We no sooner get rid of one quest than we have another."

Grinning, Mallory checked the quest. Her grin faded. *Break The Curse: Kyla of Velkden needs the curse broken that keeps her great-grandmother in the form of a harp.* How were they meant to break a curse? Not that it mattered since the harp was currently missing.

"I need her found first. I'd be willing to pay for her safe return too," Kyla said.

Brodie groaned. "Another one?"

Mallory checked her journal, the icon once again in the corner of her vision. Brodie had been right. It was another quest. *Missing Relative: Kyla of Velkden needs someone to track down her great-grandmother and bring her home. She is offering a reward for the safe return of her relative.* Yet another quest she had no idea how to complete. "Why would anyone steal, I mean, kidnap her?"

The old man Mallory had healed earlier, pushed past Brodie. "I heard that vampire asking about her. Wanted to know the story about the demon who cursed her and if you ever played her."

"I've had no training," Kyla said.

"You know that makes no difference," the old man said. "She's been cursed to play to her ability, not the ability of the one who plays her."

Mallory had a sinking feeling. "Did you show him the harp?"

The old man shook his head. "Not my place. Told him that. Told him he'd have to ask when everyone wasn't so busy."

"He knew no one was in the farmhouse?" Rodina asked.

The old man shrugged. "Possibly. I never straight out told him that."

"Surely Deneg wouldn't have stolen the harp," Danae said.

"Why not?" Brodie asked. "Because he's played for the Duke?"

Rodina strode towards the door. "We don't have time for this right now. If a musician has her, she's safe. We have others who aren't. We need to get shelter sorted and everyone in out of the weather."

"It's done. They're moving everyone," the old man said.

"Then I'd best help them." Rodina collected the bucket then strode outside.

Mallory stared after her, wishing she could believe Danae's words. She turned to Kyla. "Are there any musicians living here?"

Kyla shook her head. "None of us followed in her footsteps. Not even my son is interested in learning."

"So there's no travelling bard who lives here?" Mallory persisted.

"That was my great-grandmother. Pelga. Her music was amazing. A pity she told the demon who demanded she play for him that he could wait until she'd finished her meal."

"He cursed her because she wouldn't play for him straight away?" Brodie asked.

"Yes." Kyla nodded. "My father was travelling with her, back when he wanted to see the world and become a warrior. That ruined his taste for adventuring and he returned to Velkden and bought this farm."

As much as Mallory wanted to learn more, she had people she needed to heal. "I'm sorry about your great-grandmother." She took a step towards the door.

"I am willing to pay," Kyla said. "I don't have a fortune, but there's some money left from when Pelga played her music for nobles."

"How much money?" Brodie asked.

Mallory hurried towards her brother, speaking before Kyla could. "We need to rescue people from Cutthroat Harbour."

"Are you crazy?" the old man demanded.

Mallory grinned. "I'm beginning to think we are."

She stepped outside, glancing at her brother to let him know to follow. She waited until they were out of hearing before she spoke, Brodie on one side of her and Danae on the other, Fang checking out the area as she ran from one smell to the next. "We can't get distracted. We have to go to Cutthroat Harbour soon."

"Then why are we here healing everyone?" Brodie asked.

"Because it's the right thing to do." Mallory looked up as a raindrop fell on her. "We need to help get everyone in out of the rain." She turned to Brodie. "Not you. Go back to camp."

"I made dinner. I only came to let you know it's ready." Brodie took the empty bowl from Mallory and called Fang, heading towards the wagon that was visible from out the front of the farmhouse. His movements were awkward as he struggled to carry the bowl and use his crutches.

"Are we having dinner now or later?" Danae asked.

"Later. We need to get everyone out of the rain." Mallory headed for the nearest person reclining by a campfire, helping them to their feet and supporting them to the shelter rigged up behind the farmhouse.

It took a couple of hours to get everyone settled and a few more hours of healing before Mallory ran out of mana potions and Brodie found her, handing her a plate of venison and vegetables, currently only using one of his crutches. She ate it as she walked towards her next patient, her steps slow.

"It's midnight." Brodie stayed beside her.

She handed the plate back to Brodie, only half the food eaten.

"Are you planning to sleep?"

"How can I?" She surveyed the makeshift shelter. They'd had to place everyone close together so they could fit them in. The same in the shelter next to this one. Reaching her next patient, she crouched beside the child, placing her hands on her arm. "I need more of the poultice." She healed the child twice. It didn't help. The health dropped again. She sensed it, her hands remaining on the child's arm. "Hurry."

"Mal-"

"Hurry." She looked up at Brodie. "The kid is slipping away." She healed the child again.

She was still trying to keep the child's health up when Brodie returned with the poultice. Even applying it to the wound on the child's side didn't help. The health kept dropping and the mana she drew from the essence crystal wasn't enough. She couldn't heal quickly enough or for enough health at a time. She felt the child die beneath her hands. "No."

She tried to heal the lifeless body. Nothing happened. She stared at the child, her hands remaining on the arm. She should have tried harder. Exhaustion washed over her. No, she'd done everything she could. It was her skills that had let her down.

"Mallory." Ryan crouched beside her. "Brodie's worried about you." He looked her over. "I'm worried about you too. Have you had a rest? Or have you been healing people the entire time we've been here?"

Mallory leaned against Ryan. "The kid didn't have a revive."

Ryan wrapped his arms around her. "I'm sorry."

"This one isn't the first I've lost tonight." Yet it seemed worse. The other one had been an older man. "This one wasn't old enough to have a journal." She drew back enough to meet Ryan's gaze. "The kid was too young to die."

"You should know that doesn't make a difference. Not even in our world."

"I know. But you know what the worst part is?" She didn't wait for him to answer. "There's no one to tell about the death. The parents were killed before they could escape Velkden."

Danae joined them, Rodina with her. "Are you all right?"

Mallory shook her head, drawing away from Ryan. "I couldn't save-" Stumbling to her feet, she broke off as her throat tightened. She was grateful when Ryan rose and steadied her. She was exhausted, but she couldn't stop yet. There were more she could save.

"You've done enough. More than we expected," Rodina said. "Have a rest before we're looking for a place in here for you."

Chapter Nine

Mallory again shook her head. "Just a couple more. I need to check on a few of them to see if they're still losing health or if I've managed to stop the loss of health." Her gaze was drawn back to the child. "I was so sure I could keep the kid alive."

Ryan slipped an arm around her waist, drawing her close.

"We need a revive potion. We have two days to get one before it's too late and all that can be done is bury the child," Danae said.

"We have fourteen in need of revive potions," Rodina said. "It would be impossible to find that many in so little time."

One of the women lying on a blanket nearby struggled to sit up. "The hellions had them. They were using them on their fallen companions that had no revives."

Mallory stared at the woman, the words taking a moment to sink in. "Would they have any left?"

"I don't know." The woman gave up trying to sit up, sinking back onto the blanket. "I didn't stay to find out. They weren't raising any of our people. Only their own."

"What did they look like?" Ryan asked. "The one using the revive potions. Was there anything about them that stood out from the rest?"

"He was an orc."

"Orcs aren't that uncommon," Rodina said.

"This one was wearing a mage robe," the woman said.

"Now that is uncommon." Danae turned to Ryan. "Orcs are usually warriors."

"We're going after the potions?" Mallory asked.

Ryan grinned. "What do you think?"

She threw her arms around him. "Yes."

He held her close. "Not everyone might want to join us."

"You're going into Velkden," Rodina stated.

Mallory drew away from Ryan, keeping one arm around him. "We're thinking of it."

"We were attacked by a hundred of them. I sent someone to scout the village and they said there are at least thirty of them left behind." Rodina looked at each of them. "You don't look like you can take on that many and survive."

"We've survived terrible odds before," Ryan said.

Rodina didn't speak straight away. "If you take back our village for us, we can pay you in essence crystals."

Mallory checked her journal when the icon appeared in the corner of her vision. It was a quest.

Free Velkden: Rid the village of those who have invaded and the elder will reward you with essence crystals from the local mine.

Brodie came towards them, Fang at his heel. "What are you doing? Stop talking to people. Go to sleep or something."

"Essence crystals are really expensive," Danae said. "They're something we wouldn't normally be able to afford at this stage and they would give Mallory a lot of mana she can use."

"Expensive?" Brodie turned to Rodina. "How expensive and how many would you give us?"

Rodina glanced at Mallory. "He's rather mercenary." She looked Brodie up and down. "Do you speak for all of them?"

Mallory spoke before her brother could. "No." Half the time she didn't agree with him so she wasn't about to let him speak for her. "We decide things as a group.

We vote on it." Yawning, she covered her mouth. "I need to finish up here." There were a couple more people she needed to heal before she had a sleep.

"What about bed?" Ryan asked.

"Soon." She smiled wearily at him. "If we're going after revive potions, I will need a sleep."

"I'll stay with you until you're finished." Ryan walked at her side.

Mallory checked over her shoulder to find Brodie continued to talk to Rodina. She was too tired to care about what he was planning. As soon as she'd finished she was going to bed.

It didn't take her long to heal the last few people she needed to tend and she headed to the wagon. Ryan held a piece of canvas over their heads to keep the light rain off them, the thunder and lightning having moved off into the distance once the initial downpour had eased. As much as she wanted to go straight to sleep, she wrote in the leather-bound notebook, using the previous day's date to keep things simple. She fell asleep the moment she lay down.

Day came too soon for Mallory, Brodie shaking her awake to heal his knee. She sat up, trying to focus her blurry vision. "It's seven?" She stared up at the overcast sky, relieved it had stopped raining.

"Yeah. Time to heal my knee."

"I wanted to check on everyone before now." She stumbled out of the wagon, smiling at Callum calling out to keep the noise down. "I need to make sure no one else has died." A glance around showed the ground was damp, but not muddy, which was a relief since they did most of their travelling either on foot or by wagon. She hated to think what it'd be like travelling if it rained enough to turn the ground muddy. She started towards the shelters.

Brodie grabbed Mallory's arm, dropping one of his crutches. Fang jumped back out of the way, whining.

"Let me go. Someone might die."

"It'll only take you a few seconds to heal me. Come on, Mal. I can't do anything while I'm like this."

She slowly shook her head. "Hurry up and sit down then." She waited impatiently for him to sit on the end of the wagon before she healed him, sensing the moment the break was mended. Turning away, she scanned the area. "Where's the bag I had last night."

Brodie jumped off the wagon. "Under the front seat. You left it by the fire. I didn't think you'd want the bandages wet."

"Thanks." She grabbed the bag and headed to the shelters, checking each of her patients, relieved none of the poultices seemed in need of changing. A few of them needed healing to keep up with the very slow health loss, but most of them seemed to be on the mend. Reaching Herena's side, she smiled to see her grandfather with her, holding her hand and talking softly to her.

He grinned up at her. "How can I thank you?"

Mallory crouched beside the two of them. "You can let me heal you without any complaints."

Herena laughed. "Grandpa always complains. About everything. Pa used to say he'd scare off the customers and for him to go loiter somewhere else." Her laughter faded. "Did someone see them die? Are they really dead?"

Mallory placed her hands on the girl, relieved to find her on the mend. "I arrived after the fight."

"Someone said you're going to take Velkden back," the old man said.

She turned to him, placing her hands over his broken bones. "I need to talk to my companions." Hopefully, she could convince everyone to go with her

"If they haven't stripped the village of everything, I can pay you for all you've done. I've a chest of coins and jewellery hidden. I know it can't compare to saving the life of my granddaughter, but it's all I can offer."

"That isn't necessary," Mallory said.

Ryan chuckled, joining them. "It might help to convince everyone. Most of them want to travel on to Cutthroat Harbour today." He drew her to him, briefly kissing her. "Brodie said breakfast is ready. Blueberry pancakes."

"I wish I could have some," Herena said.

Ryan grinned down at her. "With the amount he's cooking, I'd say there'll be plenty to go around." He turned to Mallory. "He insulted Kyla's cooking and she told him to do it himself if he thought he could do better. She's been cooking for everyone as well as running her farm."

Chapter Ten

Mallory and Ryan returned to the wagon to find people lined up for the food Brodie was cooking while he spoke to one of the villagers about some of the recipes he'd love to have. The simple campfire, that had been between the wagon and tents, was now twice the size with two cast iron hotplates set up over coals.

Brodie beckoned them forward, serving them breakfast as he nodded towards the man he'd been talking to. "He's got half a dozen recipes I can have if we can take Velkden back. Said they're no use to him and that you saved his wife's life. They're no use to her either."

The man nodded, then glanced over his shoulder. "Don't go telling her I said that though."

Ryan grinned. "Wouldn't dream of it." He turned

to Mallory. "Now we just have to figure out how to convince the rest of them."

Danae joined them. "Convince who of what?"

"We want to take back Velkden," Brodie said.

"I've already convinced them," Danae said.

"You have?" Brodie nearly dropped the pancake he was putting on a plate. "How?"

"Ninette and Kruth are willing to join us or stay here and protect the wagon." Danae took the plate of pancakes Brodie held out to her. "Jorgen didn't take much convincing when I talked about family and home. If it wasn't for his family being prisoners I don't think he would have hesitated at all. And Emica threatened bodily harm to all of us if her father isn't at Cutthroat Harbour when we arrive."

"I wouldn't let her hurt you," Brodie said.

Danae smiled at him before looking from Mallory to Ryan. "So what is the answer?"

Callum joined them by the fire, Smudge in his makeshift sling. "What is the question?" He grabbed a pancake before Brodie could serve it to one of those waiting, smiling when Brodie glared at him. "And how about making me a coffee. Probably your turn to run after us considering all the running around after you we did."

"The question is if we should take back Velkden," Danae said.

"There should be no question about it," Callum said. "Of course we should."

"Is that your answer?"

Mallory spun to find Rodina behind her. After a glance at her companions, she nodded. "Yes."

"Then you'll need this." Rodina held out a rough drawing. "These are the main roads in and out of the village." She pointed out four thicker lines then ran her finger along a thinner one. "This is where you should enter. The path we take to the river. We don't use the road that takes you to the bridge. Terrible fishing there." She gestured towards the river. "You travel along until you come to a large tree with sprawling branches and a rope swing hanging over the river."

Ryan took the map. "Thanks."

Rodina shook her head. "No, thank you." She glanced at each of them. "Thanks to all of you."

"When are we going?" Danae asked.

"I'm still cooking." Brodie handed Callum a cup of coffee. "I didn't need you to tell me to make coffee. Like we don't hear you complain about it all the time."

Mallory barely managed not to laugh at her

brother's comment. She also managed not to point out that he was the master of complaints.

Roast came forward. "I'll stay here and help protect the wagon." He nodded towards the hotplates. "I can do the cooking too."

Brodie reluctantly agreed, giving numerous instructions on how to do the job.

This time Mallory turned away, unable to prevent a smile. Her smile faded when she saw some of those in line waiting for food. There were a few that looked like they were more dead than alive. She couldn't resist walking down the line and healing some of them.

Rodina stopped her when she was on the way back to the campfire. "You can use the jewellery until you're ready to go to Cutthroat Harbour. And use up the last of the mana in the crystal if you need it."

"Thanks. That should help."

Rodina stepped out of her way. "I wish I could come with you." A wry smile formed. "My people protested when I suggested it. They've been through more than enough so I gave in."

Mallory rested her hand on Rodina's arm, more to see how she was doing than to reassure her. "We'll be okay. You stay here and protect your people." She grinned. "You've stopped losing health."

"Seems like your poultice works."

"Good." She lowered her hand, glancing over her shoulder. "I better get ready." She turned away.

"Mallory." Rodina waited until Mallory faced her before she spoke again. "I'm glad you turned up here. You'll always be welcome in our village, regardless of the outcome of your attack on those holding it." A grin momentarily formed. "Or welcome in our camp if we're unable to take our village back."

"Thanks." Mallory returned to the campfire to catch the last of Ryan's words.

"We'll meet back here in ten, ready to leave."

Mallory grabbed a pancake before getting ready to go. Not that she had much that she needed to do, which meant she was one of the first back at the campfire.

They set out along the river, Emica and Jorgen with them, reaching the tree quicker than Mallory had expected. She looked from the rope to the water. "I bet this is nice in the middle of summer."

"Reminds me of a few creeks back home." Ryan turned his back on the river. "Let's take back Velkden and find some revive potions."

"What if we find more than the villagers need?" Emica stepped up beside him, staring in the same direction.

"Then they're ours," Ryan said.

Emica drew her swords, her ears becoming fox ears. "Then how about we find the orc mage and take them from him. I want to get to Cutthroat Harbour."

They started towards the village, keeping to the shelter of the trees that edged the path. "We have a reputation in Velkden now," Brodie exclaimed. "Only ten though. You'd think it'd be higher than that after all we've done."

"We don't want it too high," Danae reminded him.

"Why not?" Emica asked.

"We don't want a high world rep," Danae said.

"Then you get a negative rep in dark forces villages and towns to balance it out," Emica said.

As they neared the village, they slowed, moving further back from the path. Emica was the one that heard enemies coming towards them, telling them to hide, Smudge hearing them a few seconds later and softly making his warning sound.

Mallory pressed herself against a tree, her wand in hand as she watched the path. Two archers came into view, their bows slung across their backs. She couldn't believe how little attention they were paying as they chatted to each other. Were they that confident that they'd taken out everyone in the area? She thought of all the villagers, sighing. She supposed they should be confident. None of the villagers were in a state to fight back.

The two archers walked past them, one laughing, slapping his companion on the back. The other one joined in the laughter.

"Now." Ryan, who stood next to Mallory, drew back an arrow, aiming it at one of the archers.

Chapter Eleven

Mallory threw a fireball, hitting the one on the right at the same time as Ryan's arrow struck him. Two more arrows struck him, bringing him to his knees. Emica and Jorgen burst out of cover, going for the second archer as the rest of them attacked the other one again. He landed face first in the dirt and they focused on the one Emica and Jorgen attacked.

The two shapeshifters stood over the still bodies, scanning the area. Mallory glanced around too. Nothing else moved. She stepped closer to Ryan. "Do you think anyone in Velkden heard us?"

He shrugged. "Let's get them out of the open and see what they have before we continue to the village. If we can take them out a couple at a time, we'll easily manage this."

"If there's only thirty in the village, then we've got

twenty-eight left." Callum strode towards the bodies lying on the dirt path.

Mallory joined them, grabbing the leg of one of the archers and helping carry him to the side of the road, dropping him behind some shrubs. Ryan, Brodie and Jorgen dropped the other body next to the shrubs too.

Ryan scanned the area. "Emica, Danni and Callum keep watch. Brodie and Jorgen search the bodies and Mallory help me hide signs of the fight from the path." He broke off two branches with plenty of leaves, handing one to Mallory. "It doesn't have to be perfect. Just enough that if more come along this way they won't immediately notice."

She brushed the leaves across the dirt, hiding the scuffles and bloodstains. She spotted something shiny and crouched for a closer look. It was a silver coin. Picking it up, she dusted it off, frowning when she realised it wasn't a coin. Or at least not a coin from Ruby Isle.

"What did you find?"

She held the coin out to Ryan, taking his hand when he held it out to help her up. "I thought it was a coin."

Emica ran over to them. "Someone's coming." She took the coin Ryan examined. "Why do you have a silver piece from Eswen?" She glanced along the path, before handing it back to Ryan. "Never mind. Hurry before they reach us."

Mallory took the coin back from Ryan, following Emica. "What is Eswen?" She hid behind one of the trees with the kitsune.

"One of the countries at the bottom of the world. I've been told it snows all year round. Not sure if that's true, but it's meant to be really cold down there," Emica said.

Mallory slipped the coin into her belt pouch. "Why would a coin from Eswen be here?"

Emica shrugged. "Maybe the archer was from there."

Ryan joined them. "Three archers this time. We'll take out the one in the lead."

Emica drew her second sword. "Make me invisible. I'll attack from behind." She glanced towards where Jorgen and Brodie hid behind a nearby tree. "You should make Jorgen invisible too. Invisibility suits rogues." She grinned.

Mallory cast vanish I on Emica, crouching low before heading for the next tree, remaining below the height of some shrubs. She straightened when she reached Brodie and Jorgen. "Want to be invisible?"

Jorgen nodded, about to speak.

Brodie spoke first. "Hell yeah."

Mallory laughed, trying not to be loud. "Done." She used mana from the essence crystal, making them both invisible. She only had to wait a few seconds before she was able to throw a fireball at the archer in the lead. She really needed jewellery of her own to speed up her mana regen.

The fight was over quickly and Mallory checked everyone's health. Brodie needed healing. Unable to check Emica and Jorgen's health since they weren't part of their group, she joined them in the middle of the path, resting her hand on Jorgen to sense how he was.

"Is something wrong?" Jorgen looked at her hand resting on his wrist.

She healed him three times. "Not anymore."

He chuckled. "I'd only lost five. It didn't seem worth mentioning."

"It's better to regularly heal rather than try and do it all at once." Mallory turned to Emica, checking her health. She needed healing four times.

Brodie helped Ryan and Callum shift one of the archers off the path. "Are you lot going to help or stand around?"

Fang tried to tug one of the bodies by the leg, growling low as she did so.

"Even Fang is trying to help while you all stand around," Brodie said.

"Keep your voice down." Jorgen grabbed one of the archers under the arms, waiting until Emica and Mallory had him by the legs before he lifted him.

Once the bodies were off the road, Ryan picked up the branch again. "Same positions as earlier, everyone."

"Do you think if we wait here more will come?" Brodie asked.

"I think if we wait too long these ones will be missed." Ryan dropped the branch beside the dead bodies.

"What did we get?" Mallory tossed her branch onto Ryan's.

"We've replaced all the arrows we used and have another three spare," Callum said.

"Studded leather vambraces. Archer armour," Jorgen said. "It would have been nice if we could have found ones that can be worn by the rogue class."

Brodie held out some coins. "Thirteen silver and twenty-seven copper pieces."

"We should split it between the nine of us," Ryan suggested.

"Who gets the extra silver?" Emica asked.

"Group money for when we need to buy things," Ryan said.

Mallory shared out the coins, giving everyone a silver and three copper pieces, putting aside Ninette and Kruth's share. She added the other four silver pieces to the group money. "Did we get anything else?"

Brodie shook his head. "They don't seem to be carrying much."

"Soldiers often don't," Emica said. "They only take what they need with them. So they're not weighed down with unnecessary things."

Callum kept his bow in his hand, an arrow in the other. "Are we going into Velkden now? Before someone comes looking for the missing archers."

Ryan nodded. "We should split into two groups."

Mallory took a step towards him, holding out her hand. "No. Not again. Look what happened last time we split up when we were wandering around. You were bitten by a chameleon viper."

Ryan captured her hand. "This is different."

"Jorgen can be in whichever group I'm not in," Emica said.

Callum chuckled. "I can be in Jorgen's group."

"I'll be in Danni's group," Brodie said.

"Danni can go with Emica. We need a mix of range and close weapons in each group," Ryan said.

Mallory wanted to protest. She wanted to keep an eye on both Ryan and Brodie. That would be impossible with the way the groups were being split. "Who gets four in their group?"

Ryan looked from Jorgen and Callum to Emica, Danae and Brodie. His grip tightened on Mallory's hand. "You go with Callum." He grinned. "I'll try and keep your brother out of mischief." He laughed when Brodie protested.

Mallory clung to his hand for a moment, eventually forcing herself to let go. "Okay." It didn't feel in the least bit okay.

Ryan drew her to him, kissing her. "It will be." Letting her go, he stepped back. "No one kill the orc mage. If they have a revive, we won't be able to get the potions off them."

"We have to take an orc alive?" Brodie demanded.

"Impossible," Emica said. "They fight to the end."

Chapter Twelve

Mallory started to agree, her lips curving into a smile instead, her hand resting on her satchel.

"You have a plan?" Ryan asked.

Mallory nodded. "Sleeping mist."

Ryan took out the roughly drawn map of the village. "Okay. We search the place and meet back here." He pointed to a spot just outside and to the left of the path. "Try and stay out of sight. There are approximately twenty-five enemies left in Velkden."

"What if we're spotted?" Danae asked. "What do we do?"

"Fight if you can do so without alerting the entire village or retreat if you can't," Ryan said.

"Then they'll know where we're going to meet up," Emica said.

"Maybe we should leave someone as lookout to

take out any of the enemies that follow if we need to retreat," Danae suggested.

"It'd have to be either Danni or Callum," Ryan said. "Or both."

"We're splitting into three groups?" Mallory glanced at each of her companions. "That sounds worse."

"It actually makes better sense." Emica slowly nodded. "A lot better sense. Two archers to cover our retreat if we should need to run."

"But I was going to be in Danni's group," Brodie protested.

Ryan clapped his hand on Brodie's shoulder. "And now you're not." He looked from his brother to Danae. "You two get in a position to cover our retreat if we should need it." His gaze rested on Smudge for a moment. "No one should be able to sneak up on you."

Callum patted Smudge on the head. "Not with Smudge listening for danger."

"Mallory can go with Jorgen and search towards the left while the rest of us can head to the right," Ryan said. "Try and count how many are left in the village. But don't get caught in the process."

"This doesn't feel right," Brodie muttered.

Mallory wanted to agree with him. "How long do we search for?"

Ryan shrugged. "Half hour or so. Less if you find the orc."

"We better get moving. Someone is sure to come looking for those archers soon." Emica glanced over her shoulder to where the bodies had been dumped.

Mallory moved close to Ryan. "Be careful." She slid her arms around him, holding him tight, her lips meeting his. She drew back slightly, keeping hold of him. "Do you want some of the invisibility potions?"

"I'll take one." Ryan slipped the potion into his belt pouch when Mallory handed it to him.

"What about the rest of us?" Brodie demanded.

"One should be enough." Ryan slung an arm around Brodie's shoulders. "Time to move out." He guided the protesting Brodie along the side of the path.

Mallory followed, Jorgen at her side. When they drew closer to the village, the two of them headed to the left.

Jorgen nodded, indicating an area further to the left. "That orchard should give us better cover and we can work our way around the outskirts of the village, hiding amongst the fruit trees."

She followed Jorgen, continually scanning the area.

There wasn't a great deal of cover. "How are we meant to enter the village? We'll be spotted."

"We might have been better waiting for dark. You said you had night vision potions?"

"I'm trying to keep them for Cutthroat Harbour." They reached the end of the orchard and Mallory pressed herself against a tree, peering around it. An archer patrolled past them on the road directly across from them, heading towards a timber house. "This is impossible."

"You could make us invisible."

She started to protest, stopping when she remembered all her current bonuses for mana regen. Vanish I only cost twenty-five mana and lasted a minute. She'd be able to continually cast it on the two of them every time it ran out. And have a little mana to spare. "Okay. Shall I cast it now?"

"We'll head along this road towards the tavern and make our way behind the house before we reach it. The minute the spell lasts should give us enough time to get out of sight before you need to cast it again." Jorgen gestured towards each building as he mentioned it.

Mallory eyed the distance. "Okay. Cast it now?"

Jorgen smiled. "Cast it now."

She cast vanish I on herself first and then Jorgen.

The moment she had, she hurried towards the building Jorgen had indicated. She tried to be careful where she stepped, but didn't manage to be as silent as she would have preferred. Not that there was anyone close by to hear. Reaching the building, she checked how much time she had left as she pressed herself against the back of it. The lower half of the building was made of stone and the top was made of timber. From what she'd seen, there seemed to be quite a few buildings made like that in the village. She supposed something had to be done with the rock that came out of the mine.

She became visible seconds before Jorgen. "Where to now?"

"I've been worried about how we'll manage at Cutthroat Harbour. Maybe it won't be as bad as I feared."

"I won't have the jewellery with me."

"Maybe not." He shrugged. "Or maybe they'll be willing to sell them to you."

"I'm pretty sure something like these wouldn't be cheap." She glanced at the rings and bracelet.

Jorgen smiled. "Or they might give them to you in payment for rescuing their village."

Mallory shrugged rather than argue like she

wanted to. She doubted they'd give away such valuable items. "Where to now?"

"Behind the tavern."

With a nod, Mallory cast the spell first on herself and then on Jorgen. She hurried towards the tavern, wishing she could move as silently as him. She had no idea where he was and could only assume he was with her. She kept a check on the time, relieved to see the spell should last long enough for them to make it around the back of the tavern. Which was good since the archer who'd walked past before was coming towards the tavern along the main road that led out of the village.

She was partway along the building, when the back door was flung open and three men came out, two of them dragging the third. She froze. She couldn't retreat and there wasn't time to get past the building.

The two men slammed the third one against the back wall of the tavern. "I'll teach you not to cheat at cards," one of them warned.

"It wasn't me," he argued.

Not knowing what else to do, Mallory pressed herself against the back wall, watching as the time counted down. Her name being whispered from beside her on her left, nearly made her miss recasting as soon as the spell ended. She stared at the space beside her, waiting for the next five seconds to pass. Jorgen reappeared as the man pressed up against the tavern wall called out and she hurriedly cast a spell on him.

"Did you see that? And again. There's two people watching us. Using invisibility spells."

"You're going to have to try better than that to distract us," one of the men said.

Not knowing where to go, and not wanting to stay where she was, Mallory headed across the back of the tavern and past the three men. She almost stumbled when she heard the next words.

"That revive potion the mage used on you was a waste."

"Mage. Orcs aren't meant to be mages. They're warriors," the second man sneered.

The first man grinned. "I dare you to go over to that fancy house and tell him to his face."

This time, Mallory did stumble.

"Did you hear it?" the man pressed against the tavern wall demanded.

The two men let him go, looking around the area. The second man shrugged. "Probably those goats. Stupid creatures. Only good for goblin bait. Who'd want to farm goats?"

"Cows. That's what they should be farming. Be

glad to get home and off this island," the first man said. "Sick of eating sheep. There are too many sheep farms on this island."

"At least they also breed pigs around here," the second man said.

Chapter Thirteen

Mallory reached the end of the tavern, checking up the side of it. No one was there. She was torn. Did she keep moving or remain where she was and possibly learn more information? She peered around the corner at the three men.

The one who'd been pressed against the wall started to move away. The first man spun, catching him. "It was a trick. I knew it."

"It wasn't. I swear." He tried to pull away from the first man.

"Like you swear you didn't cheat?" the second man asked.

"It wasn't me," he protested.

The spell wore off and Mallory glanced around, making sure no one had spotted her. Before she could recast the spell, Jorgen appeared beside her.

He placed a hand on her arm. "We need to find out which one is the fancy house."

"By searching the village?"

"No. We should go back and ask one of the villagers. We aren't that far from the farm."

"Okay. Do we return the way we came? Maybe across the front of the tavern rather than behind it," Mallory suggested.

"No, go behind, but further out. You're not very quiet. I was able to easily follow you."

Mallory started to protest. She sighed. As much as she wished he hadn't pointed it out, it was true. "Okay. Ready for me to cast the spell?"

Jorgen nodded, smiling.

She was tempted to ask him what was so funny, but had a feeling he was amused by her. Casting the spell on herself first, she headed out past the back of the tavern once they were both invisible. She kept her journal open, glad it was easily seen through, and watched the timer count down the invisibility buff. As the time started to run out, she headed behind a tree, pressing herself against it. She wasn't in the least bit surprised that Jorgen was with her when he became visible. Not after his previous comment. "Ready again?"

Jorgen nodded.

She had to cast the spell twice more before they reached Callum and Danae, Smudge making soft chattering sounds as they drew near. She grinned when Callum asked him what he was trying to say. She appeared in front of Callum, causing him to jump back. "He might have been trying to tell you we were here."

Smudge nodded, continuing to chatter softly.

Danae reached for Smudge, who was still in the makeshift sling, rubbing him under the chin. "You are so clever. As well as utterly adorable."

"Is everything okay?" Callum looked past Mallory before meeting her gaze. "Did you see Ryan?"

"No. But that's a good thing. If I'd seen him then there's a chance one of the enemy would have seen him too," Mallory said.

"How many did you see?" Danae asked.

"Oh." She'd been so busy trying not to be caught that she'd forgotten to count.

"Twelve. We weren't able to see all the village though," Jorgen said.

"Why did you come back?" Callum asked. "It's not time."

"We learned where the mage is. The orc mage," Mallory said. "We overheard a conversation and need to find out where the fanciest building is."

"That would probably be Rodina's house," Danae said. "It's usually the elder's house that's the fanciest."

"We need to ask her. Or one of the other villagers." Mallory glanced in the direction of the river. "Have any others gone this way?"

Danae nodded. "A few minutes ago. Two warriors. They went looking for the patrols that were meant to be back by now."

"We should try and go after them and take them out before they discover the bodies," Jorgen said. "One can wait here while three of us take them on." He grinned. "You could make me invisible again and they wouldn't know where the attacks are coming from."

Callum looked from the village to the direction of the river. "I'll wait here. Let the rest know what's happening."

"Will we meet back here once we learn which building or do you want to meet at the farm?" Danae asked.

"We should meet back here," Jorgen said. "It makes more sense than wasting time at the village. If we get finished here quickly enough, we can continue our journey to Cutthroat Harbour today."

Mallory was tempted to sigh. Very heavily. They still needed to find time to return to their world. "One thing at a time. We need to focus on getting those revive potions first."

"So what's the plan?" Callum asked.

Mallory looked between the village and the direction of the river. She wanted to say they'd wait until the rest returned. She wanted to make sure everyone was safe. She took a deep breath, slowly letting it out. "We'll meet back here. Jorgen, Danni and I will return to the farm. And take out the two warriors along the way."

They remained to the side of the path, staying amongst the trees, hurrying towards the river as they continually scanned the area. It wasn't until they were nearly at the river that they spotted the warriors.

"Cast it now," Jorgen said.

She made him invisible, turning to Danae. "Do you want to be invisible too?"

Danae smiled. "It might help."

She made Danae invisible, but there wasn't enough to make herself invisible too. Not unless she used some of the stored mana. Which she didn't want to do. This wasn't exactly an emergency. There was enough mana to cast a fireball at each of the warriors and she was generating more each second. She didn't use all the mana as it regenerated, letting some build up so she'd have enough to cast vanish I on Jorgen again when his wore off. He appeared for a couple of seconds before she made him invisible. She nearly laughed at the expressions on the warriors' faces.

The urge to laugh faded when the two of them looked in her direction. Maybe she should have kept enough mana to make herself invisible too. They obviously now knew who was making it impossible for them to see Jorgen. They tried to run towards her, staggering and stumbling from Jorgen's attacks. She slowly backed up, letting her mana build up and casting the occasional fireball at each of them. But they were getting closer.

Another arrow, coming from amongst the trees along the path, pierced one of them and he collapsed to the ground. The second warrior took out a vial and tried to drink from it. The object was plucked from his hands before he could.

Mallory cast a fireball at him following it up with poison dart. Jorgen became visible and she didn't have enough mana to cast vanish I. Before she could decide if she should draw some of the stored mana, an arrow struck the warrior at the same time as Jorgen attacked with a stiletto, the vial in his other hand.

The warrior dropped to the ground and Jorgen searched on the ground for the lid of the vial.

Mallory hurried forward. "What was he trying to drink?"

Jorgen slipped the vial into a pocket. "Health potion." He grinned. "Invisibility is a very handy skill."

Danae laughed softly. "Not for those trying to find you."

Mallory scanned the area. "Let's get these bodies moved off the path and search them so we can find out where the orc mage is."

It didn't take them long and they also broke off some branches to brush across the ground in an attempt to hide the signs of the fight. Danae slowly shook her head. "Not as well hidden as when Welby does it. Maybe we should have asked him to come along instead of leaving him behind to guard the wagon."

"It doesn't have to be perfect, only good enough to slow them down as they try and figure out if anything happened." Mallory searched one of the bodies.

Between the two bodies, they found seven copper pieces and a utility knife. Mallory put the coins in her belt pouch and the knife in her satchel while Jorgen kept watch. He scanned the area again before glancing skywards. "Are you finished?"

Chapter Fourteen

Mallory nodded, also glancing skywards. The day was overcast, but at least it hadn't begun raining again. "Let's go find Rodina."

They hurried towards the farm, spotting those on guard before they reached it. They were waved through into the camp after being told Rodina was at the farmhouse. She was speaking to several villagers, breaking off as they entered the house. "You have the potions already?"

"No." Mallory wished she could have said yes. "We need to know which is the fanciest building in the village and where it is."

Herena's grandfather chuckled. "That's easy. Rodina's place. It's the last building on the road that takes you to Deadman Cove. You can't miss it."

"What's at my house?" Rodina asked.

"The orc mage," Mallory said.

Rodina's hand went to the hilt of her sword. "I'm going with you."

The old man rested a hand on Rodina's shoulder. "We need you here. It's only a house. Not important in the scheme of things."

"It's my house," Rodina stated.

One of the other villagers stepped forward. "You promised us you'd stay."

Rodina kept her hand on the hilt of her sword a moment longer before she lowered it. "If you're taking him alive, keep him for me."

The old man chuckled. "You're a respectable elder, not some adventurer."

Rodina's lips twisted into a smile. "I'm whatever I want to be. And he will soon learn that."

The old man shrugged, turning to Mallory. "Circle around the village to the east. You'll know it's time to turn back towards the village once you're past the goat farm."

"They were talking about the goats," Mallory said. "They didn't seem impressed by them."

Rodina chuckled. "It was originally a sheep farm. They all sickened and died and the farmer decided to try goats instead. We've been telling him for years to go back to sheep. Those goats are impossible to keep out of trouble. He'll be glad to hear the goats are causing problems for the invaders."

"He was attacked too?" Danae asked.

"Some of the farms are on the edge of the village," Rodina said.

Mallory glanced towards the door. "We better go. We left the rest of our companions over near the village." And she wanted to make sure everyone was okay. Regularly checking the journal wasn't good enough. Just because they were alive and unharmed didn't mean they weren't in imminent danger.

"Good luck," Rodina said.

Mallory followed Danae and Jorgen outside, smiling in thanks to Rodina. She couldn't help glancing in the direction of the shelters, tempted to check on her many patients. But it was more important to bring back revive potions before the dead ran out of time.

The walk back to where they'd left Callum was quiet. Not only because the three of them didn't talk, but they also didn't run into any enemies or creatures.

Mallory was relieved to find Ryan, Brodie and Emica were with Callum. She quickly went over the information Rodina had given them, looking Ryan and Brodie over, glad to see they appeared to be as fine as the journal had indicated.

Ryan took out the roughly drawn map, running his finger in an arc around the village to a larger rectangle. "I guess this is her place."

Mallory looked at the buildings they'd need to pass as they circled around the village. Then it struck her. There were a lot of buildings in the village. If this drawing was accurate in amounts. Those that had survived wouldn't come close to filling all the buildings.

"There's someone coming this way, from the direction of the river." Emica drew one of her swords.

Mallory turned, her wand still in her hand, ready to attack. She lowered her hand. "It's one of the villagers." From the look of him he appeared to be only a few years older than her and when she'd treated him last night, she hadn't wanted to ask. He'd been too close to death. She stepped out of the shelter of the trees, catching his attention before hiding again.

It didn't take him long to join them. "Rodina sent me with a message."

"Should you be walking this far?" Mallory rested her hand on his, smiling when she discovered how much he'd recovered. She healed him three times just to make sure he wouldn't run out of health if he encountered anything.

He nodded. "I'll live. Thanks to you." He gestured towards the village. "One of our miners arrived at the farm just after you left. There's a bunch of them, and some of the villagers, being held hostage in the mine and made to work. There are two guards at the entrance to the mine and six inside."

"How did he escape?" Jorgen asked.

The villager shrugged. "He looks near dead. We're all amazed he made it to the farm."

"That's Rodina's message?" Ryan asked. "That a miner escaped and some are still in the mine."

The villager shook his head. "She's trying to rally those at the farm, but most of them have never held a weapon in their life. Not that she has any weapons to put in their hands. If they had attacked later in the day, there would have been some who were armed and ready to face them. But they surprised us as we were rising for the morning and no one was prepared."

"So the message is that Rodina and some of the villagers might attack?" Danae asked.

The villager shook his head, sighing. "She should have sent someone else. I'm not good at this."

"What is the message?" Brodie demanded. He patted Fang when she growled softly at the anger in his tone. "It's okay, girl."

"She asked that you rescue the villagers before attacking the invaders. She doesn't want to risk them being killed. She says she has no idea what has been stolen, but she will find a way to reward you if most of them survive," the villager said.

"Of course it'd have to be a quest," Brodie muttered.

Smiling, Mallory checked her journal since the icon was in the corner of her vision. Not that she would have needed that to tell her after her brother's comment. *Free The Miners: Rescue the miners and villagers of Velkden who are being forced to work in the essence crystal mine and you will be rewarded.* "At least we have two quests that are related and in the same location."

Brodie's expression brightened. "Double the reward and twice the XP. That doesn't sound too bad. I've barely been earning any XP lately. All the cooking I've done hasn't given me much."

Ryan chuckled. "Then we better get on with it." He showed the map to the villager. "Where's the mine?"

It took him a few seconds to make sense of the drawing. "This is Rodina's place." He pointed to the rectangle and slid his finger back towards a nearby square. "This is the mine."

Mallory looked between the two shapes. They didn't appear that far apart. But according to the lines on the map, that she assumed were roads, they were on completely different roads. "Is there anything between the two of them?"

The villager shrugged. "Maybe some trees and shrubs. There aren't many trees in the village."

"Is the entrance to the mine open or closed?" Callum asked.

"It's a shaft mine. We have a platform that is winched up and down," the villager said.

"That makes it a little harder," Ryan said.

"I've got a brother down there," the villager said. "I'm willing to do anything to help him escape."

"What we need is a diversion," Emica said. "Something to draw the guards away. And probably the rest of the invaders who are wandering around."

"Not before we get the potions off the mage." Mallory tried not to think about the child who'd died. It was impossible to keep the image from appearing in her mind. "We can't save some just to let others die."

"We might not be able to rescue everyone," Jorgen said softly.

"I can create a diversion," the villager said.

"What sort of diversion?" Ryan asked.

The villager shrugged. "Tell me what sort you need me to make and I'll make it."

"We can't stand around here all day," Emica said. "We've killed seven of them. People will miss them soon."

"They already have." Jorgen glanced in the direction of the river. "Two warriors were looking for the archers. Soon others will come looking. A larger group that we might not be able to face."

"We need to know how many invaders are in the village," Ryan said.

"I can find out," the villager offered.

"There's no point risking yourself. How will that help your brother?" Ryan asked.

"It's nothing like that." The villager gestured towards a tall building. "One of the farms south of the village has a tunnel leading to the granary. It was once a grain farm, but they changed over to small crops years ago. The tunnel is no longer used, but it's still in good shape. There are windows at the top of the granary to let in the light when workers carry the grain to the top of the stairs to tip it into the silo."

"What if the invaders are using it to keep an eye on things?" Danae asked.

"Then we take them out." Ryan held the map out. "Which farm?" He put the map away once the villager had shown him. "That's a better plan. It'll take us past fewer buildings with less risk of invaders coming unexpectedly out of them."

Chapter Fifteen

Mallory looked in the direction of the tavern. She didn't need any more close calls. "That sounds good to me."

"Okay. This way." Ryan led the way, keeping to the trees and circling around the village, passing in sight of a couple of buildings and going close by a grain farm. They also passed a small crops farm, before approaching the farm the villager led them to. They slowed as they drew near, open ground between them and the farmhouse, an archer walking past the back of the building.

"How are we meant to get over there without being spotted?" Brodie demanded.

Mallory smiled. "Vanish."

"You don't have enough mana to make all of us invisible at the same time," Brodie said.

"I don't need to make everyone invisible at once.

Two can go over at a time." Mallory glanced around the group. "Who wants to go first?"

"I will," Ryan said. "Wait until you see me move the curtain in that window before anyone else comes over. There could be someone inside."

Mallory's smiled faded. She hadn't thought of that. Taking a deep breath, she managed not to beg him to let someone else go first. "Okay. Who else?"

"I will go too," the villager said. "You won't know where the tunnel entrance is."

"Are you both ready?" Mallory asked. When they nodded, she cast the spell, trying to see, or hear, where they were.

"I bet I could be quieter than them," Brodie said.

Callum laughed. "I don't think you've got that many points in dexterity."

Mallory stared at the curtain, willing it to move. "How long should it take for them to reach the farmhouse?" She held her breath when the archer walked past the door. "Is he guarding the building?"

"What if they know about the tunnel?" Danae asked.

Mallory wished Danae hadn't said anything. She took half a step forward. "Should we attack the-" She broke off when the curtain shifted, falling straight back into place. "That was them, wasn't it?"

"Yeah, that was them," Callum said. "Send me next."

"And me," Emica said.

"Are you both ready?" Mallory waited for them to nod before she cast the spell, needing to draw on some stored mana so she could make Smudge invisible too.

Danae and Brodie went next and if she hadn't been so worried about everything, Mallory probably would have smiled at how quickly Brodie had said he'd go with Danae. She also needed to draw on some stored mana to make Fang invisible. Her and Jorgen went last. Like the previous times, she couldn't hear his footsteps.

As they neared the back door, the archer stopped in front of it and fumbled in his belt pouch. Mallory checked how much time she had left. It continued to count down. The archer remained where he was, searching in his belt pouch. She couldn't stay where she was much longer or she'd appear in front of him. She started to step to the side when he drew out a piece of jerky and closed his belt pouch. Mentally urging him to move, she held her breath as she watched him take a step in the same direction she'd been about to go in.

She took a step in the opposite direction, wincing

at the soft sound her foot made. The archer spun to face her. A sound further across to her left caught the archer's attention and she hurried for the door, barely making it inside before the spell ended. She sagged against the wall beside the door, trying to steady her breathing.

Jorgen appeared in front of her. "Keep moving. The pebble I threw might have him checking the area a little more carefully."

"The noise that distracted him was you?" Mallory pushed away from the wall, wishing she could sit down. Her limbs felt shaky. Actually, her entire body felt shaky.

Before Jorgen could answer, Ryan entered the room. "This way. The trapdoor is in the bedroom. We had to move a large chest. It'll be impossible to hide it."

Mallory followed him into the next room. Besides the chest, there was a double bed made of carved timber and a small, narrow table with a water jug and wash bowl on it. She recognised the curtain at the window as the one she'd stared at, waiting for the signal from Ryan.

Brodie handed Fang down through the opening of the trapdoor. "Careful."

Mallory moved closer to the trapdoor, peering past her brother. "There was a light down there?"

Ryan shook his head. "We found a lantern in the living area."

Jorgen peered out the window, the curtain only slightly moved aside. "A warrior has joined the archer. It looks like he's taking over from the archer that's been patrolling."

Mallory hurried to the window and peered past the other side of the curtain. "Where is he going?" She kept her voice low.

"In the back door." Jorgen stepped back from the curtain, drawing his stiletto, striding to the bedroom door that was closed.

"Wait." Mallory hurried after him. "We need to attack all at once."

Callum and Danae came out of the trapdoor, neither Smudge nor Fang with them.

The bedroom door started to open and Mallory cast vanish I on Jorgen and Ryan who were closest to the door. She moved back from the door, out of view, watching her mana regen as she waited for enough so she could cast the spell on Brodie.

The archer stood in the doorway, opening his mouth as he reached for his bow. Before he could make a sound, two arrows struck him and he was attacked by invisible blades.

Mallory cast vanish I on her brother, not sure if she should draw on the stored mana again. At the rate she was using it, there'd soon be none left. She drew her sword, heading towards the archer, throwing a fireball the moment she had enough mana. Before she could reach him, he was dead. She stood halfway across the room, heart racing, both weapons out.

"Do you think the warrior heard?" Emica asked.

Spinning, Mallory hurried to the window, sheathing her sword. She peered out past the curtain, barely daring to breathe. She couldn't see the warrior. About to step away from the window to check that he hadn't entered the living area, he came into view, striding towards the farmhouse. Letting the edge of the curtain go, she sagged against the wall next to the window. "He wasn't nearby. I'd say he's patrolling a larger area than the archer was."

"In the tunnel then." Ryan closed the bedroom door. "Before another one comes in."

Callum rose from the body he'd searched. "I got a sheathed hunting knife and a tin of bowstring wax." He held out the tin that fit in the palm of his hand.

It reminded Mallory of a shoe polish tin. "What do you need that for?"

"It increases the durability of bows and crossbows, like a whetstone does for bladed weapons," Danae said.

"Is there something that does that for wands?" Mallory asked.

"Timber weapon polish. It can be used on shields too." Danae entered the trapdoor.

Callum gave the hunting knife to Ryan to put in his backpack and put the tin in his satchel. "How much can it increase the durability by?"

"Not past its maximum durability. It just brings it back to normal. But it can only do it so many times. Eventually, even the bowstring wax won't be enough and you'll either need to have it repaired or replaced," Jorgen said.

Chapter Sixteen

Mallory waited for Callum and Jorgen to climb down the ladder to the tunnel below before she went down. The air was cool and damp and smelled stale. "How long is it?"

The villager held the lantern, waiting for all of them to enter and close the trapdoor before he walked along the tunnel. "Not long. It was a way for the farmer to check on the grain during bad weather. Make sure it wasn't going mouldy or anything during rainy periods."

"What did he do if it went mouldy?" Mallory eyed the damp walls, not sure if she wanted to scrape off the moss that had a faint glimmer to it letting her know it could be gathered. She supposed they could return later and gather what was likely an alchemy ingredient.

"Different potions or spells can be used, depending

on the type of mould, or problem." The villager stopped at the other end of the tunnel, gesturing to a ladder and trapdoor above. "It opens up in a corner of the granary, half hidden by the silo. Sometimes there are sacks of grain stacked on it, but there shouldn't be today. The last lot of sacks were sent to the capital last week along with a shipment of essence crystals. Which is a good thing or the invaders would have had plenty of crystals to take. They might not have wanted to keep anyone alive to mine them."

Mallory looked back the way they'd come. The tunnel was a lot shorter than she'd expected. When Ryan started up the ladder, she hurried forward. "Do you want me to make you invisible?"

"When I start to open the trapdoor." Ryan continued to climb up the ladder, pressing a hand against the trapdoor when he reached the top.

Mallory waited until she could see light around the edges of the trapdoor before she cast the spell, keeping her wand ready in case she needed to use it again.

Ryan lowered the trapdoor before he spoke. "There are two up here. A mage and an archer. With where they're standing, they'd see the trapdoor if I open it fully."

"I can go out there and create a diversion," the villager suggested.

"No." Mallory was tempted to slowly shake her head. He seemed determined to get himself killed. "Do you want to die?"

"I shouldn't have lived." The villager stared at the stone floor. "My cousin should have lived, not me. She saved my life."

Ryan became visible, standing beside the villager who jumped back. Ryan clapped him on the shoulder. "Has she been dead two days yet?"

The villager shook his head.

"Then there's still time to bring her back. But getting yourself killed won't help." Ryan glanced at the trapdoor. "Stay at the top of the ladder and keep watch. Let us know when they move out of sight. Make sure you don't open the trapdoor much."

The villager handed the lantern to Ryan before he scrambled up the ladder.

Emica gestured in the direction they'd come from. "Should we return to the farmhouse and find another way in?"

Before anyone could answer her, Smudge made soft warning sounds, looking in the direction of the farmhouse. Fang joined him, growling softly.

Mallory took a step towards the farmhouse end of

the tunnel, light entering through the open trapdoor. "Do you think someone found the trapdoor?"

"Only one way to find out." Ryan drew his cutlass. "Make me invisible."

"I'll go with you." Jorgen turned to Mallory. "Make me invisible too."

She cast the spell on both of them, listening to only one set of footsteps move away. "How does he manage to be so silent?"

"It's a shapeshifter thing. Even in human form we have some of the abilities of our animal self. Not to the same extent." Emica gestured in the direction Ryan and Jorgen had taken. "Someone is opening the bedroom door."

"We should go help them." Mallory took a step towards the farmhouse direction.

"They're out of view," the villager called down.

She looked from one direction to the other. Surely the two invaders in the granary would be out of view again later.

"You go help Jorgen and Ryan," Emica said. "The rest of us can take out the ones above us."

"I can make two of you invisible." Mallory started backing away, glancing over her shoulder several times.

"Me," Brodie said. "Make me invisible."

Emica nodded towards the villager on the ladder. "Better make him invisible too since he's going out first."

As soon as Mallory had made the two of them invisible, she ran in the direction of the farmhouse. Reaching the end, she found the tunnel empty and the trapdoor open. She scrambled up the ladder. About to enter the room, she had to duck when an arrow flew overhead. She peered over the edge of the floor, casting poison dart at the archer Ryan and Jorgen fought.

The archer glanced at her before making a dash to the door.

Mallory threw fireball after fireball at him, some of them missing their target. They couldn't let him escape. He'd warn the rest of the invaders. The archer made it through the doorway and out of her sight. Mallory scrambled into the room, running after Ryan and Jorgen who followed the archer. She threw another fireball at the archer as he reached for the handle of the back door that was now closed.

An arrow pierced him, Ryan having used his hunting bow. He thudded against the door, slipping to the floor. They all remained where they were, staring at the archer.

Mallory lowered her wand. "You think anyone heard?"

Jorgen shrugged. "I'll check out the window to see if anyone is headed this way."

Mallory stepped out of the doorway, looking between Ryan, who searched the body, and Jorgen, who looked out the window. "We need to see how everyone else is doing."

Ryan put a dark green shirt in his backpack and handed Mallory three copper pieces. "I'll put this body in the bedroom with the other one first."

Jorgen turned away from the window. "There's no one nearby."

"Hopefully that means no one ran off to warn the rest of the invaders." Ryan hoisted the body onto his shoulder and carried him to the bedroom, dumping him next to the other body.

Mallory entered the room and closed the door. "We've taken out nine. Eleven if the others took out the two in the granary. If the information is correct, we've taken out about a third of them."

Ryan stood by the trapdoor, waiting for Jorgen to climb down the ladder. "That's still too many for us to face all at once."

She tried not to think about being attacked by

twenty enemies. The image filled her mind anyway. "Did you have to mention it?"

Ryan grinned, gesturing towards the trapdoor. "You can go next."

"We can't face twenty. We wouldn't survive." She climbed down the ladder, still trying to rid her mind of the image. It would be a slaughter. They'd take a few out, but not all of them. There was only seven of them, eight if you counted the villager who had no weapon. It'd be an impossible fight.

Ryan came down the ladder, closing the trapdoor, plunging them into darkness. "We have revives."

"Smudge and Fang don't." She took a hesitant step in the direction she needed to go. "We need a lantern." When someone took her hand, she flinched. "You could have warned me."

"I'm sorry," Jorgen said. "I can see better in the darkness than you can."

Ryan chuckled. "Lead the way. Should I hold Mallory's hand instead of both of us holding one of yours so we can be in a line rather than crowded in the tunnel like this?"

"If you like." Jorgen placed Ryan's hand in Mallory's before starting along the tunnel.

Seeing the light of the open trapdoor at the other end, Mallory was able to walk faster. She checked her journal as she healed Ryan and Jorgen for the health they'd lost. Brodie and Callum were both down five health each. "They've been fighting." As she watched, Brodie lost four more health. "They're still fighting."

Reaching the ladder, Jorgen let go of Mallory's hand. "Can you make me invisible?"

She waited until he neared the top of the ladder before she cast the spell. "I need to level it up. Or get one that lasts longer."

"We'll see what we can find next time we're in a decent sized village or town." Ryan gestured for her to go up the ladder first.

"This place would have been a decent sized village." Clambering up the ladder, she made herself invisible before she entered the granary. Turning, she watched for Ryan, doing the same to him before he left the safety of the tunnel. A glance around the area showed the archer was dead and the mage was struggling against the overwhelming odds. About to cast a fireball at him, she caught movement near the door. "Rogue trying to escape." She threw two fireballs at him, following them up with poison dart.

The rogue half opened the door, unable to fully open it when Jorgen turned into a wolf and leapt across the room to land on him. The door slammed shut.

Chapter Seventeen

Mallory looked from the door to the mage, who crumpled on the floor. It felt like everything stopped for a split second. Then they all burst into action, helping Jorgen attack the rogue, arrows sinking into him.

Ryan ran forward, glancing over his shoulder to Callum. "Get up the top and see what's in the area." He attacked the rogue who was once again on his feet.

"Intr-" The rogue's cry was cut off mid-word.

Brodie looked up at Callum. "Do you see anyone?"

"Give me a minute." Callum checked the other windows. "There's no movement out there. Or at least no movement out of the ordinary. I can only see eight." He started down. "I'll show you where they are on the map Rodina gave us."

"Fang levelled up," Brodie exclaimed. "She finally levelled up."

Callum reached the floor. "I gained a CAS point when we took out that rogue."

"I'm never going to catch up," Brodie muttered.

Emica grinned at him. "I've gained a CAS point while we've been in this village too."

"So have I," Jorgen said.

Laughing, Mallory continued to heal her companions, able to heal Callum now he was closer. By the time Callum had pointed out all the locations, and the path each enemy seemed to be taking for those on patrol, they were all at full health. "What do we do next?"

"We get the potions." Ryan put the map away. "Someone needs to check to see if the orc mage is at Rodina's house and if he is, activate the sleeping mist so we can take all the potions from him."

"Talking of searching, we should search this lot before we go." Callum gestured to the three bodies scattered around the granary.

"If Mallory comes with me, I can go the last part of the way on my own and put the sleeping mist balls next to the orc mage," Jorgen offered.

"I can do that," Mallory said.

"How will we know when to come after you?" Brodie asked.

"You won't." Mallory took a step towards the door. "You can all work on taking out the rest of them before they can give the alarm. Particularly the ones guarding the mine."

"If we wait until the end of the work shift the guards will bring the miners up with all the crystal they've mined," the villager said. "The miner who escaped said they started at six and were brought up every five hours for a water break and to unload the crystal."

"What's the time?" Callum asked.

Ryan took out the pocket watch. "Do those five hours include the time they take to unload and their water break or does it start after their break?"

"Includes the unloading and break. Their final knock off time is nine in the evening," the villager said. "They only have time to eat a meal in the morning and one in the evening and sleep. The rest of the time they spend mining. He didn't know if they'd continue to work them like that, but that's what they've been doing since the village was captured."

"It's a quarter to eleven." Ryan returned the pocket watch to his belt pouch.

"No wonder I'm getting hungry," Brodie muttered.

"We need to get started if we want to rescue the miners when they're brought up. We have fifteen minutes to take out eight enemies and whatever might be in the buildings and take the potions from the orc mage."

Callum rose from the bodies he'd searched. "Another two spare arrows, belt pouch, two silver and five copper pieces, small essence crystal, a ring worn by the rogue and a mana potion." He handed the coins, crystal and potion to Mallory and the ring to Brodie.

"I wonder what it does." Brodie slipped it on his finger. "It does nothing."

"Just because it doesn't have a buff doesn't mean it doesn't do something," Danae said. "It might work with another skill or ability."

"Worry about it later. We need to get this done," Ryan said.

Mallory turned to Jorgen, who nodded before she could ask him if he was ready. She cast the spell on the two of them, heading out the door when it half opened. It was easier making their way towards Rodina's house now they knew where all the enemies were and she followed Jorgen's whispered instructions of each destination they were to head to. The last instruction brought them to a window along the side of Rodina's house.

Mallory cast vanish I on the two of them before she peered in the window. The orc mage was standing in front of an archer, a finger pointed at him.

"Find out."

"Yes, sir." The archer backed away. "But how–"

The orc strode towards the archer, finger still pointed at him. "Do you expect me to do your job for you?"

The archer continued to back towards the door. "No, sir."

"Order the slaves brought up out of the mine. That should draw in whoever is targeting us."

"We have to do something now." Mallory fumbled in her satchel for the tin containing the sleeping mist balls and vial of activation potion.

"Give me the sleeping mist balls and I'll set one beside the two of them." Jorgen placed an invisible hand on her arm.

Mallory put the tin in his hand, half wishing she could hear him so she knew when he moved away. But that would mean an enemy might hear him. She crept towards the front of the house, careful not to make a sound. She wanted to be at the front of the building to cast Vanish I on Jorgen when he reappeared. She peered around the corner of the house.

The archer stepped out the door. "I'll take care of it. I swear."

The orc remained in the doorway. "You better."

An invisible hand dragged Mallory away from the edge of the house and out into the open. Before she could protest, a cloud of mist rose from the ground near the doorframe. The orc and archer collapsed.

Jorgen appeared beside Mallory. "Wait for the mist to disperse before you go near them. And make us invisible." He glanced around the area.

She quickly cast vanish I, also scanning the area. No one was nearby. "I thought it was meant to take five minutes to activate." She stared at the prone bodies. "That wasn't even a minute."

"Adding a second drop speeds up the activation process. Reduces it to thirty seconds."

"How long will it take to disperse?" Mallory asked.

Before Jorgen could reply, there was a shout behind them. "You'll know. I'll help everyone else. Stay here with the orc. Someone might steal the potions if you leave them."

"Jorgen?" When he didn't answer her, she assumed he'd left. She faced the bodies, watching as the mist faded away. When there was none left, she took a step forward. Was that what he'd meant? That she'd no longer be able to see the mist. She moved closer to the house, recasting vanish I when she became visible again.

Chapter Eighteen

Taking another step, Mallory breathed deeply. Nothing happened. She made her way to the orc and archer, spotting a satchel. She slipped the strap off the orc, rolling him so she could pick the satchel up. It didn't take her long to realise the satchel wasn't all she could take. Removing the longsword, belt and belt pouch, she set them aside. There was also fifteen silver pieces in the belt pouch along with a letter demanding five chests of essence crystals be shipped to Cutthroat Harbour by the eighteenth. A sound drew her attention and she turned to see a herd of goats run along the road.

Behind the goats ran two archers, yelling threats as they chased after them. Mallory crouched lower, dragging the bodies inside, all the time expecting to be spotted. She brought the gear inside too, startled by movement in her peripheral vision. Spinning, she saw Jorgen enter the room.

"What's going on?" She gestured out the front.

"One of the guards at the mine entrance spotted your brother. We convinced them it was goats." Jorgen nodded to the satchel. "Are the potions in there?"

"I haven't checked." Mallory picked up the satchel and looked inside. There was a variety of vials. She moved over to a table that was in the middle of the room and carefully set the potions on it, sorting them into groups.

"I'll find rope to tie up these two." Jorgen left by the door he'd entered through.

Mallory counted the various potions. Three health potions, four mana potions, two invisibility potions and eight revive potions. She rested her hands on the table, the timber cool beneath her palms. They didn't have enough. Turning, she faced the orc. Maybe he carried more in a pocket or something.

Jorgen returned at the same time as Mallory finished searching both the bodies. She watched him tie them up. "I can take everything on them if I want."

Jorgen nodded. "Their items haven't lost all

durability in a fight. You can't take items that have no durability left."

Brodie stepped inside the house in time to hear the comment. "We should knock them out instead of killing them in future. We'd get more loot."

Mallory rose to her feet. "Are the villagers safe?"

"Ryan said we need you." Brodie turned to Jorgen. "Both of you. There's one rogue left and he's threatening to drop a potion he calls poison mist if anyone moves. He wants us to leave. Ryan is slowly backing away to keep him busy, pretending to negotiate with him."

Mallory returned all the potions to the satchel and slipped the strap over her head and arm. There'd be time enough later to share the bad news. She gathered up the rest of the items she'd taken from the orc. "I didn't have the chance to search the other body."

Brodie took the belt and belt pouch from her. "This way."

Not knowing what else to do with it, Mallory added the longsword to her belt before following her brother, Jorgen beside her. "Where are we going?"

"Where Ryan said would be the best place for you to attack from." Brodie glanced over his shoulder. "There's enough cover that the rogue won't see you and you'll be able to get close before you need to go invisible."

Jorgen strode ahead of Brodie. "I see where you mean. You can stay back here. The fewer going close to the rogue the less chance we have of catching his attention."

Brodie remained where he was. "I'll search the bodies to make sure you didn't miss something."

Mallory nodded, continuing to follow Jorgen. She checked everyone's stats, grinning when she noticed Brodie had gained a CAS point, as had Ryan and Danae. No wonder her brother had been so happy. He was gaining experience points again.

Jorgen glanced over his shoulder, nodding to her.

Mallory cast vanish I on him, creeping closer so she could cast it again if she needed to. She peered around the edge of the building.

A rogue was surrounded by wounded and dejected people, holding up a potion vial. "I mean it. Keep moving or I'll smash this against the ground. I've got a revive. I doubt any of these slaves have one."

Mallory's grip tightened on her wand. She wanted to attack him, but wasn't about to risk killing the villagers surrounding him. She tried to figure out where Jorgen would be. Not having a clue, she stared at the potion. It was plucked from the rogue's hand.

He spun to face the people around him, drawing out a stiletto. "Who took it? Answer me now."

Before he had a chance to attack, lines of blood appeared across his body and the villagers scattered. Jorgen became visible, darting in and out.

Mallory cast vanish I on him before throwing a fireball at the rogue. Several arrows struck him at the same time. Before Emica could come close to attack, the rogue dropped towards the ground, vanishing before he hit it. Mallory came away from the building, taking a step towards where the rogue had been. Was that it? Had they taken out all the enemies?

One of the miners came forward. "Who are you?" He looked from Mallory to Jorgen then to Ryan who stood with the rest of them except for Brodie.

The villager Rodina had sent with the message, came out of hiding. "Rodina sent them. Some of us escaped and made it to Kyla's farm."

The villagers crowded forward, asking about various people.

Ryan interrupted the noise. "Are there any more invaders here?"

The miner, who'd initially come forward, stepped away from the crowd. "The rogue has a demonic spider. It's roaming the mine."

Brodie joined them, Fang following him. "Is that

it? A spider?" He carried a cloth bag, bulging with items. He glanced over his shoulder. "Someone might want to guard the two in Rodina's house so they don't try and escape."

"Why bother guarding them? We should kill them," one of the villagers called out, several agreeing with her.

Mallory hurried forward. "Rodina wants to deal with them. I told her we'd leave them for her."

The angry mutterings died down. The miner who'd first spoken gestured towards the mine entrance. "Who's going to deal with the spider? It's going to be angry someone took out its companion. And I for one don't want to face a seven and a half foot tall spider."

Brodie's mouth dropped open. "Seven and a half feet tall. You've got to be kidding."

"I'm sure all those who have a share in the mine would be willing to reward some adventurers for dealing with it," the miner said.

Brodie groaned, shaking his head. "No way. I don't care what the reward is, we're not completing that quest."

Smiling, Mallory brought up her journal and read over the quest. *Angry Companion: The owners of the Velkden Crystal Mine would be willing to pay to have something done about the demonic spider wandering the tunnels and shafts.* She had to agree with Brodie on this one. There was no way she wanted to face a seven and a half foot tall spider. Huntsman spiders were bad enough and they were the size of her palm. She shuddered, trying not to picture what it would look like. An image formed and she shuddered again.

"We should search the village to make sure we cleaned it out of invaders then return to the farm," Callum said.

"I can run over and let Rodina know you've rescued everyone," the villager offered.

Callum shrugged. "If there are any left, it shouldn't be too many."

"We'll help search." The miner turned to those who'd been held captive with him. "We'll grab picks from the storehouse."

"Let Rodina know," Ryan said to the villager.

With a nod, the villager ran in the direction of the farm.

Mallory watched him go, smiling at Ryan when he joined her. "Are you okay?" She checked his journal before he could speak, slipping an arm around his waist and healing him. "We should go home before Brodie has the chance to break another bone."

"I heard that." Brodie strode towards her. "It wasn't

like I wanted to be shot in the knee. It could have easily been one of you."

Callum smiled. "I doubt it. You were the one running into danger."

"You're going home tonight?" Danae asked.

Callum glanced around. "It doesn't have to be tonight. We could go for a couple of hours. If we returned after school not much time will have passed here."

Emica and Jorgen joined them, Emica gesturing south. "What about rescuing my father?"

"It'd be better leaving for a few hours while everyone is somewhere safe than returning home while we're on the road," Ryan said.

"We could help move the injured villagers while you're gone," Danae said.

"We don't even know if the village is empty," Emica said. "For all we know, there could be invaders hiding in one of the buildings."

"I doubt they'll survive long." Ryan looked in the direction of the storehouse. "Those villagers looked ready to take on anything when they came out of the storehouse with picks."

"Except seven and a half feet tall spiders," Brodie muttered.

"Cutthroat Harbour is less than three hours from

here," Callum said. "We could leave at daylight tomorrow and arrive well before lunch."

Chapter Nineteen

Mallory drew away from Ryan, scanning the village. From where she stood, she saw the freed captives searching the nearby buildings, easily spotted. "We have night vision potions."

"What about them?" Emica demanded.

Mallory faced the group. "Cutthroat Harbour is their base in the area."

Several of them nodded.

"What are you getting at?" Emica asked.

"There were approximately thirty here," Mallory said.

Callum interrupted before Mallory could continue. "Twenty-six. Unless you count the ones we ran into at the wayshrine."

"So it's logical that there will be more than thirty at Cutthroat Harbour," Mallory said.

"Are you trying to get out of going after my father?" Emica demanded.

Mallory shook her head.

Ryan grinned. "We go at night."

Mallory nodded. "Yes. We go at night."

Emica frowned. "We'd be at a disadvantage. They'd know the area."

"Maybe someone around here knows Cutthroat Harbour or could tell us something about it," Callum suggested.

"If we arrive when most are asleep, we can get in, search the place and get out with any captives before they realise we're there." Jorgen nodded to Mallory. "With the help of a spell or two."

"I won't be able to cast vanish as often," Mallory said. "I need to return the jewellery."

"Not all of it. You can keep the bracelet."

Mallory turned to see that Rodina strode towards them, several villagers with her. "I can?"

Rodina nodded. "It will generate one mana every fifteen seconds. Not the best regen, but I'm sure it'll help."

Mallory tried to return the essence crystal first, surprised at how little colour there was in it.

Rodina shook her head. "You keep it. There's very little mana left in it. Ninety at the most. Then it'll crumble into a clear, gritty dust only good for artists and potters who use it to give a shine to their work."

Mallory dropped the crystal into her satchel then slipped off the rings, returning them. "Thank you." She ran a finger across the plain, silver bracelet before opening the satchel from the orc. "We didn't get enough potions." She took out the eight revive potions, handing them over.

Rodina took the potions. "This is good. A half dose of a revive potion can be used to lengthen the amount of time the body will last before the rest of the dose needs to be administered. It will give us a week. There's an apothecary in Wrentville who can make revive potions. We'll be able to mine enough essence crystals to afford doses for everyone. The miners can work overtime to pay back the share that goes to the owners since the village is only entitled to ten percent of the profits."

"You need to use a full one on the child and the cousin of the one you sent after us," Mallory said.

Rodina inclined her head. "I'll see to it personally."

"I think you're forgetting something," Callum said.

"An overgrown spider," Brodie muttered.

"Spider?" Rodina looked at each of them.

Ryan was the one who explained what Callum meant.

Rodina sighed heavily. "I don't suppose you're interested in taking on a demonic spider? I daresay my villagers would complain if I chose to go after it. I also have no idea what we have left of value and how much damage the invaders have caused. We might be able to scrape together the funds to buy the potions, but I'm not completely certain."

"Why don't you see what you can manage first?" Ryan asked.

Rodina stared at him for a moment, her brow furrowed. "Give us a few hours to sort ourselves out and then I'll see that you're paid for rescuing those trapped in the mine and taking our village back from the invaders."

Ryan grinned. "Sounds like just enough time." He glanced at Emica who glared at him.

Rodina looked between the two of them. "I'm missing something, aren't I?"

Danae laughed softly. "Yes, but I think you're better off not knowing."

"We need somewhere to shower." Mallory glanced down at herself. There was no way she could turn up at school dirty, sweaty and streaked with the blood of her enemies. That thought made her think of Rass. It was nice not to have needed to face him for a change.

Then she was certain there would have been a lot more blood on her.

"I have a washroom you can use," Rodina offered.

Mallory started to thank the elder. She was interrupted by a villager running up to them.

"There are two naked invaders tied up in your house."

Mallory turned to her brother. "Brodie!"

Grinning, he shrugged, glancing at the cloth bag he carried. "Not like they need the stuff."

Ryan chuckled. "Let's get sorted out and cleaned up so we can be back here in a few hours."

"We need lunch too. I bet it's midday," Brodie said.

Fang barked, as if in agreement.

"See, Fang is hungry too."

"You're as bad as each other." Mallory looked from Brodie to Fang and back again. Her brother didn't look in the least bothered by her comment.

"Where is it you're going?" Jorgen asked once Rodina and the villager had left.

"To our world," Callum said.

"Can I go there too?" Jorgen asked.

"Why would you want to go to their world?" Emica made a sweeping gesture. "I bet you haven't even seen all of this one."

Jorgen shrugged. "I'm a traveller." He spoke the words like they explained everything.

Mallory guessed they probably did. "You look like someone from our world."

"So I could travel with you?" Jorgen asked.

"I wish I could go back with you," Danae said wistfully.

Mallory glanced at everyone. Callum shrugged, Ryan grinned and Brodie was busy patting Fang and telling her they'd eat soon. "Ryan could keep an eye on you. But I have to warn you, our world is nowhere near as interesting as Inadon."

Jorgen's lips slowly curved into a smile. "Every world, every location, is interesting to those who've never visited before." He held out a hand. "Did you wish to add me to your group now?"

Mallory placed her hand on his. "Accept party member Jorgen." She was half tempted to ask him to share journal information with them so she could see exactly how high his stats were. He had to be at least character level six since he was able to dual wield stilettos. Instead, she lowered her hand, words unspoken. Turning to her brother, she nodded to the bag he carried. "What did you take?"

"Mage robe, a brown pair of trousers, a khaki shirt, leather belt, two pairs of leather boots, a hunting knife and six copper pieces. And they weren't naked. I left their undergarments on them. As if I was going to take them off." Brodie muttered the last few words.

"Time to get moving." Ryan started for the farm, glancing over his shoulder. "We don't have all day. Not if we want to eat before we leave."

Brodie hurried after Ryan, first handing over the coins to Mallory that he took out of the bag. Fang darted back and forth, checking out the area and attempting to chase anything that moved, returning to Brodie each time he called her back.

Brodie glanced at Smudge asleep in Callum's makeshift pouch. "I'd try and put Fang in one of those, but I doubt she'd stay in one for long. Not with how active she is."

Chapter Twenty

Arriving back at the farm, they packed away the items they'd gained and Mallory gave everyone a silver piece from the fifteen she'd taken off the orc mage, putting the other six with the group funds. She also put all the potions in her satchel and gave the orc's satchel to Jorgen, as well as giving him and Emica a belt pouch each. Jorgen handed over the vial of poison mist, warning Mallory it would kill her too if she used it near herself. It was the type of weapon you threw from you so it smashed several metres away.

"How much health does it take?" Callum asked.

"Sixty," Jorgen said.

Mallory took two calico cloths out of one of the panniers and nestled the potion vials in amongst them in her satchel. She really needed a more secure way to carry the potions. Although the vials seemed to be fairly durable. Closing the satchel, she rummaged through their gear for her clothes to wear home.

They returned to the village with their change of clothes, leaving Ninette and Kruth to help pack up the wagon and escort it to Velkden. Brodie was the first to have a wash, winning the roll of the dice. When he came out, he asked to borrow the nib pen and ink from Mallory.

"What for?" She longingly watched Callum head to the washroom. She'd ended up with the worst roll and would be last.

"To write some of my recipes on my arms. I'm sure I can figure out how to make them back home," Brodie said.

She stared at her brother for a moment. "You do know not all the ingredients will be available in our world."

Ryan chuckled. "I'm sure he can substitute normal crab for coastal crab and beef for bear."

"I was thinking about the blueberry pancakes. They turned out good." Brodie took the pen and bottle of ink from Mallory.

"Don't use it all up or I will need to buy more ink," she warned him.

When Callum came out, he took the pen from

Brodie once he was finished and drew demonic runes on his arms.

"Make sure you don't draw actual words," Danae warned. "You can never be too careful when it comes to demonic runes."

"What if I leave plenty of space between each letter?" Callum looked up from his arm.

"That should work," Danae said.

Once Mallory had washed, she came out to find the wagon was set up beside Rodina's house and Brodie had cooked venison steaks along with some finely diced vegetables. While she ate some food, Mallory checked everyone's health and stats. Or at least those whose journals she could see. She only had five more experience points before she'd reach level five. A smile escaped. Brodie wasn't going to be impressed with that. Especially since he needed a hundred and eleven experience points for his next CAS point and needed a total of five CAS points before he reached level two.

Everyone else was well ahead of him. Ryan had seventeen of the hundred and fifteen experience points of his next CAS point and only needed three CAS points to reach character level two. Callum had the same amount of CAS points as his brother, but he had twenty-four of the hundred and fifteen experience points needed for his next CAS point.

Danae was nearly halfway through character level two with six of the hundred and twenty-two experience points needed to reach halfway. With everyone so far ahead of him, Mallory was pretty certain Brodie would be focused on wanting to level up when they returned to Inadon.

They weren't ready to leave until one, putting most of their gear in the wagon.

"You will be back in a couple of hours," Emica said.

Mallory nodded, smiling reassuringly. She had a feeling it hadn't made a difference. Emica continued to look worried. "For every hour we're in our world, only ten minutes will have passed here. We'll be back in plenty of time to go to Cutthroat Harbour."

"I hope so." Emica returned to the fire. She sat beside Fang who rested her head on her paws, her gaze following Brodie, occasionally whining. Smudge was curled up on one of the blankets in the wagon, having already scolded Callum when he said he was going home.

Mallory went through the usual spiel, making sure she left behind those of the party who weren't going with them. Like always, the world went black with sounds, smells and sensations fading. Smells returned first, followed by sound, sensations and light. They were back at the apartment.

"Hey." Brodie swiped at a cockroach scurrying across the bench, grabbing his backpack. "There better not be any of them in our gear."

Jorgen did a slow turn. He wore his trousers, shirt and boots, having left the rest of his gear behind, including his belt and weapons. "This is your world?"

Ryan chuckled. "Certainly not the best of it."

Mallory took the disc out of the laptop and put it in its case. Grabbing her backpack, she put the disc case in it. "I need to get changed for school."

"So do I." Brodie hurried to the bedroom.

Mallory headed to the bathroom at a slower pace. She couldn't help thinking about everything that had happened this time and the things they still needed to do. Her phone made a noise, indicating an incoming message, quickly followed by a second one. She left it in her backpack. They would only be messages from the guardians. She'd check them on the way to school.

Once they were ready, they headed for the van. Mallory walked beside Ryan, her fingers entwined with his, smiling as she listened to Brodie's explanation to Jorgen's questions.

Callum came alongside her. "Should we rescue him?" He glanced at Jorgen.

Mallory laughed. "I think someone needs to or he'll have no idea about anything." She grinned at her brother when he glared at her.

Callum started to move away, coming closer to Mallory instead. "Did you realise that only two people would be able to have the full dose when you said who the revive potions should be given to?"

"Why didn't you say something?" Mallory asked.

Callum stopped at the front of the van to face her. "Would it have made a difference?"

She started to say yes, but ended up shaking her head. She let go of Ryan's hand when he started to walk around to the driver's side. "No. I still would have chosen them. It was the right thing to do." She shuddered. "I really hope we don't need to face a seven and a half foot spider."

Brodie opened the back door, Ryan having unlocked the van. "It's not happening. Not at all." He got in the van. "Can I borrow your notebook? I need to write down my recipes and I probably shouldn't write them in any of my school books."

"Don't you carry scrap paper?" Mallory dropped her backpack on the floor of the van as she sat on the front passenger seat.

"I have scrap paper." Once Callum was seated, Jorgen next to him, he took out some paper and handed it to Brodie, along with a pen. He kept some paper for himself and took out another pen. "I need to write down the runes."

Mallory checked the messages on her phone as Ryan started the van, reading the news headlines aloud. "Members from a notorious gang taken down, family reunited, well-loved companion rescued, grave looters prevented from getting away with their crime, man's search for idol ends in tears."

"That last one doesn't sound good," Callum said.

"Did we get paid for it?" Brodie asked.

Mallory shrugged, checking the other message. "Danni was paid two gold, eight silver and two copper pieces and the same amount has been deposited into the Inadon International Bank for Jorgen of the crystalline wolf clan. Temporary code to access the account is five thousand two hundred and forty-eight. A new code will need to be set upon initial access."

"That's not fair," Brodie exclaimed. "Now we hardly get any money."

"I forgot about that," Ryan said.

"I can pay it back to you when we're near a bank."

Jorgen leaned forward. "Was that exactly what it said? Only my clan. No reference to parents."

Mallory checked again, turning in her seat to face him. "Only your clan."

"They didn't make it." Jorgen momentarily closed his eyes, lowering his head.

"Who didn't make it?" Callum asked.

"My parents."

Chapter Twenty-One

Silence filled the van and Mallory tried to think of a way to break it. "Are you certain?"

Jorgen nodded. "We are always referred to as the child of someone and then our clan. Until our parents have passed on."

"Maybe demons do things differently," Callum suggested.

Jorgen met his gaze, slowly shaking his head. "No. Everyone knows how to address us."

"We didn't," Brodie said.

Jorgen smiled sadly. "You aren't of my world. I wouldn't expect you to know."

"Do you have any other family?" Callum asked.

"I hope so," Jorgen said.

Callum rested a hand on his shoulder. "We'll be in Cutthroat Harbour soon and find out if any of them are there."

Jorgen rested his hand over Callum's for a moment. "Thank you." He glanced at each of them. "And thank you for the opportunity to visit your world. It means a great deal to me."

Mallory nodded, having no idea what to say. She checked her bank account balance. "I was paid a hundred and forty-four dollars."

"I guess that's one way of splitting up the extra," Callum said. "If we were paid for all the quests mentioned, that means we were paid four hundred and fifty dollars for taking out members of the dark forces. Approximately fifteen if you average it at three levels each."

"I don't remember seeing that many hellions," Brodie said.

"Not all members of the dark forces are hellions," Jorgen said.

"Jorgen is right," Mallory said. "The payments are for members of the dark forces. Nothing was said about them needing to be hellions."

Ryan pulled up out the front of their school, leaving the engine running. He drew Mallory to him. "I'll see you this afternoon."

She returned his kiss, nodding when she drew back. Grabbing her backpack, she glanced over her shoulder before getting out of the van. "See you this afternoon, Jorgen."

Jorgen once again leaned forward, staring at the view through the windscreen. "Yes. I will see you then."

Callum slid the back door open, jumping out. "Hop in the front. You'll get a better view of everything and my brother won't have to look like a chauffeur."

"What is a chauffeur?" Jorgen joined them on the footpath, slowly looking around.

Callum chuckled. "Ryan will have to explain that to you. They don't appreciate it when we're late to class and I still need to change into my uniform." He hoisted his backpack onto his shoulder and waved. "See you this arve."

Mallory followed Callum onto the school grounds, Brodie beside her, glancing over her shoulder several times. The van was still parked on the side of the road when she was far enough on the school grounds that she couldn't see when it left.

"Do you think we should have said no?" Brodie asked. "I mean, not just because of the money, but he doesn't know this world."

"We didn't know anything about his world when we first arrived. I think he'll do better than us." She nodded in the direction she had to go. "I'll see you later."

"Yeah, I guess."

She stood where she was, watching her brother walk away. Surely he was wrong and there'd be no problem from having brought Jorgen with them. Mentally shrugging, she headed to her first classroom.

The day dragged, and as it came closer to the time for school to end, Mallory found herself starting to nod off. They were going to need a nap before they returned to Inadon. They'd obviously not thought everything out properly and taken into account time for sleeping. They'd been too focused on how long it had been since they'd come home because of Brodie's injury.

She couldn't resist a smile, relieved when the bell went, giving her a reason for her smile if someone should ask what she was so happy about. It wasn't that she was happy her brother had been injured, it was more the situation. Gathering her books, she rose to her feet along with the rest of the students, the teacher raising their voice to be heard over the commotion.

Outside the classroom, someone tapped Mallory on the shoulder and she spun to face them, automatically reaching for a wand that wasn't there. She forced a smile to her lips. "Andrea."

"Have I done something wrong?"

Mallory frowned, trying not to glance in the direction of the school grounds exit. "No. Why would you think that?"

"You keep making excuses not to do anything with me."

"Oh." She'd been so focused on Inadon. "Ryan and I–"

Andrea interrupted her. "You've thrown our friendship aside for a boy?"

"It's not like–"

Andrea interrupted her again. "I didn't think you'd be like that. Well, fine then. Don't come complaining to me when you break up."

Andrea strode away before Mallory could correct her. She sighed heavily. It was too late to go after her. She'd already disappeared amongst the crowd of students keen to leave for the day. Not knowing what else to do, Mallory collected the rest of her gear and headed for the exit, relieved to find the van parked out the front, Ryan leaning against it.

He pushed away from the side of the van and came to meet her, taking her backpack and sliding an arm around her waist. "Are you okay?"

"Yeah. Just a misunderstanding with a friend." Not that she knew how to fix the problem. Andrea obviously wasn't interested in what she had to say and had already made up her mind about the situation. "How was your day?" She smiled up at him. "You weren't overwhelmed by all the questions?"

Ryan laughed. "No, but there were a few." He stopped by the passenger door, holding it open for her. "I've got another surprise for you." He took a folded envelope out of his pocket and handed it to her, striding around to the driver's side before she could open it.

Mallory looked between the envelope and Ryan who opened the driver's door. "This is for me?"

"Hop in." Ryan closed the door once he was seated.

"Why does she get a present?" Brodie demanded from the back of the van.

Mallory sat in the front passenger seat and glanced over her shoulder as she buckled up, her backpack on the floor and the envelope on her lap. "What do you think of our world?"

"Messy, smelly, noisy, busy and surprisingly intriguing for all of that," Jorgen said.

Laughing, Mallory faced forward and picked up the envelope. She felt something small and hard inside. "What is it?" She slipped her finger under a corner and ran it across the back to break the seal.

"Look inside and see." Ryan started the van and pulled out onto the road.

She tipped the item into her hand, staring at a shiny, silver coloured key. She stared at it, a smile slowly forming. "We have a place?" Grinning, she faced Ryan. "You rented a place."

"Which one?" Brodie asked. "Is it the shop?"

"Yeah. It's the shop," Ryan said. "Did you want to visit it now?"

Mallory desperately wanted to say yes, but Andrea had slowed her down. "We'll be home late and Mrs Torres will tell Mum."

"Five minutes," Brodie pleaded.

Mallory ran her thumb back and forth over the key she held. "You know it will be longer than that."

"Is it normal to get a place that quick?" Callum asked. "Didn't they need to check references?"

Ryan grinned, glancing at the rear view mirror. "Apparently a guardian knows the owner and told them to let us rent it."

"That's handy," Callum said.

"When can we move in?" Brodie asked.

Ryan glanced at the key Mallory continued to hold. "As soon as we want."

Chapter Twenty-Two

Mallory tried to hand the key to Ryan when he pulled up on the side of the road. "I wish we could move now."

"That's for you," Ryan said. "I already have one."

"What about us?" Brodie demanded.

Ryan chuckled. "Don't worry. You won't miss out. I need to get more cut. I only picked them up about half an hour before school finished."

"I wish we could see it." Brodie slid open the back door, pausing before he exited. "Does this mean you can return the van and get your car back?"

Ryan laughed. "Once we've shifted in. I might need the van to cart furniture and stuff."

Jorgen looked past Brodie who remained in the doorway. "Why have we stopped on a corner?"

Mallory grabbed her backpack and briefly kissed

Ryan before getting out. "We have a nosey neighbour. She tells our mum everything we do."

Brodie slid the back door closed once he was on the footpath. "She needs to get a life."

"I'll see you soon. Come in the laundry door. I'll unlock it for you." Mallory closed the door when Ryan nodded, striding along the footpath towards home.

"It feels odd being back here." Brodie looked up and down the street. "And Jorgen is right. It's smelly and noisy."

Mallory smothered a yawn, slipping the new key into her backpack. "I wonder how many guardians move to Inadon."

Brodie yawned, glaring at Mallory. "Did you have to? Now I'm going to be yawning all afternoon."

"We should have a nap before we return. A couple of hours. Otherwise we're going to be too tired to face Cutthroat Harbour." Mallory stepped up onto the concrete patio, unable to resist glancing across the road to see if Mrs Torres watched. The curtain twitched and she turned her back on the woman before she smiled.

"I'm sick of her always getting me into trouble," Brodie muttered.

Mallory unlocked the door, swinging it open as she laughed. "I think you manage that all by yourself."

"I do not." Brodie dumped his backpack on the floor beside the door, swinging the door closed.

"I'll get the laundry door." Mallory headed towards the kitchen, leaving her brother rummaging in his backpack.

"I'm going to make some pancakes. I'm sure there are berries in the freezer."

Mallory unlocked the laundry door only seconds before Ryan, Callum and Jorgen arrived, all of them coming inside. When the other two continued through to the kitchen where Brodie was making a lot of noise, Ryan remained with her and she slid her arms around his waist, leaning against him. "I'm so tired."

"Is that what was wrong earlier?" Ryan's arms tightened around her.

"No. It was a misunderstanding with a friend. She thought I'd dumped her over you."

Ryan chuckled. "Probably better to have her think that than try and figure out what the alternative is."

"I guess." She yawned. "We didn't think things through this time. This was a terrible time to return. We're going to be so tired when we go back to Inadon."

"I was going to suggest a nap. We've got time before your mum gets home from work." Ryan glanced towards the kitchen. "What is your brother doing? Other than making a lot of noise."

Mallory laughed. "Apparently cooking."

"I heard that," Brodie called out from the kitchen.

Letting go of Ryan, she stepped over to the doorway. "You were meant to."

Jorgen examined everything Brodie took out. "And you say none of this is magic." He opened and closed the fridge.

Mallory entered the kitchen. "How about we all cook so we can get the food made and the kitchen cleaned up. I don't know about the rest of you, but I need a nap before we return."

"That would be a good idea," Jorgen said. "Especially if, as you've said, only a short amount of time will have passed in my world by the time we return."

"We can leave at five." Callum cracked eggs into the bowl Brodie placed on the bench. "Your mum won't be home until six so we'll have plenty of time. And providing we get finished up here and have the food eaten by four, we'll get an hour's sleep and return to Velkden an hour and a half after we left it."

Mallory took out her phone and checked the time.

"Half an hour. We can eat them as they come out of the pan." She washed her hands at the sink. "What do you need me to do?"

The food was cooked and eaten and the kitchen tidied up only a couple of minutes after four. The five of them sprawled out in the lounge room, Brodie bringing a pillow from his bed and the rest dragging cushions off the couch. Both Mallory and Ryan set alarms on their phones.

Mallory felt like she'd no sooner fallen asleep, than the piercing tone of her alarm was waking her, Ryan's echoing it. She tried to focus on the phone so she could turn it off.

"How long does it take you to turn it off?" Brodie demanded.

Callum staggered to his feet. "I need a coffee before we go. Another half hour won't matter."

Finally managing to turn the alarm off, Mallory staggered to her feet. "In that case, I'm going to have a shower. It might help me wake up." By the time she returned from the bathroom, Callum had finished his coffee and it was nearly half past five.

Ryan set his laptop up on the dining table and Mallory collected the disc from her room where she'd put her backpack, already dressed in the clothes she'd worn back from Inadon that morning.

Before she could put the disc in the laptop drawer, the sound of a vehicle outside caught her attention. She frowned. "That sounds like Mum's car."

Brodie headed to the lounge room to check out the window, running back to the kitchen. "It is." He closed the lid down on Ryan's laptop. "You've got to get out of here before she's inside."

"What is going on?" Jorgen asked.

Mallory placed a hand on Ryan's laptop when he would have picked it up. "Too late. She'd hear you leaving." She gave the disc to Ryan. "Put this in your backpack."

"What's the plan?" Brodie lowered his voice.

"Sit down." Mallory opened the laptop lid up and clicked on a word document. "Jorgen is an exchange student and we're helping him with his homework." She'd barely spoken the words when the front door opened.

Norine stopped in the kitchen entrance. "Why is everyone here?"

"What are you doing home early?" Brodie demanded. "You shouldn't be home until six."

"You think that makes it all right for you to have people here?" Norine came closer to the table. "And who are you?"

"He's an exchange student," Mallory said.

"I think you've been watching too many movies," Norine said.

Jorgen rose to his feet. "I am sorry, mistress." He raised her hand bowing forward slightly and touching it to his forehead. "I'm clearly not welcome here." He let go of Norine's hand.

"You have an accent." Norine stared at him.

Chapter Twenty-Three

Mallory laughed. "I did tell you he's an exchange student." She thought it was the best way to explain the reason why Jorgen sounded a little different from them. It hadn't been as noticeable on Inadon, with the various accents and races.

Norine took a step back. "That still doesn't explain why everyone is here."

"As if he wants us teaching him maths." Brodie glanced at Callum. "So we told Callum to come over."

"What's Ryan here to teach him?" Norine demanded.

Ryan chuckled. "Absolutely nothing. I just tagged along with Callum."

Norine slowly shook her head. "I don't have time for this. I need to catch your father before he goes out and isn't interested in talking to anybody."

"What are you calling him for?" Brodie demanded. "It's not like we're due to visit him any time soon."

Norine strode away, not answering.

Jorgen remained standing. "Will this cause a problem with the time we return to Ruby Isle?"

Callum shook his head. "So we turn up ten minutes later. We'll still be gone less than two hours."

Brodie stared in the direction Norine had taken. "Why do you think she's ringing Dad?"

Mallory wanted to reassure her brother, but had as little idea as him as to what was going on. "I don't know."

"I wonder how close we have to be to each other for the disc to work," Ryan said.

"I'll message Ewen and Kern." Mallory stared at her phone once the message had been sent. No reply came through.

"What if it's hours more before we can leave?" Jorgen asked.

Brodie again glanced in the direction Norine had taken, lowering his voice before he spoke. "We sneak out once Mum goes to sleep. She goes to bed every night at ten."

"We wouldn't be able to leave the moment she went to bed," Mallory said. "She'd need some time to fall asleep."

"Then we leave at midnight. That should–" Brodie broke off at the sound of approaching footsteps. He waited until Norine was in the doorway before he spoke. "Why did you ring Dad?"

"I don't have time for this. I need to pick Alicia up." Norine started towards the front door.

Brodie stepped in front of Norine. "Then why did you come home? You must have been expecting to get into an argument with him. And why do you need to pick Alicia up? Why isn't her car fixed yet? They've had all day."

"They're waiting for a part. Not that it's any of your concern." Norine attempted to step around Brodie.

Mallory rose to her feet. "They're waiting for a part." She walked towards Norine. "When will it arrive?" She had a bad feeling she already knew.

"Next week. I bet it's next week," Brodie exclaimed. "It is our concern. You're going to dump us with Dad."

"Don't be so melodramatic, Brodie, and get out of the way." Norine tried to step around him again.

"We're not going," Mallory stated.

Norine spun to face her. "Don't you start."

"We're not going," Mallory repeated.

"Why should we go there?" Brodie demanded. "He hates us."

Norine stepped to the side looking from one to the other. "He's your father. Why would he hate you?"

"We're still not going." Mallory had no idea how they'd manage to return to Inadon if they were stuck at their father's place all weekend. "Why would you even want to take Alicia to her family reunion? It's not like she's ever going to tell them about you."

"Her family are conservative." Norine took a step back from them. "I need to go. She'll be wondering where I am."

"We've got plans for this weekend," Brodie said.

Norine glanced at Callum, Ryan and Jorgen who stood near the dining table. "You can reschedule. Alicia can't." She headed towards the front door.

Brodie followed. "Tell her to hire a car."

"You know that isn't practical. It'd cost a fortune." Norine opened the front door. "Now drop it, Brodie. The two of you are going to your father's this weekend. You can catch the train after school Friday and return Sunday night." Stepping outside, she closed the door on Brodie's protests.

Mallory stood by her brother. "An entire weekend."

"Fang will miss me," Brodie said.

Ryan joined them, Callum and Jorgen following. He slipped an arm around Mallory's waist, drawing her against him. "We'll figure something out. We can do a heap of quests so we've got more than enough money to pay the rent for our place and accommodation on the Sunshine Coast for the weekend."

Mallory looked up at him. "That might work."

"We'll sort something out so it does work," Callum said.

Brodie checked the time on his phone. "It's nearly six. Let's get out of here before Mum comes back and ruins any more plans."

"I need to write in my notebook," Mallory said.

"We don't have time. And I don't think either of us is going to forget Mum has ruined our weekend and is sending us to Dad's place." Brodie strode to the table, the rest of them following.

Mallory put the disc in the laptop drawer. She looked at each of them. "Ready?" When everyone nodded, Mallory clicked on yes, reaching for Ryan's hand at the same time. The world went black, eventually going back to normal, the wagon in front of them.

Fang leapt to her feet, running over to Brodie to jump up on him.

He crouched to hug her. "I missed you too, girl." He looked over his shoulder. "See. I told you she'd miss me if I'm gone too long. We can't go to Dad's. He never lets us go anywhere."

"Yes, he does. With a really strict curfew. But that doesn't matter. We only need a few minutes and then we can have all the time in the world," Mallory said.

Danae joined them. "What has happened?"

Between all of them they explained what had happened and Jorgen answered some of the questions Danae had about their world.

Danae smiled wistfully. "I wish I could have gone with you."

After giving Fang one more pat, Brodie rose to his feet. "We've got our own place. We'll be able to take you back there soon."

Danae moved closer to him. "How soon?"

Ryan chuckled. "Not this time. We're at Mallory's place. I don't think her mum would be happy having someone else there when she gets home." He paused a moment. "Although we could probably be out of there well before she returns."

Ninette came towards them from the direction of Rodina's house. She waited until she was close before she spoke. "Rodina is ready to see you."

"We're going to get paid for our quests now?" Brodie asked.

"If we're going to finalise some quests, we should add Emica, Ninette and Kruth temporarily to our party so they can gain XP too," Ryan said.

"You would do that for me?" Ninette asked.

Ryan half shrugged, half nodded. "You're helping us out too."

Emica looked at each of them. "Why didn't you do it earlier? We did help level Mallory up."

Ryan half shrugged, a wry grin forming. "I guess we didn't think of it. We'll remove you from the party once the quests have been finalised then add you in again next time we have quests that are ready to be finished up."

Emica nodded. "That sounds fair."

Chapter Twenty-Four

Mallory added each of them to the party, sending Ninette to find Kruth so he could be added before they visited Rodina. Entering the house, Mallory couldn't help looking at the place where she'd left the two invaders. They were gone. The table that had been in the middle of the room was also gone.

There was now a cluster of chairs at one end in front of a fireplace and at the other was a narrow bench running the width of the room. It contained several plates and bowls with an array of fruit, pies and sweetrolls.

Brodie stopped partway across the room, his attention on the food. "We haven't had dinner."

"What were the pancakes?" Callum asked.

"Afternoon tea," Brodie said.

"You missed the midday meal?" Rodina frowned.

Ryan chuckled. "Not exactly."

Rodina gestured towards the food. "Help yourselves. This discussion might go better with something to eat."

Brodie looked between Rodina and the food. He took half a step towards the food before turning back to Rodina. "You don't have anything for a reward?"

Rodina's deep laugh filled the room. "I'm afraid it isn't that simple."

"You plan to ask us to hunt down the demonic spider," Jorgen stated.

"Why would we want to do that?" Brodie hurried over to the food, grabbing several sweetrolls and a pie. He looked down at Fang and sighed before giving her the pie. "Going after it sounds dangerous."

Jorgen took a sweetroll from the bench. "It is worse than dangerous. It's lethal. They're extremely poisonous, have leathery skin rather than the more easily pierced one of normal spiders and they have exceptional hearing so invisibility spells won't be of much use unless you have one that silences you."

Ryan grabbed food for him and Mallory, handing her share over to her before he spoke. "Do they have a weakness?"

"The joins of their body. The skin is weaker in that area." Jorgen sat beside Rodina who used the chair closest to the fireplace.

Mallory sat across from Rodina. "I don't know if we're capable of taking on a seven and a half foot spider that is nearly impossible to kill." She had a bite of the sweetroll and turned to her brother. "You need to learn how to make these."

"I wish." Brodie had a large mouthful, grabbing another sweetroll before he sat in one of the chairs.

Kruth remained by the door. "I would be willing to help you. We had to fight off some spiders that were in the South Peak Mine tunnels. They weren't that big though. Probably half that size."

"We need to get to Cutthroat Harbour," Emica said. "Do you want the king to be woken?"

Rodina looked at each of them. "The ancestral king?"

"Why don't we sort out the quests we have completed then figure out what we're going to do next?" Callum asked.

Rodina nodded. She beckoned forward a villager who remained in the doorway leading to the rest of the house. "Have the chest brought in please."

The villager nodded and retreated through the doorway. He was back a minute later with another villager, both of them carrying a wooden chest between them. They placed it in front of Rodina. Rising to her feet, she opened the lid. She took out a cloth bag and handed it over to Mallory. "Four medium sized essence crystals. They each contain ninety mana. As promised in return for ridding the village of invaders." She took out a small drawstring bag and five potions. "Fifteen gold pieces and five antipoisons in payment for rescuing those held in the mine."

Mallory took the bag and potions, unable to resist looking at the variety of items in the chest. Scrolls, clothes, books, ink, potions, coins, cutlery, linen and two large essence crystals. The journal icon was in the corner of her vision, but she was more interested in knowing why Rodina had so many items brought out than checking to see if she'd levelled up and reading over the quest details.

"What's all the stuff in the chest for?" Brodie asked.

Rodina sat down again. "We don't have enough essence crystals or money to buy the amount of revive potions we need for everyone." She gestured towards the chest. "Even if we sold all these items and hadn't paid you, we wouldn't be able to afford enough potions. The only way we can get the potions we need in time is by mining more crystals. Which we can't do while the demonic spider is roaming the mine."

Ryan glanced at Mallory's satchel where she'd

placed the antipoisons. "Which is why you gave us those potions."

Rodina smiled fleetingly. "Can you blame me?"

"Is that what the chest is for?" Brodie asked. "Payment if we go after the spider."

Rodina inclined her head. "The villagers helped me find things you might be interested in. Crafting ability books, recipes, spells and other odds and ends that you might find useful in your travels. You can also have the chest to store your things in."

"How many recipes?" Brodie peered into the chest.

Mallory almost groaned. "It's seven and a half feet tall, Brodie."

"Yes, but…" His voice trailed off, the sentence finished by a gesture towards the chest.

"You can't be serious," Emica exclaimed. "Do you know how hard it is to kill one of them? They can hear you coming."

Callum looked from Mallory to Brodie and then to Jorgen. "What if they couldn't? We have two rogues with stealth and a mage with vanish I." He turned to Rodina. "Would Mallory be able to borrow the jewellery again?"

"Yes. She could borrow them to help hunt the spider," Rodina said.

"We can't do this," Emica argued. "We have to go to Cutthroat Harbour."

Rodina rose to her feet. "I'll leave you to discuss it. Let me know if you need more information." She strode from the room, the villagers going with her.

Brodie knelt in front of the chest the moment they left. "There's even a blank leather-bound book." He reached for one of the scrolls.

Emica knocked his hand away. "Are you listening? We have to go to Cutthroat Harbour. My father needs to be saved. The entire Green Isles need to be saved."

Ryan rose to his feet. "If we leave here at eleven tonight we'll reach Cutthroat Harbour around two in the morning. The place should be quiet." He took out the pocket watch. "Even taking into account time to pack up, we'll still have more than enough time to track down a spider and take it out."

"How will we track it down?" Emica demanded.

"We won't need to," Jorgen said. "It'll hunt us. All we'll need to do is make plenty of noise."

A shudder ran through Mallory. "This sounds like a really bad idea."

"You don't want to save the rest of the villagers?" Ryan asked. "You want to let them die?"

"I didn't say I wouldn't do it, just that it sounds like

a bad idea." She didn't know if she'd be able to face such a large spider. Normal sized ones gave her the creeps.

"So we tell Rodina yes?" Ryan asked.

Brodie held up a recipe. "Smoky honey sauce. I have honey."

Mallory laughed, echoed by Callum, Ryan and Danae. "I guess that's a yes from you."

"I think we should do it." Callum indicated the chest. "Not because of the things we'll gain, but for the people who'll die if we don't."

"I agree with Callum," Danae said.

"So do I." Ryan turned to Ninette, glancing at Kruth. "Would the two of you be willing to stay behind and help pack up the wagon if we're gone longer than expected?"

They both nodded.

"What about us?" Jorgen nodded to Emica.

"You're welcome to join us in the mine if you want," Ryan said.

"I'm willing," Jorgen said.

Emica glared at Ryan. "I'll join you. Only to get it over and done with quicker."

Callum glanced at Brodie, trying to suppress a smile. "A pity we sold that drum. It was good at catching the attention of nearby creatures. Either that or it was Brodie's playing they objected to."

"Very funny," Brodie muttered when Ryan and Mallory laughed. He rose to his feet. "Are we going now?"

"Give me a minute to sort out my level up," Mallory said.

"Unfair!" Brodie exclaimed. "I'm never going to catch up."

"I gained a CAS point too," Ninette said.

"You can power level later," Ryan said. "For now, let's get ready to take on that spider." He took the recipe from Brodie and returned it to the chest, closing the lid. "Then we can travel to Cutthroat Harbour." He faced Emica. "And rescue everyone there."

"About time," Emica said. "Anyone would think you didn't care if the Green Isles were destroyed."

"We care." Ryan strode to the doorway, calling out to Rodina.

Chapter Twenty-Five

While Ryan let the elder know their plans, Mallory checked her journal. The two quests had more than levelled her up. She now had nineteen experience points of the one hundred and forty-eight needed for her next CAS point. She read the information for the quests. *Free Velkden: You were rewarded with four medium sized essence crystals for your party. You also earned fifteen experience points each. Free The Miners: You were rewarded with fifteen gold pieces and five antipoisons for your party. You also earned ten experience points each.*

She smiled when she saw there was a quest update. *Angry Companion: You have been offered a chest containing various items if you hunt down and kill the demonic spider.* If it wasn't for those in need of revives she didn't know if she'd be willing to go after the spider. It still sounded like a really bad idea.

Finished going over quest details, Mallory levelled up her character, adding her five new attribute points in strength, constitution, intelligence, wisdom and luck. It had been tough choosing between dexterity, charisma and luck as they were all looking extremely low compared to her other attributes, but she was beginning to think they could do with a bit of luck and hopefully that one point might make a difference.

Her new attribute points brought her health up to forty-two, her stamina to seventy, her mana to sixty and her carrying capacity to a hundred and forty kilos. She now regenerated twelve mana a minute, sixteen with the bracelet. Not that mana should be a problem while they hunted down the spider since Rodina was going to let her borrow the rings again. Putting her class point in warrior, she read over the new details. *You have reached level three warrior. You can now wield enchanted dual swords.* She supposed that would be handy when they could eventually afford enchanted weapons.

Finished talking to Rodina, Ryan rejoined them, handing the rings to Mallory. "Rodina said some of the mine tunnels intersect with a natural cave system."

"It's sounding worse by the minute." Mallory slipped the rings on her fingers.

Ryan grinned. "Everyone ready?"

"I really want to say no." Mallory smiled, a wry one containing no mirth.

"Then you should," Emica said. "We could leave earlier for Cutthroat Harbour and search the surrounding area before we attack the village."

"If we're lucky, we won't need to attack Cutthroat Harbour." Ryan led the way out of the house, glancing over his shoulder at those following. "All we need to do is rescue everyone who was captured."

"I doubt it's going to be as easy as you're trying to make it sound," Emica said.

"I didn't say it would be easy. We'll probably need every single potion we have to stay undetected and get everyone out of there alive." Ryan led the way towards the mine. "Rodina said there are some miner's helmets on the platform that takes us into the mine."

Ninette and Kruth headed towards the wagon, both telling them good luck.

Brodie waited until they'd left before he spoke. "What do we need the helmets for? Are the tunnels falling apart?"

"They have lanterns in them," Ryan said. "And I have no idea about the condition of the tunnels."

"Why didn't you say they had lanterns to start with?" Brodie asked.

Ryan started to speak, shaking his head instead.

Callum laughed. "I don't blame you. Probably would have been wasting your breath." Reaching the platform, he looked down at Smudge in the makeshift sling. "Did you want to stay up here? It isn't going to be safe down there."

Smudge chattered at Callum, then ducked down beneath the side of the sling.

Danae laughed softly. "Sounds like he's coming with us."

Smudge popped his head up again, chattering once more.

Brodie crouched in front of Fang. "What about you, girl? Want to wait up here?"

Fang ran over and sat on the platform, clearly waiting for them.

Brodie followed her. "We really need revive potions or actual revives for our companions."

Everyone joined Brodie on the platform and Ryan lit the four miner's helmets. He kept one for himself and handed one to Mallory, Callum and Brodie. "Should I see if they have more?"

Danae shook her head. "We can stay together. It isn't a problem."

"Okay. Then let's get down there and find that spider." Ryan worked the pulley, slowly lowering them into the mine.

Noticing the journal icon in the corner of her vision, Mallory brought her journal up. She'd earned fifteen experience points for discovering a location.

Jorgen turned to Brodie. "We'll only have one chance to do this. If you have no points in stealth, you'll only be able to activate it once an hour."

Brodie drew his stiletto. "What if we can't kill it in the thirty seconds I have to attack silently?"

"The spider will have no way of healing. We could keep it on the move so it continues to bleed out and attack it from a distance. Providing we can stay ahead of it." Jorgen glanced at Danae, Callum and Ryan. "Same goes for the three of you. Aim your arrows where the body segments meet." He looked at Mallory. "Aim your fireballs there too."

"Why are we trying to get close?" Brodie demanded.

"Because that's the best way to get a good hit on it. Attacking from a distance with a range or mage weapon isn't as effective as close up with melee," Jorgen said.

The platform came to a stop, resting on the bottom level of the mine. Mallory took a cautious step off the timber platform and onto the rough stone ground, glancing at Smudge who made soft warning sounds and Fang who regularly growled. "Does that mean something is nearby?"

"Maybe they just don't like the place." Brodie patted Fang on the head. "I don't blame them if that's the reason."

The lanterns didn't light up enough of the darkness and Mallory had no idea what was upsetting the companion animals. Or if it was like Brodie said and they didn't like being down here. "How much noise will we need to make to catch the spider's attention?"

"What if we catch the attention of something else?" Emica asked. "Something worse than a demonic spider."

Jorgen followed Mallory, stepping past her. "I doubt there's anything worse than a demonic spider."

"Great," Brodie muttered. "That almost guarantees something worse will come along."

Ryan chuckled. "Our luck isn't that bad."

Mallory smiled. "Our luck has actually gone up a point. Or at least mine has. Surely that has to help our party in general."

"Is it worth putting a lot of points in luck?" Callum asked.

"It can be," Danae said. "Not just for general luck, but also the better quality resources and items you gain."

They reached an intersection and Mallory looked in both directions as well as ahead. "Which way should we go?"

"We should find a more open area," Jorgen said. "Fighting the spider in these tunnels will be extremely difficult. We need somewhere with more space otherwise we're not going to last long."

It took them half an hour to find a suitable area. It wasn't until they stumbled on the natural cave system that they found a large, cavernous area. The rock overhead was so far above them that even the light on the miner's helmets didn't show where it was. Mallory took several steps inside the open space. "Can anyone else hear those noises?"

Danae stepped forward too, her bow in hand and an arrow ready. "I doubt the demonic spider is all that's in the area."

Callum was off to one side. "It's some of that moss that was in the tunnel. Is it good for anything?"

Danae examined it. "It probably would be, but I don't know what it's used for. I'm afraid my alchemy isn't high enough." She took several steps away from him, pointing to a dark red mushroom with a pitted surface. "I know what that one is. It's a coral puffball, used in disease curing potions."

Chapter Twenty-Six

Mallory hurried forward to pick the coral puffballs. "That's one of the ingredients that can be used in corpse rot poultices."

Brodie stepped in front of her. "No you don't. You've levelled up more than enough."

Ryan chuckled. "I bet he won't be saying that next time he breaks a bone. He'll be wanting you to get the next rapid mend so he can be healed even faster."

"I didn't break the bones. It was that archer." Brodie picked the four mushrooms and put them in Ryan's backpack.

Danae glanced around the area. "I really need to travel to Merrow so I can level up my alchemy more." She gestured towards the moss. "All these ingredients can be turned into potions, salves and ointments and would last a lot longer than storing them fresh, or even dried."

Emica took a step further into the cavern. "Someone should go out there and start trying to attract the demonic spider's attention."

"It can't be me," Brodie said. "Or Jorgen."

"I'll go." Ryan started forward.

Mallory grabbed hold of his arm. "You're not a tank either. At least not yet." She smiled. The group was all a long way off anything like that. "But, I do have the most amount of health. I should be the one to go."

"Mallory, you need to cast–"

She interrupted Ryan. "I can just as easily cast vanish on the two of them from out there as I can from here."

Ryan rested his hand on hers that continued to hold his arm. Eventually, he nodded, grinning. "Maybe we should work on getting to Merrow. We can always come back here and finish up the things we're interested in doing."

"Come back here without Danni?" Brodie asked.

Ryan shrugged. "She could come with us, but I don't know how often she needs to attend the academy."

"It's difficult to explain. They don't expect you there every day. Even every week. But if you don't turn up for a few months and you can't prove you've made progress when you do turn up, they will kick you out of the academy," Danae said.

"What's the point of attending?" Brodie asked.

Danae smiled. "Access to their equipment, knowledge, teachers, recipes, library and also alchemy based quests."

"Are we going to stand around talking all day or is someone going to try and get the attention of the spider?" Emica demanded. "I'm going to Cutthroat Harbour tonight, with or without everyone."

With a smile for Ryan, Mallory stepped away from him. "Any suggestions for catching the attention of a demonic spider?"

"You could try calling out 'here Charlotte, come on Charlotte'," Callum suggested.

Mallory laughed. "And if we spot webs with words written in them, we know we're on the right track?"

"If this spider is as intelligent as the one from 'Charlotte's Web', I think we'll be in a lot of trouble," Ryan said.

"Yeah, let's not think about that possibility." Mallory faced the open area of the cavern, taking several steps forward. Ahead of her, everything was dark, only a small area lit up by the lantern of her miner's helmet.

"What are you waiting for?" Emica demanded.

"Do you need me to go out there and get its attention?" Emica took several steps forward, coming to a stop. "There's something out there."

Mallory peered into the darkness. "Can you see it?"

Emica shook her head. "I can hear it."

"Does it sound big or little?" Mallory took another step forward, not sure she really wanted to. Another step brought her alongside Emica. "I miss spotlights right about now."

"Spotlights?" Emica asked.

Before Mallory could explain, several spiders about the height of a Labrador came out of the darkness. They had dark red, leathery looking skin and large fangs. "Please tell me these aren't demonic spiders." She slowly backed away.

"They're demonic spiders," Emica said.

"I thought we were looking for a seven and a half foot tall spider." Not that she wanted to run into such a large spider.

"They carry their eggs sac on them and when the babies hatch, they scurry up the mother's legs and ride around on her until they can fend for themselves." Emica drew her second sword, the first one having already been in her hand.

"How many do they lay?" Mallory wanted to check over her shoulder to see how close she was to her party, but there was no way she was taking her eyes off the spiders. So far they hadn't moved much.

"Up to a hundred," Emica said.

"You've got to be joking," Brodie said. "We've got to face a hundred of these?"

Mallory ran into someone, but didn't glance behind her to check who it was. Her gaze was firmly fixed on the spiders. "How are we going to face a hundred of them and a gigantic spider too?"

"Their health is between eighteen and twenty-five," Callum said.

"We should take these ones out before more arrive." Ryan placed his hand on Mallory's shoulder. "Are you okay?"

She wasn't sure. "Maybe."

"Smoky honey sauce," Brodie said. "Smoky honey sauce."

"I don't think a sauce is worth having to face them." Emica gestured towards the spiders with her sword. "If we die down here, we won't have as many revives when we reach Cutthroat Harbour."

"If I die down here I won't have any revives for Cutthroat Harbour," Brodie said.

"How's that sauce sounding now?" Emica asked.

Ryan chuckled. "Like it'd probably go nice with

roast venison." He stepped around Mallory. "If we've got a hundred of these to face, we better get started."

"There won't be a hundred." Jorgen held both his stilettos. "At the most, there'll be fifty. Not all of them survive the birth and they tend to fight each other over the food in the area. If we're lucky, they'll be an aggressive lot and have taken out many of their siblings so we only have a couple of dozen to face."

"They don't look all that aggressive to me." Callum moved forward a few steps, putting his spyglass away and readying his bow.

"The more aggressive ones will be with the mother. These will be the weaker ones, chased off by the siblings who are more determined than them to survive," Jorgen said.

Mallory looked them up and down. "They don't look weak to me."

"Nor to me." Danae drew back an arrow, aiming at one of the spiders. "Are we ready?"

Once again Mallory was tempted to say no. She was nowhere near ready to face the spiders. She counted them. Seven. One each. That wasn't in the least bit good. "I'll take the third from the left."

They each called out which one they'd attack. Emica took another step forward. "Are we ready now?"

"About as ready as I'm likely to get," Mallory said.

Brodie nodded. "Smoky honey sauce." He took a deep breath then repeated the words.

Callum chuckled. "Brodie's fearsome war cry."

Mallory couldn't even bring herself to smile.

"Okay. Attack on three," Ryan said. "One, two, three."

Chapter Twenty-Seven

Mallory threw a fireball, rapidly following it up with another one. The spider she attacked ran towards her and she threw a third fireball, braced to attack it once more. It crumpled in a heap on the ground. It took her a few seconds to realise she should be helping the others. She attacked two more spiders, the rest taken out before she had the chance to attack any of them. She stared at the dead bodies littering the ground. "That's it? We did it already?"

Callum lowered his bow. "It wasn't like they had a lot of health." He glanced at Brodie. "Unless it was the fearsome war cry that helped."

"Very funny," Brodie muttered. "I need to collect my throwing knives." He headed for the closest spider, crouching beside it. "They're better XP than goblins and easier to fight. I gained twelve XP from that fight."

Callum collected arrows. "You were meant to focus on taking out your spider, not gaining XP. If Mallory and I hadn't helped you, your spider would have come close enough to attack one of us."

Brodie looked up from the second spider. "I think their fangs can be harvested."

Mallory took a step back. "No way. I am not harvesting spider fangs." She raised a hand as if to push the thought away. "I don't care if they're worth a hundred gold. It's not happening."

"They're probably only worth half that," Danae said.

Mallory stared at her. "What? Fifty gold?" Surely Danae was joking.

"Demonic resources are worth more than normal ones," Danae said.

Jorgen made a sweeping motion with his hand, indicating all the spiders. "If I harvest them, do I gain part of the profits?"

"Everything will be split equally amongst us, and the other two, when we're finished in the mine," Ryan said.

Emica frowned, staring at Ryan for a moment. "You do know that since this is your party and we're just helping out, we aren't entitled to an equal percentage of the profits. We're really only entitled to a hireling fee."

"They know." Danae crouched by one of the spiders, holding the hunting knife. "They often share everything out anyway."

Mallory looked away, unable to watch Danae dig around at the spider's eyes. "I'll go over here further and keep watch for more creatures." She stepped away from the dead bodies.

Ryan chuckled, joining her. "Need a hand with that?"

"We're in a dangerous area. We don't need everyone to see what they can get out of the spiders." Mallory shuddered. "I'm sure there's enough already searching the bodies."

Brodie joined them. "They probably don't need me either."

Emica looked up from the spider she was working on. "Oh, no you don't. Get back over here or give me your miner's helmet."

Danae rose from the spider she'd been crouched beside. "It probably makes more sense for someone else to have the helmet since Brodie will eventually be turned invisible."

Brodie reached for his helmet. "Did you want it, Danni?"

"Didn't you hear me say I wanted it?" Emica demanded.

Danae smiled at Brodie. "Emica can have it."

Brodie handed it to the kitsune. "Won't it make it difficult for you to hear with your fox ears?"

After glaring at Brodie, Emica gave the helmet to Danae. "It wouldn't completely keep me from hearing."

By the time they finished harvesting everything they could from the spiders, they had eight fangs and twelve eyes. They put the eyes into two empty potion vials, six in each. Mallory shuddered when Danae held the vials out to her. The eyes were large enough they touched the sides of the vials, appearing as if each row of them stared back at her. "Ryan can carry them."

Ryan chuckled, putting them in his backpack. "They aren't that bad."

Mallory shook her head. She didn't want to think about them, let alone discuss them. The light from the miner's helmet bounced across the ground. "Should we stay together for now? And do we get rid of all the baby spiders first?"

"How will we know we've got rid of all of them?" Brodie asked.

Most of them shrugged or shook their head, only Jorgen answered. "We don't."

Mallory, who'd started to move further into the open area of the cavern, turned to face him. "If we missed any, they'll grow up to be seven and a half feet tall like their mother."

Jorgen nodded.

"We need to find every single one," Mallory stated.

"We'll do our best." Ryan strode into the open area of the cavern, his light cutting through the darkness. "I've got a feeling the mine is too big an area for us to search all of it in one afternoon."

Danae followed Ryan. "As long as we take out the large spider, the miners and villagers can patrol the tunnels and search for all the smaller ones. They should be capable of taking them out."

Mallory walked at Ryan's side, scanning the area even though she couldn't see very far. She glanced over her shoulder. "Do you hear anything?"

Emica nodded. "There are a lot of different sounds. Nothing nearby."

"Should we make some noise?" Brodie asked.

"You could try your war cry," Callum suggested.

"Very funny," Brodie muttered.

This time, Mallory did smile. "It is, Brodie. Although it's probably just another one of those things you won't find funny. A bit like an arrow in the knee."

Ryan chuckled. "That's not going to get old for a very long time."

"You lot are all–" Brodie was interrupted by one of the smaller demonic spiders dropping on him from above.

Fang barked at the spider, attacking one of its legs. Mallory threw a fireball at it while Emica attacked with her swords. Before the rest could join in, four spiders dropped down from above. Jorgen rolled out of the way and Ryan was able to block one, but Danae and Emica were knocked to the ground.

"I've been bitten." Brodie sank his stiletto into the spider that still had him pinned to the ground.

Mallory backed away, casting fireballs at the spiders, hitting them one after the other. She had no idea what was behind her, but surely it couldn't be worse than what was in front. "How long do we have to give him an antipoison?"

Danae escaped the spider that had her pinned to the ground. "Usually it's until you run out of health. But I don't know a lot about demonic creatures."

Mallory continued to back away, healing her brother twice. A sound behind her had her spinning to see six spiders, one of them looking like it was ready to leap on her. She threw herself to the side and the spider missed her by centimetres. "There's more over here."

"Yes! I killed one," Brodie shouted.

They were outnumbered. The death of a single spider wasn't going to help. Mallory checked behind her, not wanting to back into more spiders. There were two down. She smiled. Maybe they weren't outnumbered after all. She cast weak reanimate on the two dead spiders. She'd barely finished casting the spells, when one of the other spiders jumped on her, knocking her to the ground. The two spiders she'd raised, attacked the one on her, taking it out and going on to another one. Mallory reanimated the newly fallen one, focusing her efforts on casting weak reanimate and healing her companions, particularly her brother.

Brodie sank his stiletto into a spider, taking it out. "Yes! Smoky honey sauce."

"Hopefully not on spiders," Ryan said. "I think that'd be a waste of a good sauce."

Danae laughed softly, firing an arrow at one of the few spiders still standing. "There's actually a dish that uses spider legs in it."

Mallory shuddered, reanimating another spider. "That's one I can do without." The last of the spiders were taken down by her reanimated spiders. The five that were still reanimated scurried off into the darkness. "Where are they going?"

"Something else must be nearby," Danae said.

Mallory looked from the darkness to the bodies scattered on the ground around them. "I have no idea what's out there, but I'm taking an army to face it." She reanimated three more spiders before handing an antipoison to her brother and striding after the spiders that had disappeared into the darkness.

"I can hear them." Emica caught up to Mallory. "Whatever they're fighting, they aren't doing too well."

Chapter Twenty-Eight

Mallory's steps slowed. "Go help them." She urged the three spiders with her to go ahead. They scurried off into the darkness.

"Do you think it's the mother spider?" Brodie asked.

"You better start chanting your war cry in case it is," Ryan said.

"You're not funny, you know," Brodie muttered.

No one laughed. Mallory glanced at each of them, seeing they were all as worried as she was. The smaller spiders had been bad enough. How were they meant to face a seven and a half foot one?

"When we're close enough, cast vanish on us," Jorgen said.

Mallory nodded. What she would have preferred to do was turn around and go back the way she'd come from.

Ryan, who was a little ahead of Mallory, glanced over his shoulder. "You might want to hurry it up so we reach her before your reanimated spiders die again."

Mallory picked up her pace. She hadn't thought of that. She slipped her hand into the satchel and took out the faded essence crystal. She had a feeling she was going to need it.

The sound of fighting became louder and they nearly stumbled upon the large demonic spider, coming around a corner of the cave. Seeing only two of her spiders were still alive, Mallory spun and cast vanish I on Brodie and Jorgen before she turned back and reanimated a couple of the spiders lying on the ground. She needed to draw on the mana in the crystal. "How many times can I reanimate something?"

"Until it's beyond use." Danae fired an arrow at the mother spider. "And that varies with your skill, their level and the type of creature."

Three small spiders leapt down off the back of the mother spider, trying to jump on them. Emica stumbled back, gaining her balance and immediately attacking. Danae focused on the spider Emica attacked while Ryan and Callum each focused on one of the other spiders. Callum had barely managed to put the spyglass away before they were attacked.

"The mother has a hundred and fifty-four health. I don't know how much she had before we attacked her." Callum blocked the spider with his bow, dodging out of the way as he reached for an arrow.

Mallory wasn't sure what to do. Eventually, she wouldn't be able to keep reanimating the spiders. Already there was less of them. She cast a fireball at each of the smaller spiders her companions were fighting, needing them to be killed so she'd have more to reanimate.

The moment the three small ones were dead, she reanimated them and sent them against the mother spider. Seeing first Brodie and then Jorgen become visible, Mallory cast vanish I on each of them. The essence crystal crumbled, becoming dust that drifted to the ground. She felt a moment of fear. What would happen if she couldn't gain mana quickly enough? Or if they took so long to kill the spider that she needed to use up all her mana potions and essence crystals. How would they survive in Cutthroat Harbour?

Mallory backed away from the mother spider. "How much health does she have left?"

Callum retreated before he took out the spyglass. "A hundred and twenty-three health."

Mallory threw fireballs at the joins of the spider's body. "I'm going to run out of creatures to reanimate before she's dead." As she said the words, another one of the small ones collapsed on the ground and she reanimated it.

Callum returned to firing arrows at the spider. "Does it have a weakness? Other than the joins of its body."

Emica darted in and out, slashing with her swords and jumping back before the spider could focus its attention on her. "Water spells."

Mallory started to wish she'd chosen a water spell when she'd had the chance. She immediately changed her mind. The ones she'd chosen had been useful. "Surely there's something else." She kept up her attacks, not using too much magic to make sure she'd have enough when she needed to reanimate another one of the spiders.

Brodie and Jorgen reappeared, Brodie calling out to her when she didn't immediately make him invisible. "Cast the spell, now. It helps." He was knocked back by the spider.

Mallory looked between Brodie, Jorgen and the two spiders that needed reanimating. She cast vanish I as she took out one of the new crystals they'd earned from the last quests. Drawing on the crystal, she reanimated the spiders. "I need more spells. More variety."

"Maybe the ones in the chest we'll earn from this quest will be useful." Ryan slung his hunting bow on his back. "Make me invisible. I can't do much damage with this bow. It's taking too long to kill her. We can't keep this up all afternoon."

Emica continued to dart in and out. "At least you have a ranged option. I don't." She dodged the spider's attack, nearly being knocked to the ground. She stumbled, gaining her balance in time to get out of the way of another attack.

Mallory cast vanish I on Emica. At this rate, she'd go through all the essence crystals. Although she supposed it could be worse. The jewellery Rodina had let her borrow was helping with her mana regen.

"How much health does it have left now?" Danae asked.

Callum fired an arrow before he took out the spyglass to check again. "Ninety-three." He returned the spyglass to its holster and readied an arrow. "There's absolutely no way I'll be able to-" The spider sprang towards him, interrupting his words as he dodged to the side, dropping the arrow he'd readied.

Mallory was also forced to jump out of the way. She reanimated the last two smaller spiders. This time, she attacked with poison dart. "What about flame? I could set her on fire."

The spider spun to attack someone it couldn't see.

"No. Don't set her on fire." Danae shook her head. "We'd risk some of us catching on fire when we attacked her from close up."

Brodie reappeared. "We should have brought Kruth and Ninette with us. Actually, we should have brought all the villagers."

Mallory cast vanish I on both him and Jorgen. "I doubt there'd have been room for that many down here." The section of the cave they were in wasn't as narrow as the mine tunnels, but it also wasn't as spacious as the large cavern.

"I really want to ask how much health it has left," Danae said. "Except it hasn't been long enough."

Mallory knew exactly how Danae felt. "Can you figure out how much I'm hitting for, between my two different attacks?" She needed to know which spell was the better choice to use. They needed to take the spider's health down as quickly as possible. Before she ran out of essence crystals and baby spiders.

Callum took out the spyglass. "I'll give it a go."

"I hope you don't expect the rest of us to stop attacking," Brodie said, still invisible.

"Absolutely not." Mallory couldn't think of anything worse. She reanimated the last small spider.

"Attack a few times so I can figure out which is your attack." Callum held the spyglass to his eye.

Mallory cast fireball four times. "Is that enough?"

"A couple more," Callum said.

She cast another two. "Well?"

"Mostly two, occasionally three."

"From my fireball attack?" Mallory asked.

Callum lowered the spyglass. "What should it normally be?"

"Since I levelled up, a low attack of four, normal of six and crit of nine."

Ryan became visible again. "Can you stop talking and start attacking?"

Mallory cast vanish I at him, stunned to realise she had no more spiders to reanimate and the last one was now dead. She made the other three invisible too. "I'm going to attack with poison dart."

Callum raised the spyglass to his eye. "Hurry up before she targets us."

Chapter Twenty-Nine

Mallory threw poison dart at the spider, needing to wait three seconds each time due to its cooldown. "Well?"

"It's a bit harder to judge because of the damage over time and everyone's attacks." Callum put the spyglass away. "The damage over time seems to be six a second and you attack for five with your initial attack."

"Poison dart it is then." Mallory attacked again.

Callum readied an arrow. "And she's down to thirty-nine health. We seem to be doing better now."

"You should have used poison dart sooner," Brodie said.

Mallory tried to pinpoint where he was, but it was hard when he was invisible. About to attack again, she threw herself to the side when the spider jumped towards her.

"I think she knows who's doing the worst damage out of the ones she can see," Callum said.

Mallory crashed into the wall of the cave when she tried to avoid the next attack. She couldn't do anything while the spider was focused on her. Using up the last of the mana in the essence crystal she held, Mallory went invisible, diving out of the way and spinning to face the spider. She cast poison dart.

The spider spun to face Callum, leaping towards him. Before she could reach him, she dropped to the ground in a heap.

Mallory stared at the spider. "She's dead?" It didn't seem possible. She'd been certain the spider would attack Callum before he could move out of the way.

Callum took out the spyglass, putting it to his eye. "Completely."

Emica, becoming visible, sheathed her swords. "Well, not completely. At least not for a couple of days. Her companion could use a revive potion on her."

"How do we prevent that from happening?" Callum asked.

"Burn the body," Jorgen said.

Danae looked around. "Where are you, Mallory? If you're thinking of using flame on her, wait until we've had a chance to see what resources we can gain from the body."

Mallory took a step back from the spider, running into the wall of the cave. "There is no way I'm looting the body. Someone else can have that job."

Ryan chuckled. "Probably my turn." He took out his skinning knife.

"You should be doing it anyway. Don't you get a bonus for looting the bodies of the creatures you kill?" Brodie asked.

"One percent more likely to get rare resources from wild animals I've hunted. But I don't know if this would be considered a wild animal." Ryan held up a large fang, one the length of his forearm. "I have no idea what this is used for, but it's big enough for a weapon."

Danae took the fang from him. "That would be a waste. They're used for alchemy. One this size would go for a really good price."

Ryan managed to gain another fang, handing it over to Danae while he worked on trying to remove the eyes.

Becoming visible, Mallory hurriedly looked away when Ryan managed to get an eye, the object far too large for her liking. "Tell me when you're finished and you've put them away."

Danae laughed softly. "They aren't that bad. I've handled worse when it comes to alchemy ingredients. Some of the strange items that have come into my father's shop over the years have been worse than this."

Mallory shuddered. "I'm rethinking wanting to have anything to do with alchemy right about now."

Ryan chuckled. "I only ended up with two eyes and they're away now."

Hearing his voice coming closer, Mallory turned to face him. Seeing him reach for her, she sidestepped. "You've been touching spider eyes. There's no way you're coming anywhere near me until you've cleaned off any spider…" Shrugging, she tried to think of what to call it. "Goo."

Ryan grinned. "Is that the technical term?"

"Yes, it is."

Ryan chuckled again. "Okay. Let's get out of here and get cleaned up." He glanced at his hands. "Callum might have helped me wash them with water from the waterskin, but they still feel like they're covered in spider goo."

"Are we going to burn the spider first?" Danae asked. "So it can't be revived. Any decent revive potion will be able to bring it back to the state it was. At worst, there'll be scar tissue where it had to regenerate the missing parts."

Mallory shuddered. "We're burning it." She cast flame at the creature several times, remaining where she was until it was ashes, tugging her tunic up over her nose at the smell.

As they headed back towards the platform, Brodie frowned. "Why didn't we get location XP when we entered the cave? We got it when we entered the mine."

"It's probably considered one location with how it's all together now," Danae said. "Not all mines will give location XP. Some are considered part of the town or village they're in. It depends on how they're set up."

"It would have been nice if we could have looted all the little spiders, but at least we ended up with a nice lot of XP for killing the big spider," Brodie said. "Twelve. No wonder it was so hard to kill. It gave us almost as much as a mine location."

"It felt like a boss fight." Callum stepped onto the platform, moving out of the way so Ryan could use the pulley to take them upwards.

"We wouldn't have managed without the mana regen rings." Mallory glanced at her hands. "Or the essence crystals. I wonder how much they cost to buy."

"I wonder how much we can sell the spider fangs and eyes for," Callum said.

"The fangs will last, but the eyes will rot if we don't find somewhere to sell them within a few days." Danae stepped off the platform the moment it came to a stop.

Mallory smiled at Fang and Smudge who'd finally stopped making regular growling and warning sounds now they were above ground. She was just as glad as them to be out of the mine.

"Is there anywhere on the way to Cutthroat Harbour that we can sell the eyes?" Brodie hurried after Danae who headed towards Rodina's house.

Mallory's smile widened into a grin. If anyone could figure out a way to get the spider eyes sold before they rotted, it would be her brother.

Callum walked beside Ryan. "Can I have the map of Ruby Isle? I don't recall anything nearby, but…" He let his voice trail off.

Ryan handed over the map, striding ahead to collect Kruth and Ninette before they went to Rodina's house.

Callum was still looking at the map as they stepped inside the house, the elder welcoming them inside when she saw them coming. She nodded towards the map, taking the jewellery Mallory returned to her. "Are you looking for somewhere in particular?"

"Somewhere to sell the demonic spider eyes before they rot," Brodie said.

"How many do you have?" Rodina asked.

Mallory winced, looking away when Ryan took them out of his backpack. "Couldn't you have just said how many?"

Ryan chuckled. "There's nothing quite like a visual when it comes to something like this."

"Some visuals are better off not being seen," Callum said.

Mallory was glad someone agreed with her. Before she could tell him that, Rodina spoke.

"Would you be willing to trade essence crystals for them? We could trade these directly to the apothecary and not have to find someone else to buy the essence crystals first. The apothecary will only take so many essence crystals in trade."

"We don't know how much they're worth," Ryan said.

"Give me a minute." Rodina left the room, heading further into the house.

Mallory started to face the rest of her group,

turning away again when she caught a glimpse of the eyes. "Can't you put them away?"

"I'm with Mallory on this," Callum said. "It feels like they're watching me."

Before Ryan could put them away, Rodina returned with Herena's grandfather. He took the vials of eyes from Ryan, examining them. "They look to be in good condition."

"You're a trader?" Brodie asked.

"I was. My son took over a few years back. Guess it's time for me to return to work." He gave the vials to Ryan and examined the larger eyes.

Mallory couldn't resist occasionally checking to see what was happening. A shudder went through her each time she caught a glimpse of the eyes. She was glad she wouldn't be the one trying to get the smaller eyes out of the potion vials with how they'd been pushed in. She doubted it'd be a pleasant process. "How long will this take?"

"The apothecary would give us forty gold pieces for each small eye and two hundred for each larger one. Eight hundred and eighty gold pieces in total," the trader said.

Chapter Thirty

Mallory stared at the trader, mouth open. She tried to speak, but she couldn't make a sound.

"Do you have the same value in essence crystals?" Brodie asked. "We can take an equal trade. At the lowest price, we'd be likely to get for them. And in whichever size sells the best."

"We'd need a few hours to send the miners down there to get more," the trader said. "But I've been told you're not leaving until late tonight anyway."

Mallory nodded, still trying to comprehend the amount of money the spider eyes were worth. "How much are demonic spider fangs worth?"

"Do you have fangs too?" the trader asked.

"We're not interested in selling them," Brodie said. "We don't want all our trade items to be the same type."

The trader nodded. "Smart. That's a good plan."

He turned to Mallory. "A small fang would be worth fifty gold pieces and a large one would be worth two hundred and fifty gold pieces." He smiled. "Demonic varieties are always more valuable than the common variety. Part of the reason why higher level adventurers tend to visit demonic lands. Better profit."

"Demonic lands," Brodie said. "Like Hellfire."

"Yes." The trader glanced at each of them. "Do we have a deal with the eyes? We can offer equal trade if you're willing to wait a few hours for our miners to collect enough essence crystals."

Mallory nodded when her brother looked towards her before looking at everyone else. She would have been willing to take a lower offer just to get rid of the eyes.

Brodie held out his hand. "We have a deal."

The trader shook his hand after glancing at Rodina. "I'll let the miners know." He took the eyes with him.

Mallory felt like cheering the moment he'd left the building with them. She somehow managed to contain herself.

Rodina gestured towards the chest that remained in front of the chair she'd been sitting on earlier. "I take it you've killed the demonic spider."

"It had babies," Mallory said. "We killed twenty-one babies, but we don't know if there are any more down there."

Rodina inclined her head. "We only expected you to kill the adult spider. Thank you for dealing with so many of the babies. I'll send guards and miners to search for any more before they're old enough to be a real problem." She again gestured towards the chest. "Are you happy with our offering for your services?"

"Hell yeah," Brodie said. "Smoky honey sauce."

Mallory laughed, more at the look of confusion that crossed Rodina's face than her brother's comment. "We accept." The moment she spoke the words, the journal icon appeared in the corner of her vision.

"Do you need help taking the chest to your wagon?" Rodina asked.

Ryan shook his head. "We can manage." He took hold of one handle and Kruth took hold of the other. "Thanks though."

Mallory led the way to the wagon, checking over the notification in her journal along the way. *Angry Companion: You were rewarded with a chest containing various items for your party. You also earned fifteen experience points each.* Her lips curved into a smile. She couldn't wait to see all the contents of the chest.

Brodie remained at the side of the chest. "Are we going to see what's in it now?"

"Wait until we put it down." Ryan nodded to a spot beside the wagon.

Once he'd lowered his end of the chest, Kruth turned to Mallory. "Thank you for including me in all the XP. It was generous of you."

"Yeah, it allowed me to gain a CAS point," Emica said.

"I gained a CAS point too," Callum said. "Only another two CAS points until I gain a level."

Brodie turned to Kruth. "It was fair." He faced Mallory. "Kruth'll get some of the essence crystals to sell too, won't he?"

Mallory nodded before removing all the extras from the party. She half wished she could say they were keeping the crystals to use at Cutthroat Harbour, but as her brother had said, it was fair they shared them out. "Maybe we should have asked for all little crystals. There might not be enough to share around. I have no idea how many we'll end up with for eight hundred and eighty gold pieces."

"A lot if they're little ones," Ninette said.

Danae laughed softly. "Small ones are more common than medium and large ones so we're more likely to be given small or medium than large. My father sells the small ones for sixty gold, the medium for two hundred gold and the large for six hundred gold pieces. But that's shop prices. You asked for lowest prices so they should give them to us for the price shops would pay them. Which would be ten less gold for the small ones and twenty less for the other two sizes."

Brodie glanced in the direction of Rodina's house after a long look at the chest. "Do you want me to tell Rodina we want small ones?"

"You can wait until we've had a look inside the chest." Mallory was surprised he'd managed to offer to tell Rodina with how much he obviously wanted to see what they'd earned from the quest.

"Hell yeah." Brodie flung the lid open. "There better be more than one recipe."

Mallory joined Brodie in front of the chest, moving him aside. She took the linen out so she could see what was underneath. The linen themselves were two sheets, the crisp white material soft to the touch.

Ninette took them from her. "Did you want them put in one of the panniers?"

Mallory shook her head. "They can go back in here eventually." Her gaze was drawn to the two large essence crystals. Now she knew what they were worth, the two of them alone were probably all that the village had needed to pay. They'd obviously been desperate to have them agree since they'd put together a chest full of items to entice them. Now the linen was out of the way, Mallory spotted two bottles of black ink, a nib pen, a leather-bound notebook with blank pages, six silver knives, forks and spoons, a pack of cards tied together with a ribbon and a miner's helmet.

Brodie picked up the helmet, putting it on his head. "Is it one size fits all or have we been lucky?"

"They make a few different sizes, but there isn't a great deal of size difference between them," Danae said.

Mallory took the helmet off Brodie. "It should come in handy in the future."

"Tonight," Ryan said. "When we travel to Cutthroat Harbour."

Mallory checked the potions. There were two mana, two health and a cure disease potion. She returned them to the chest. Picking up a small drawstring bag, she tipped ten silver pieces into her hand, returning them to the bag once she'd counted them.

"What books did they give us?" Callum came forward to peer over her shoulder. "Rodina said crafting ability books. Are they ones we don't have?"

Mallory picked up the three books, looking at their titles. "Understanding The Crafting Ability Fishing as well as brewer and thatcher." She handed the books to Callum.

"Hell yeah." Brodie victory punched the air. "Brewer."

Ryan chuckled. "You do know you won't be able to do any brewing while we're travelling around."

"My people manage to brew their alcohol while on the road. Some clans have a caravan dedicated to brewing, some have different parts of the process set up in the caravans of a few of the people," Jorgen said.

"What recipes do we have?" Brodie asked. "Other than smoky honey sauce."

Mallory picked up the recipes. "Tropical island fruit drink, herb stuffed chameleon viper, sugar blossom and strawberry tea, bacon and pineapple fritters and of course the smoky honey sauce."

"Cool." Brodie took the recipes from her, slipping them into his satchel. "I can't wait to make some of them."

Chapter Thirty-One

Mallory looked through the small pile of clothes set to one side, leaving the spells till last. There were two dresses. One a pale blue and the other a deep red. There were also two pairs of black trousers, a brown pair and a beige shirt. Returning the clothes to the chest, Mallory picked up one of the scrolls. She frowned when she read it. "Beacon. What is that for?"

"It creates a column of light to mark your location," Danae said. "It is often used to show sailors the way home in bad weather." She took the spell from Mallory. "This one will only last for ten minutes, but higher level ones last longer. Some of them for hours. Levelling this one up will also make it last longer." She returned the spell.

"Could it be used for a light?" Mallory put it in her satchel to learn later. She was too tired to try and learn a spell.

Danae nodded. "It could be, but it's stationary. You wouldn't be able to move it around. You'd need to recast it."

Mallory picked up the next scroll, grinning when she read what it was. "This is better. Magelight. Exactly what I've needed for ages." She put it in her satchel with the other one.

"Aren't you going to learn it?" Brodie asked.

"Not when I'm so tired." Mallory picked up the last scroll. "Lightning Strike. A pity it couldn't be the basic water one." She added it to her satchel too. Yawning, she stood up, taking the bag of coins with her. "I know it's not much compared to what's in the chest, but the ten silver pieces can be shared between Ninette, Kruth, Emica and Jorgen, with Kruth and Ninette getting an extra silver piece each since they didn't gain as much XP." She smiled. "Unless one of you are interested in the sheets."

"You don't need to give me any of the money," Ninette said.

"You've already paid me more than I was expecting," Kruth said.

Mallory held the bag out to Ninette. "You can share them out." Another yawn escaped. "If I don't get some sleep soon, I'm going to pass out." She looked at Emica and Jorgen. "Are you both happy with that?"

Jorgen smiled. "I would have spoken up if I was displeased."

Emica shrugged. "I'll be home soon and have access to my own money. The XP is more important to me than a few coins. Especially since I haven't had to worry about accommodation or food along the way." Her hand rested on the hilt of the sword at her right hip. "And I have weapons that are good enough to get the job done."

Ninette handed out the coins, holding the drawstring bag out to Mallory.

She waved the object away, taking a stumbling step towards the wagon. "Keep it." She staggered the last few steps to the wagon and although she didn't recall getting in the wagon or falling asleep, she assumed that somehow she'd managed since she was woken in the darkness by Ryan.

His shadowy figure leaned over her, flickering light behind him highlighting his body. He chuckled when she tried to roll over again. "It's time to get up. We leave in an hour."

She drew him down beside her. "Then I can sleep for another half an hour."

His lips brushed across hers. "No, you can't. Not

if you want something to eat. At the rate the stew Welby cooked is disappearing you might want to get out there fast."

Groaning, Mallory sat up, rubbing at her eyes. "You could save me some and let me have a bit more sleep."

Ryan tugged her towards the end of the wagon. "The villagers want to thank you for all you've done."

Mallory drew back from him, glancing past the canvas over the wagon, lowering her voice before she spoke. "I'm definitely not going out there. The entire village must be waiting for me." She had another look, drawing back again at the sea of faces past the campfire.

Ryan chuckled. "Come on. At least it's not as bad as spider eyes."

"I think it might be worse," Mallory mumbled.

"Aren't you hungry?"

"Yes, but…" Again she peeked outside. "There are hundreds of them."

"Twenty at the most."

"I don't know what to say to them."

"You're welcome?"

Mallory sighed. "Okay. Let's get it over and done with." She staggered out of the wagon, glancing back at it when she saw everyone watched her. She recognised all of them. They were people she'd treated. People she'd kept from dying.

Ryan nudged her forward. "They're waiting."

Her steps were slow as she approached them. Crowds didn't bother her, but having so many people all focused on her at once made her feel uncomfortable. She tried to smile, but had the feeling it was more a grimace than anything even remotely like a proper smile.

People shook her hand, some clapped her on the shoulder. They all had something to say. Some a simple thank you, others wanted to gush with gratitude. A few gave her gifts in appreciation. Ninette came over, bringing with her a cloth bag and taking the gifts. She put the gifts in the bag, slowly sending the crowd away until only the child who'd died was left. Even Brodie was given five recipes from the man who'd told him he had recipes for him, apologising it wasn't the dozen he'd thought he had.

The child clasped Mallory's hand. "How can I repay you?"

"I don't need you to repay anything," Mallory said. "You weren't the only one who had a revive potion." The two cousins had been amongst the crowd, offering their thanks too.

"I can travel with you and serve you," the child offered.

Mallory sent a pleading look to Ryan, having no idea what to say without giving offence.

Ninette stepped closer. "That's my job. Your elder already paid for our services. You don't owe Mallory anything."

Mallory wanted to demand when that had become Ninette's job, but thought it best to wait until the child had left. She didn't want the child getting any ideas. "I'm glad you lived. I'm glad I was able to save so many. None of you owes me anything. Like Ninette said, your elder paid us for what we did to help your village."

The child held out a ring. "I want you to have this."

"What is it?" Mallory stared at the plain gold band.

"I should have been wearing it at the time. It has a revive on it, but you have to be wearing it for it to work. It's too big for me so I didn't have it on."

Mallory shook her head. "You keep it."

"If I'd been wearing it, even on a necklace, I would have used it up. Take it to replace the revive potion you gave me." The child continued to hold the ring out.

Ninette took the piece of jewellery. "This more than repays Mallory."

Nodding, the child hurried away, giving Mallory a smile before leaving.

Mallory stared at the ring. "What am I meant to do with it?" It didn't feel right leaving the child without a revive.

"If you don't want it, I'll have it for Fang," Brodie said.

"What about Smudge?" Callum asked.

Brodie took the dice out of his belt pouch. "We can roll for it." He held one of the dice out to Callum.

Ryan, who'd remained beside Mallory, grinned. "Better check Brodie doesn't have a loaded die."

"As if," Brodie muttered. He paused a moment. "How would you make loaded dice?"

Mallory laughed. "Okay. One of the companion animals can have it. They're going to need it with some of the areas we take them to."

Brodie rolled the highest number, victory punching the air before he took the ring from Ninette. "Hell yeah." He crouched in front of Fang, showing her the ring. "Look what I got for you, girl." He laughed when she licked his face. Standing up, he frowned. "Where would I get a collar for her?"

"You could cut down one of those spare belts we have," Ryan suggested.

Callum headed towards the panniers. "I'll help you.

We'll make it big enough to give her some growing room."

Ninette gave Mallory the cloth bag then pointed to a log in front of the campfire, three books sitting on one end of it. "Everyone except you has read the crafting books. If you want to get started on them, I'll get your bowl of stew."

Chapter Thirty-Two

Mallory stopped Ninette before she could move away. "We didn't invite you to come with us so you could become some sort of servant."

Ninette stared at her for a moment. "I just thought…" Ninette's voice trailed off and she glanced away.

"What did you think?" Mallory asked.

Ninette continued to stare at the ground. "I thought I could help."

"You are helping. You've stayed with the wagon so it's not left unprotected. And you're going to do that while we're in Cutthroat Harbour."

"What about when you've rescued everyone?" Ninette glanced up from the ground. "When you no longer need anyone to guard the wagon."

Mallory smiled, finally understanding the problem. She rested a hand on Ninette's shoulder. "There will always be other adventures, other jobs needing to be done."

"I can stay with you after you see the wagoner home?" Ninette asked.

Mallory nodded. "You can stay with us until you're ready to leave."

Danae laughed softly from behind Mallory. "I don't blame you if you want to stay. We've been to a lot of interesting places and have plenty of exciting plans ahead of us."

Mallory continued to rest a hand on Ninette's shoulder. "Then you stay. If that's what you want, we don't mind." She smiled at the thought of what Brodie might have to say. But she was pretty sure that once Danae said she was happy for Ninette to stay, Brodie would be too.

Ninette grinned. "Really? I can stay with all of you as long as I want?"

Mallory nodded.

Ninette threw her arms around Mallory, hugging her tightly before letting go. "I'll get the stew for you while you read the crafting ability books."

Mallory slowly shook her head. "Did she understand what I said?"

Ryan chuckled. "I'm sure she did." He slid his arm around her waist. "You better eat while you have the chance. We'll be leaving soon." He walked with her to the campfire and sat beside her on the log.

Mallory read the start of the two books she hadn't unlocked the crafting abilities for, taking the bowl of stew from Ninette when she brought it over. Once she'd read the start of the books, she checked her notifications. *You have unlocked brewer, a crafting ability that allows you to make various alcoholic beverages. You have unlocked thatcher, a crafting ability that allows you to use reeds, straw and rushes to repair and make structures and buildings.*

Ryan rose from the log. "Did you want more stew?"

Mallory shook her head. "This will be enough." She watched as he put a couple of spoonfuls of stew on a nearby rock, stepping back. Before she could ask him what he was doing, a skinny cat crept forward and hunched in front of the food, poised to run if anyone should move towards it. The short black fur was missing in a few places, but other than that, it appeared unharmed.

Ryan put the spoon down and returned to the log. "I guess the invaders didn't care about feeding any of the pets."

"Probably not." Finished the stew, she put the bowl beside her and took out the three new spells and read them over. The scrolls for beacon and magelight vanished in a flash of light. Lightning strike went in the same flash of light, but was accompanied by the faint crack of thunder. She felt like she should apologise to the cat that had been scared away, but she hadn't expected the light or the noise. At least it had managed to finish the food. Unable to resist, she cast magelight. A ball of white light hung just above her head and behind her, lighting up the campsite.

Brodie strode towards her, Fang at his side with her new collar, that looked large on her, the ring tied to the leather. "About time you got another decent spell. How much mana does it take?"

"Twenty and it lasts for fifteen minutes." Mallory's fingers brushed across the hilt of her sword. She wouldn't need to worry about carrying a lantern next time she fought in the dark.

Brodie nodded towards the bag she'd set beside her when she sat on the log. "You going to find out what's in there? I've already looked at the recipes I got. Fiery tomato chutney, salty sea serpent soup, venison in a mushroom sauce, strawberry jam and adventurer's savoury biscuits."

"I've not long finished eating." She picked up the bag and tipped the contents out onto her lap. There were three gold, twenty-seven silver and forty-two copper pieces, along with a letter of introduction to a trader in Shadhurst requesting she always be given a discount. There were also several patterns from various crafting abilities. A pair of cloth slippers for cobbler, a simple table and chair for woodworker, a leatherwork pattern for an apron and a red glaze recipe for potter.

"What are we going to do with all that stuff?" Brodie asked. "And why should you get paid and not the rest of us?"

Mallory handed the patterns to her brother. "Make yourself useful and put these in the chest Rodina gave us."

"Why should I run around after you?" Brodie took the patterns.

"Did you want me to put them in the chest?" Ninette asked.

"I've got them, haven't I?" Brodie headed towards the wagon.

Smiling, Mallory added the three gold pieces to the group funds and took out twenty-seven silver and thirty copper pieces so she could split the money between the nine of them. After putting the letter of introduction in her belt pouch, she went to find everyone and give them their share of the money. Six silver and eight copper pieces each. For a moment she wondered if she should have split it with the wagoner, Welby and Roast too, but they hadn't done much. She'd give them a share of the crystals.

Kruth shook his head when Mallory held out the coins to him. "I don't think you know how much guards are paid a day. And they're usually paid at the end of a journey. Not part of the way through it. Not that you're meant to be paying me. We had an agreement."

Ryan joined them, chuckling. "What other guards are paid doesn't make a difference to us."

"A silver piece a day. Travelling guards are also given two copper pieces a kilometre," Kruth said.

Mallory continued to hold the coins out. "I know. The wagoner told us when we escorted him to Surith."

Kruth took the coins. "Did you want me to stay with you longer? Is this payment in advance for after this agreement has ended?"

Brodie came over, having already received his share. "She shouldn't be left in charge of the money. We'll end up with none at this rate."

"Really?" Mallory looked pointedly at his knee. She turned back to Kruth. "We don't always earn a decent amount. Enjoy it while we can afford it." She smiled at him. "And you'll probably more than earn that money when we reach Cutthroat Harbour and we leave the two of you to guard the wagon." Their finances also weren't so bad now. They had sixty-two gold, twenty-five silver and a hundred and eight copper pieces in their group funds. She also had some money of her own. Nine silver and fifteen copper pieces.

Kruth slipped the coins into his belt pouch. "I'll make sure no harm comes to it or the wagoner."

While they were packing up the last of the things, and Danae refilled the waterskin with health tea before putting out the campfire, Rodina arrived with the essence crystals. She handed over a cloth bag. "There are eighteen small ones." She glanced at Brodie. "As requested. It's a little more than the value of the alchemy ingredients, but after all you've done for us…" She let her words trail off, finishing them with a smile.

Mallory took the bag. "Thanks."

Rodina inclined her head. "If you ever come through this way again, call in. You're welcome to stay at my house. There's plenty of space." She turned to Brodie. "And thanks for all the herbs and vegetables you gave us earlier today. I'm afraid the invaders didn't leave much like that behind. And we couldn't keep expecting Kyla to feed us."

They all thanked her, striding to the wagon that was packed and ready to go. Before everyone clambered on, Mallory offered each of them an essence crystal, after putting aside six to use while they were at Cutthroat Harbour.

Welby shook his head. "You keep it. You might need it while we're rescuing everyone."

Roast took the one offered to him. "Thank you. It'll be nice to know I have extra mana to draw on at Cutthroat Harbour."

Nearly everyone else declined the crystals. Only the wagoner and Jorgen also took them. The wagoner also lit the miner's helmet and put it on in preparation for the journey ahead, nodding when Mallory asked him if he'd finished doing business in the village and had managed to buy the essence crystals he'd been interested in.

Chapter Thirty-Three

Mallory put most of the essence crystals in the chest since nearly everyone had declined them, leaving six in her satchel. Once they were all on the wagon and headed towards Cutthroat Harbour, Mallory having recast magelight, she faced Brodie who sat beside her on the wagon. "You gave Rodina some herbs and vegetables?"

Brodie shrugged. "Wasn't like we could sell them anywhere and there were too many for us to eat. You gathered tonnes while you were levelling up."

She smiled. "I'm glad."

"It would have been a waste," Brodie muttered.

Still smiling, she took out her notebook, wanting to write in it before the day ended. It didn't take all that long to write in her notebook and she put it away, being careful not to disturb all the potion vials that were carefully wrapped in the calico cloths.

Staring out the front, through the gap between the canvas and the wagon, she tried to see past the wagoner, Welby and Roast. "Can I send the magelight ahead so I can see an area better?"

Danae looked up from Smudge who she was brushing with the horse brush, causing him to make contented sounds. "That is a different type of spell. Magelight always remains in the same position. Behind and above your head."

"Don't recast it when it goes out," Callum said. "We should probably get more sleep. Otherwise, it's going to be a long morning. Not all of us need to stay awake to watch for enemies."

"As if I could sleep." Brodie rubbed Fang's stomach. She was stretched out on his lap, asleep. "We're going after the dark forces. Going to one of their actual villages. We should make a fortune when we return home, getting paid for every member of the dark forces we take out."

Welby glanced over his shoulder. "Not every person at Cutthroat Harbour will be a member of the dark forces. Some will be those paid to do a job. In it for the money and not caring who it is that pays them."

"Oh." Brodie's expression fell. "But there should be more of them there, shouldn't there?"

Danae laughed softly, returning the brush to the saddlebags that were not far from her, patting Smudge when he protested. "There'll be plenty there."

Smudge scampered over to Callum, clambering onto his lap and chattering at him, stretching a paw out towards the saddlebags.

Callum laughed, patting Smudge on the head. "I think you've been brushed enough." He smiled when Smudge berated him.

Brodie glanced at Jorgen. "We need to make sure we earn a lot more money before we go home again. So we should take out every dark forces member we can."

Ryan chuckled. "Considering we're usually only home for a day, we do earn good money each time."

"In total, we've earned six hundred and fifty-seven dollars each and only a week has passed in our world," Callum said.

"See," Ryan said. "That isn't bad. Especially since we've only had four trips back home from here."

Emica looked at each of them. "Who pays you?"

"Guardians Of The Round Table," Brodie said.

"You're members of their faction?" Emica asked.

"Working on it." Ryan grinned. "Or at least that's the plan."

"Is that why you're helping us?" Emica asked.

Mallory shook her head. "We're helping you because it's the right thing to do." It seemed like so long ago that she'd once thought all this was a game. At times it still felt like one and death might not always be permanent, but with how serious the rest of the consequences were, it was more dangerous than a simple game.

When her magelight went out, Mallory didn't recast it, lighting a lantern instead and keeping it turned down low. She was too worried about what was ahead of them to sleep. Checking the time with Ryan, and learning it was just after midnight, she decided to sort through her satchel to help pass the time. It was starting to get full. And it wasn't like she needed to carry everything with her now. They had plenty of storage containers between the panniers and the chest Rodina had given them.

She put three of her five mana potions in the chest, both the water breathing potions, the hairbrush, the tooth powder, all six bone dust of the undead, the twenty knuckle bones of the undead, four of her seven health potions, the boneset salve, one of the cure disease potions, two of the four antipoisons and all three of the medium essence crystals. The six small ones she'd left in her satchel should be enough. She stared at her leather-bound notebook for a moment, finally deciding to put it, along with the nearly empty bottle of ink and nib pen, in the chest. She didn't need to cart them around with her.

Setting the satchel down next to her, she smiled. It was now far lighter and less bulky. She decided to do the same with her belt pouch, putting some of the money in the chest from Rodina, hiding the coins in one of the corners, beneath all the contents. She put fifty gold, twenty silver and forty copper pieces in the chest. Closing the lid, she sat beside Ryan, leaning against him. She stared out into the night, able to see a few stars through the gap between the top of the trees and the arch of the canvas at the rear of the wagon.

Ryan slipped his arm around her shoulders, drawing her close. "We need a base for those things we don't always need to cart around with us."

"One of the travellers' caravans would be better," Callum said. "Then we could take more things with us and not have to worry about leaving something behind that we might have needed."

Jorgen smiled. "No matter what you take with you, or how well you plan, there'll always be something you should have taken instead."

Callum shrugged. "I still think it would be useful."

"It is, but you can't plan for everything. The unexpected always occurs," Jorgen said.

Emica glanced at Jorgen before returning to staring out the back of the wagon. "We'll be at Cutthroat Harbour soon. Then we'll be able to rescue your people and my father." She glanced towards the front of the wagon. "And everyone else."

Jorgen's reply was interrupted by the wagoner calling out. "There's a bear ahead of us."

Mallory barely managed to jump out of the wagon and cast magelight before the bear was dead, its body riddled with arrows. "It didn't stand a chance."

"Yeah, they better watch out at Cutthroat Harbour," Brodie said.

Ryan chuckled. "The dark forces are a little harder to take out than a bear." He dragged the body to the side of the road and waved the wagoner on. "I'll see what I can get from this then catch up."

Mallory stayed with Ryan so he could see what he was doing with the help of her magelight. He managed to get a pelt and two canines. She helped him clean up when they returned to the wagon, tipping water from the waterskin onto his hands.

Clambering back onto the wagon, she sat beside Callum, watching Ryan put the items away. "What if we can't sell the bear pelt for a few days? Will it become useless?"

Welby, who was still sitting on the front seat, turned to look at them. "We're not going to want to stay in this area for long. Once we rescue everyone, we'll need to leave in a hurry. There's absolutely no way we'll be able to take out every single enemy at Cutthroat Harbour. There'll be too many of them. The aim will be to get in and out as quietly as possible, rescuing all the captives."

"What about killing members of the dark forces?" Brodie asked.

Welby met his gaze. "I'm sure there'll be plenty of them for you to kill."

"I wonder if Rass is there," Callum said.

Mallory shuddered, the image of Rass' eyes and the look that had been in them, filling her mind. "I really hope not."

Ryan sat beside Mallory again, slipping an arm around her shoulders and drawing her close. "If he is, we'll take him down like we've done every other time."

Mallory started to protest that none of the other times had been easy. She remained silent. She didn't need to tell him something he already knew. The monotony of the journey had her falling asleep, snuggled against Ryan, his arm remaining around her.

Chapter Thirty-Four

Mallory had no idea how long she'd been asleep when the lack of movement from the wagon woke her, but she woke to nearly complete darkness, a blanket draped over her. Not even the miner's helmet or a lantern was lit. She reached for her wand.

Ryan placed his hand over hers, his other arm remaining around her. "We're too close to Cutthroat Harbour for a light."

"What are we doing? Other than sitting here." Mallory stared out the back of the wagon. It was too dark to see anything other than shadows against shadows.

"Welby and Jorgen have gone to scout the area to find somewhere for the wagoner to wait," Emica said.

Mallory stared at the area in front of her, trying to see Emica in the darkness. "We're not going to have enough night vision potions. It's impossible to see anything around here. We can't go stumbling around in the darkness or we'll have everyone in Cutthroat Harbour knowing we're on the way."

Danae laughed softly. "It'd make a good decoy to cover the rest of us sneaking in."

Mallory stared in Danae's direction. "Decoy."

Ryan straightened, sitting away from her slightly, his arm remaining around her shoulders. "You've thought of something."

"How close do I need to be to the beacon that I cast?" Mallory asked.

"I don't know," Danae said.

"I should have tested it out earlier," Mallory said.

"Quiet," Callum mumbled. "Want a few more minutes sleep."

Mallory grinned. She bet he wouldn't be saying that if someone offered to make him a coffee. She nearly laughed. "You do realise we're about to attack a village filled with the dark forces and possibly lots of coffee."

"Wake me when we're ready," Callum mumbled. "Till then, quiet."

"I think you have to see the ground," Emica said.

Mallory frowned. "The ground of what?"

"Where you want to cast the spell. I've seen it cast before. At Shadhurst. I don't know if they were able to cast it so far away from them because they'd levelled it up, or if that's the way the spell works," Emica said.

"If you cast it on the beach, they'll think you're signalling a ship," the wagoner said.

Mallory stared at the front of the wagon. The shadowy figures of the wagoner and Roast were a little easier to see with the night sky behind them. "What if I cast it on one side of the village and then race to the other side and cast another one? I can ride Bug and make sure it's a few minutes away from Cutthroat Harbour." She grinned. "It might make them split their forces."

Ryan chuckled. "Sounds good to me. But you're not going on your own."

"I'll go with you," Emica said. "Bug can take both our weights and I won't need a night vision potion."

Ryan tangled his fingers with Mallory's. "I can come with you. I'm sure Danni won't mind if I ride Augusta."

Mallory squeezed his hand, smiling up at him even though he couldn't see her expression. "You'll need to help rescue the captives. Who knows how many they'll have. We'll figure out a place to meet at the village so Emica and I can help once we've finished with the decoys."

"Just remember you're not a tank," Ryan said.

"Neither are you." Before Mallory could say anything else, a wolf howled nearby. It was followed up by another two calls, equally spaced apart.

"They're back."

Mallory's gaze followed the sound of Emica's voice as she jumped down from the wagon, remaining by the rear of it. "Welby and Jorgen?"

"Yes," Emica said. "We didn't want to accidentally attack them when they returned. Or let an enemy sneak up on us thinking it was them returning."

"Can we turn a lantern on yet?" Brodie asked. "I hate not being able to see anything."

"Mallory might as well cast beacon if you're going to light a lantern," Emica said.

"We're too close to Cutthroat Harbour," Danae said.

"We've found a location for the wagoner to stay," Welby said from behind the wagon.

Mallory tried to see if Jorgen was with him. It took her a moment to realise he was the larger shadow down lower. He was still in wolf form. The blanket slipped down off her and she shivered at the cool night air. "Why isn't your fur standing out against the darkness?"

"He rolled in the dirt," Welby said. "After he went in the ocean."

"Does that mean he'll still be muddy when he becomes human again?" Brodie asked.

"Where are we taking the wagoner?" Ninette asked at the same time as Brodie asked his question.

"An abandoned orchard," Welby said. "The farmhouse has been burned to the ground, but the barn is intact and there are plenty of trees for cover."

"How will we see to find our way there if we're not allowed to use a lantern?" Brodie asked.

"I can see enough to drive us there. If someone can tell me where to go," Emica said. "A wagon can't be that much different to driving a carriage."

Jorgen made a soft, low bark, his shadow moving towards the front of the wagon.

"I'll assume he's telling me he'll show me the way." Emica joined Roast and the wagoner on the front seat.

Mallory shifted over to make room for Welby. "How far away is it?" She took the coat Ryan pressed into her hands, pulling it on.

"A little closer to Cutthroat Harbour, then we take a left along an overgrown road," Welby said. "There's plenty of space in the barn for the wagon and they can stay in there out of sight. The barn is in a good state of repair. Dirty, but solid and they can use a lantern or have a small fire without risking anyone seeing it."

"We can all meet up there after we've finished in Cutthroat Harbour," Ryan said. "It'll be good to have a location to head to in case we get separated." He paused a moment. "Or don't manage to meet up again at the village."

"We managed to have a bit of a look around Cutthroat Harbour," Welby said. "If you head directly down from the orchard, and around the sheep farm, it takes you to the coast near a pig farm. It's on the outskirts of the village." He paused a moment. "Where the main road enters the village, it goes between two small crops farms and there's the lumberyard on the left as you come into the village. North of Cutthroat Harbour is a grain farm and a couple of houses along the road that heads along the coast. Including a large, fancy house. There are quite a few trees scattered throughout the village and a lot of different sized buildings and houses from what we could see without actually entering Cutthroat Harbour. We also saw a sailing ship at the dock."

Mallory tried to picture the layout as Welby described it. "Emica and I will set the first beacon south of Cutthroat Harbour then circle around and set one to the north. I want to see what's in the large house. Maybe it's where their village elder lives."

"Yeah, take out the head of the village first," Brodie said.

Mallory smiled. "That wasn't exactly what I was thinking. I thought it might be a good location to start searching for the captives. After all, Rodina kept her prisoners at her place."

"Did you see any prisoners?" Ryan asked.

"No, but we didn't get too close to the village. We were more focused on finding somewhere safe for the wagoner," Welby said.

"Are the rest of us splitting up into groups?" Brodie asked. "Or just Mal and Emica?"

"We'll split up–"

Brodie interrupted Ryan. "I'll go with Danni."

Ryan chuckled. "Of course you will. The two of you can take Augusta and Jorgen can go with you. Come into the village from the south."

"We should get a closer look at the ship," Callum said. "Make sure there are no captives on board."

"I'll go with you," Ryan said.

Chapter Thirty-Five

Mallory searched for Ryan's hand, holding onto it when she found it. "Don't go on board the ship. You'll end up getting caught."

Ryan lightly squeezed her hand. "We've got this. Stop worrying." He paused a moment. "Welby and Roast can come in from the east. We'll figure out where all the captives are and try to meet up near the lumberyard to organise taking them all at once."

"We should have some sort of signal in case plans change and we need to get the captives and get out of there in a hurry," Welby said.

"Mal could put her beacon down in the village," Brodie suggested.

"Somewhere near the dock," Welby said. "A central location."

"What if there are captives on board. Won't that make it difficult to get them out?" Callum asked.

"A bit north of it," Welby said.

"We've arrived," Emica said as the wagon slowed. "If someone wants to open up the barn so we can go straight in."

"I've got it." Welby jumped out the back of the wagon, landing lightly on the ground.

It didn't take them long to ready Bug and Augusta while the wagoner, Kruth and Ninette set up a basic camp and lit a small campfire. Ninette gestured towards the fire. "I'll get a venison stew cooking. I bet the captives haven't been fed properly in ages."

"Make sure there's enough for us too," Brodie said.

Mallory glanced at everyone. Ryan, Brodie and Callum wore one of the brown coats they'd bought in Surith while Danae wore her own jacket, a black one that was a lot fancier than theirs. Roast and Welby were dressed in warmer clothes too. Only Emica and Jorgen had nothing warm to wear, but since he was still in crystalline wolf form she assumed he'd be warm enough. She turned to Emica. "Did you want a blanket to keep you warm? We could cut a hole in the middle and you could slip it over your head."

"I'm fine. That would hampen my movements too much if I need to fight."

Mallory nodded, glancing once more around the group. "Are we ready to go?"

"I am," Brodie said. "I need the XP. We didn't get any for finding this place."

"It's probably too close to Cutthroat Harbour to be considered separate from the village, even though it's abandoned," Danae said.

"Then why didn't we get XP for discovering Cutthroat Harbour?" Brodie asked.

"You need to be closer to the more populated area of a town or village, or the centre of it if it's abandoned, to gain XP," Danae said.

Emica swung up onto Bug. "I'm ready to go." She held out a hand to Mallory.

"Wait." Callum stepped forward, taking the spyglass and holster off his belt. "You might need this. Make sure the area is clear before you put a beacon down."

"Thanks." Mallory put it on her belt.

Ryan stepped up close, resting his hands on her hips. "Don't forget you're not a tank."

She smiled up at him. "Neither are you." Her lips met his and she slid her arms around his neck, holding him close. Reluctantly loosening her grip, she took a step back. "I'll see you soon." Letting go of him, she took another step away, glancing around the group. "Does anyone need any of the night vision potions?"

"I'll shapeshift and remain a deer until I reach

Cutthroat Harbour. There's enough light once in the village I won't need a night vision potion." Welby turned to Roast. "You're not that heavy. I can carry you there."

Jorgen gave a soft bark and went to stand beside Brodie and Danae.

"I guess that means he can show us the way," Brodie said.

"Just Callum and I will need a night vision potion then," Ryan said. "One will be enough."

Mallory handed over one of the night vision potions before joining Emica on Bug. Emica headed for Cutthroat Harbour the moment Mallory mounted. It didn't seem as dark once they reached the shore with the wide open beach and the sparsely growing trees behind them, even though the moon was little more than a slither. Finding a suitable location, Mallory retreated to the treeline.

She glanced at Emica who stood beside her. "Are you ready?"

"Cast it."

Mallory stared at the sand close to the water's edge, drawing her wand from the canvas loop it hung in at her side. The moment she cast beacon, she remembered she was meant to check the area with the spyglass. It was too late now. The beacon rose into the sky, a white pillar of light that would be clearly seen in Cutthroat Harbour. As well as a long way to the south of the village. About to put her wand away, she grinned, casting lightning trap on the sand near the beacon. A white circle appeared on the sand with symbols around the edge of the circle that reminded Mallory of demonic runes. The centre contained an image of forked lightning. "Can you see that?"

"See what?" Emica asked.

"The lightning trap that I cast."

Emica swung into Bug's saddle. "Only those in your party will be able to see it." She held out her hand. "Hurry before they come to investigate."

After casting another two lightning traps, she returned her wand to the canvas loop and took hold of Emica's hand, swinging up onto the horse. She held onto the kitsune as they raced through the trees, circling around the village to reach the beach north of the place. Everything was silent and Mallory dismounted, taking out the spyglass.

She didn't see anything. Not that there was enough light for her to see much other than the shadowy outline of the trees edging the beach. "It's too dark."

"Give me that." Emica took the spyglass from her. "Maybe you should have had a night vision potion before you tried to see what's around us."

Mallory took out her wand, scanning the beach for a likely place to cast beacon. She took the spyglass from Emica when she held it out. "Anyone?"

"It's all clear." Emica mounted Bug. "Hurry up so we can find my father."

Mallory cast beacon at the water's edge and set three lightning traps around it before putting her wand away. She mounted the horse behind Emica.

The kitsune rode towards the village, staying amongst the trees. Off to the left was a green farm, ahead was a scattering of lights in a few of the buildings of the village, including what Mallory assumed was the large, fancy house Welby had mentioned.

"We'll leave Bug in that cluster of trees behind the large house and take a closer look at the building. It seems like a good place to start," Mallory said.

Emica changed her course, heading for the trees. "Cutthroat Harbour is bigger than I thought it'd be. It wouldn't surprise me if there are as many as two or three hundred people living here."

Mallory stared at the back of Emica's head. "Two or three hundred?" How were they meant to face that many people?

Emica laughed. "There will be some who are just villagers. Traders, craftspeople, farmers and such.

Some will be the sort to hide rather than fight. It won't be as bad as it sounds."

Mallory dismounted when Emica stopped amongst the trees. "I hope not. Getting ourselves killed while trying to rescue everyone seems pretty lame." She checked her journal since the icon had appeared in the corner of her vision as they approached the cluster of trees. It was a notification that she'd earned experience points for a new location. Ten experience points. While she had her journal open, she checked everyone's stats. They were fine.

"Did you want to wait here while I have a look? I can shapeshift so I'm less noticeable," Emica offered.

Mallory shook her head. "I'll go with you too." She took out her wand, in case she needed to use it, and followed Emica to the large house that had been built facing the road intersecting with the one that went along the coast.

There were no lights shining in the buildings around it, only in one well off to their left that appeared to be a tavern and one over towards the docks that also seemed to be a tavern. Mallory couldn't tell for certain with the trees and other buildings that were in the way. Before she left the cover of the trees, Mallory cast vanish I on herself,

Emica having shapeshifted so she was a lot harder to spot.

Chapter Thirty-Six

Reaching the large house, Mallory peered in a window while she was still invisible. Shock arrowed through her. Rass was in the room along with the woman who'd held a blade to Brodie's throat and two other men. She remained where she was, staring open mouth at the scene in front of her, only moving away from the window to press herself against the outside wall when she became visible.

Emica shapeshifted, her ears remaining that of a fox. "What did you see?"

"Someone I would have preferred not to see." Mallory made herself invisible again to peer through the window.

"I'll check out the houses around here." Emica shapeshifted and ran towards the closest house before Mallory could say anything.

Not that she knew what she would have told the

kitsune. Don't leave me here alone sounded pathetic, even though they were the words that had come to mind as she watched Rass slam his hand against a map spread out on the table in the middle of the room.

Rass raised his voice. "I don't want to hear any excuses. Send a group to rescue the orc. He will answer to me for his failure to send the rest of the essence crystals we need. We're meant to be leaving for the border in less than a week." He turned to the woman. "You better not have lost the potion from the frog mage, Zorlla."

The woman raised her chin, meeting Rass' glare with one of her own. "Don't tell me how to do my job. It's in my room. You're the one responsible for the security here. So if something goes missing, it's on your head."

"Nothing is getting in here. Not with the security measures I have in place," Rass said.

"Two pathetic guards at the front door and a few hidden traps around the place," Zorlla sneered.

"If you're so concerned, why-" Rass broke off when two men came running into the room. "Why aren't you at the front door?"

"Beacons were spotted along the beach in both directions," one of the guards said.

"There were traps around them," the second guard

added. "Some warriors were left by the beacons to watch for ships."

"It took two of you to come in and tell me this," Rass demanded.

Numerous plans rushed through Mallory's mind, most of them too dangerous. She needed to do something while the guards were no longer at the door. What she needed were spells with an area of effect. She drew in a sharp breath as the answer hit her. Grabbing out the poison mist potion, she threw it at Rass' feet as the two guards backed away towards the door, apologising to him.

Before she could recast vanish I, Rass looked in her direction, anger in his eyes, the woman doing the same. Rass took a single step towards her, mist rising up around him and the other inhabitants of the room. Not knowing if she was far enough away, Mallory cast vanish I and backed away from the window. How long did it take for the poison to disburse? Was she far enough away? She kept moving, her gaze on the window.

"Mallory."

She spun at hearing Jorgen's voice behind her. It took her a few seconds to spot him pressed up against a building a few metres away. She hurried forward, noticing that his hair was wet. "Is everything okay?"

"Yes. We found a wagon in a barn on the south side of the village. We can use it to help us get the captives out of here. The ones we've seen are in poor condition."

Mallory glanced over her shoulder. "How long does it take for a poison mist potion to disburse?"

"Five minutes at the most." Jorgen glanced in the direction Mallory had come from. "Who did you use it on?"

Mallory checked over her shoulder. No one had come out of the building. Did that mean she'd taken all of them out? And how would she know considering Rass and possibly Zorlla's bodies wouldn't be there if they both had revives. "Rass. And some of his people. How will I know if they're dead if they have a revive, like Rass does?"

"Check your XP. How many were with him?"

"The woman who held a blade to Brodie's throat when we visited the demonic shrine, two guards that came in from the front door and two men."

"The woman was level five, I doubt she's levelled up in the meantime. Were the guards hellions?"

Mallory shrugged even though he couldn't see the movement. "I didn't see any tattoos." She checked her journal. "I gained thirty-one XP." She smiled. Only another six experience points and she'd gain a CAS point.

"It sounds like you took all of them out."

Before Mallory could ask about the traps, she became visible and Emica ran out of the shadows towards her, becoming human.

"Make me invisible. I found my father, but there are guards nearby." Emica grabbed hold of Mallory's arm. "Please. He's lying on the floor of a cage in front of the guildhouse, in front of a cluster of trees. There's a crystalline wolf in the cage next to him." Emica gestured in the direction she'd come from.

Mallory looked from the direction of the large house to where Emica had indicated. "I need to get the frog mage's potion back before they learn it's a fake. Except there are traps in the house."

"What sort of traps?" Jorgen asked.

Still holding onto Mallory's arm, Emica turned to Jorgen. "Don't you want to rescue one of your clan people?"

"Not while it means putting another at risk," Jorgen said.

"They look half dead," Emica said.

Mallory was torn. She didn't want anything to happen to Hisoki or the traveller, but she also didn't want to have the dark forces hunting the frog mage down. "Let me check their health. I can heal them from a distance." Or at least from two metres away from them. Taking out the spyglass, she made herself invisible before she moved closer to where the cages were. Seeing the two collapsed in the bottom of the cages, she feared they were dead. Bringing the spyglass to her eye wasn't at all reassuring. Hisoki had three health while the traveller, in crystalline wolf form, had two. Hisoki reminded her of Emica with his long, russet coloured hair and dark brown eyes, looking like he was only in his mid-twenties, late twenties at the most. And like Jorgen, the crystalline wolf had a snowy white coat with a crystal blue tinge to it.

After moving even closer, and putting the spyglass away, Mallory healed each of them twice. An extra four health points weren't much, but they had to be better than what they had.

Hisoki raised his head off the floor of the cage, the movement barely noticeable. He looked directly at where Mallory stood.

Mallory took a step back. Could he see people who were invisible? Or was he able to hear where she was? She didn't have time to figure it out, turning away, she returned to where she'd left Emica and Jorgen. "Can your father see people who are invisible?"

Emica shook her head. "Where is the potion we need to collect?"

"The house contains traps." Before Mallory could step away from the building they stood beside, Ryan and Callum came out of the darkness to join them.

"We looked through the windows of the house, but only saw dead bodies." Ryan chuckled. "We assumed you'd been there."

"How many dead bodies?" Mallory asked.

"Four. All in the one room," Callum said.

"The frog mage's potion is in one of the bedrooms," Mallory said.

"Then we better go find it." Ryan led the way, keeping to the shadows.

They entered through the window Mallory had peered through earlier, keeping below the level of it so that no one walking past would see them. Callum went to the table, picking up the map. "This is Inadon." He folded it up and put it in his satchel. There was a book on the table beside the map that he put in his satchel too. Lost And Powerful: Myths Of Misplaced Staves.

"We should split up," Emica said.

"What about traps?" Mallory asked.

Jorgen nodded towards the dead bodies.

"Reanimate them and send them out to trigger any traps in the house."

"I can do that?" Mallory took out her wand.

Emica nodded. "Raise them and send them to find the traps so we can find the potion and get out of here."

Chapter Thirty-Seven

Mallory reanimated three of the dead, using up all her mana. "Now what do I do with them?"

"Tell them what you want them to do," Emica said.

Mallory looked at each of the reanimated enemies, about to tell them to search for traps, when Ryan spoke.

"We'll split up. Send one with Emica, one with Jorgen and one with me."

Mallory gave them their orders.

Emica strode from the room, the reanimated enemy going ahead of her. Jorgen and Ryan left too. Mallory hurried after Jorgen, leaving Callum to search the room. She hurried between the three of them, reanimating the enemy until the traps were found. It didn't take long to search the house. It had a main living area, four bedrooms, a kitchen and the room with the table they'd already been in.

But running between the reanimated corpses kept Mallory's stamina low. Emica was the one to find the potion, giving it to Mallory and asking to be made invisible.

"You can't set them free yet," Ryan warned.

"I know. But I want to let him know I'm here." Emica headed for the window, all of them back in the room with the table. She paused at the window, looking back at Mallory. "Cast it on me once I'm out?"

Mallory nodded, waiting until Emica had climbed out the window before she cast vanish I on her. She slipped the potion into her satchel. "What do we do next?"

"I'm going to see what's in the kitchen. There was nothing else of use in here." Callum strode towards the door.

Ryan grinned. "Don't take too long looking for your coffee. Someone is sure to come looking for Rass." He turned to Mallory as Callum left the room. "We should search his room. See what we can learn about Rass."

Mallory returned to the room that was probably the one being used by Rass. It had a change of clothes, a longsword, a whetstone, a letter and three silver pieces. The letter was addressed to Rass. She looked around the room. There was a double bed with a chest at the foot of it and a washstand against the far wall. "He doesn't have much here." She took the letter and coins, leaving the rest of the items behind.

"He doesn't seem like the sort to carry any unnecessary items." Ryan headed for the doorway. "We should search the other rooms to see what we can find out. And to take a few things so it doesn't look like all we came for was the potion."

"We've already taken a few things and I'm not sure I want to find out anything else. Last time we learned something relating to Rass it was about the ancestral king," Mallory said.

Ryan glanced over his shoulder with a grin. "We ended up with a few quests out of it. Which is always good for levelling up."

Sighing, Mallory followed him. The only other bedroom that was in use was the one used by Zorlla. There were several changes of clothing, six steel throwing knives set out on the washstand next to the washbowl and jug, a towel folded neatly and placed on the end of the washstand. The bed was neatly made and a book had been left on the chest at the foot of it. Mallory collected the throwing knives and put them in her satchel for Brodie.

Ryan picked up the book. "Lost And Powerful:

Myths Of Misplaced Staves. It's the same book that was in the other room."

"I wonder why they have two copies of the book."

Callum burst into the room. "Two archers have come looking for Rass. They're still in the main room, trying to figure out which one is to tell Rass the bad news that no one has discovered who cast the beacons."

"We can't let them find out he's dead," Mallory said. "We've still got to find everyone."

"I spoke to Jorgen before I came in here." Callum glanced back the way he'd come. "He ran into Welby and Roast. They've found their people." Again he glanced over his shoulder. "We should leave while we still can."

"What about Jorgen? Did he find more of his clan?" Mallory asked.

"There was only one here." Callum stepped out of the room, heading towards the room with the table.

"Did you find any coffee?" Mallory followed him, keeping her voice low so as not to catch the attention of the enemies in the front room.

"Two full pottery jars." Callum's hand momentarily rested on his satchel. "I have no idea how many cups are in each one, but it has to be at least twenty cups."

Mallory followed Callum to the window, Ryan beside her. "I'll go cast beacon to let everyone know it's time to leave."

Emica climbed in the window. "We can't. The key for the cages is in here."

Mallory wanted to close her eyes. What were they going to do about the archers about to look for Rass? They couldn't let them escape and fighting them risked one of them escaping and sounding the alarm.

"There's a key in the main room," Callum said. "I saw it when we were searching earlier."

"Make me invisible." Emica clutched Mallory's arm. "Please."

"You don't know where it is." Callum took Smudge out of the sling and handed him to Ryan. "Make me invisible. I'll meet you near the building next door."

Mallory cast vanish I on Callum before turning to Ryan. "I'll meet you there too." She cast the spell on herself and climbed out the window, hurrying towards the docks and heading north of them. Other than noise coming from the tavern on the corner before the docks, the place was quiet. She stopped in front of the next building along, about to cast beacon.

A man came out the door, muttering under his breath about people not able to wait until morning to collect their gambling debts, closing the door behind him as he spun to walk down the road.

Mallory stumbled back, having been too close to the door. She held her breath, trying to step lightly away after the slight noise she'd made.

The man froze. "Is someone there?" He glanced around.

Mallory brought up her journal, watching the time count down. Twenty-eight seconds.

"Anyone?" When no one answered, the man shrugged and strode towards the tavern.

Mallory recast vanish I as the time ran out, waiting until the man entered the tavern before she cast beacon on the beach in front of her, placing a lightning trap near it before hurrying away. Behind her she heard people call out, telling others to come look at the beacon.

Callum, Ryan and Emica were at the side of the building, waiting for her, Smudge once again in Callum's makeshift sling. "We have the key." Callum gestured towards Emica. "Emica has it now. We'll meet you at the cluster of trees behind the cages. We'll circle around while the two of you help Hisoki and the traveller."

Mallory nodded, then worried they might not have seen the movement clearly in the shadows, spoke.

"Okay." She made Emica invisible, casting the spell on herself again too. She headed towards the cages, not sure if Emica was beside her. She was as silent as Jorgen. Walking well around the guards, who'd remained where they were rather than check out the beacon they stared at, Mallory stopped by the cages, healing each of the occupants. This time the traveller also raised his head to look in her direction, no longer in wolf form as he'd been earlier. He reminded her of Jorgen.

There was a click as Emica unlocked the cages. "It's time to go." She swung each of the doors open.

Mallory glanced at the guards. Both still had their backs to them. Crouching in front of the cage with the traveller, she rested her hands on him. She immediately gained a sense of his injuries. Besides low health, he had a broken arm and was suffering from adventurer's malady. At least the disease was simple to cure. They had two cure disease potions. One in her satchel and one in the chest from Rodina. When he moved his head, she caught sight of thin plaits in the bottom layer of his pale blond hair, the occasional bead along them. She looked into his blue eyes, seeing they were filled with pain.

Chapter Thirty-Eight

The time was running out on her invisibility so Mallory cast it on herself again, resetting the time. She did the same for Emica the moment she reappeared. "Our friends are hiding amongst the trees behind the cages. I'll make you invisible and you can join them." When the traveller nodded, she drew mana from one of the small crystals in her satchel and cast vanish I on him.

"What about my father?" Emica asked from beside Mallory.

Moving to stand in front of the open cage, Mallory ran into the invisible kitsune, Emica moving away from her. Mallory placed her hand on Hisoki, gaining a sense of his injuries. He was in a similar state to the traveller, but instead of a broken arm, he had broken ribs. Again she drew on the mana crystal. It became dust, not giving her enough mana. She needed to take eight from another crystal before she could make Hisoki invisible.

The three of them barely made it to the cover of the trees before vanish I wore off on Mallory and Emica. Mallory didn't want to cast it again. She might need her mana before they reached the barn where the rest of them waited. "I need to collect Bug." Mallory gestured towards the north.

"I told Jorgen where she was," Emica said. "They needed her to help pull the wagon they found."

"Then let's get out of here," Ryan said.

He'd barely spoken the words when a shout went up behind them. Mallory faced the direction of the cages, the two guards running towards them. "Hurry. Get them to the barn while I try and slow the guards down."

"Not on your own." Ryan readied his hunting bow.

Emica drew her swords. "See that my father reaches the wagon, Callum."

Hisoki put a hand on her shoulder before she could step forward. "I am not about to run and leave you to face them on your own."

"I'm not on my own," Emica said.

"We might want to move in a hurry," Callum said. "More enemies are joining them."

"If it wasn't for the crystalline wolf, I would have been able to create an illusion," Hisoki said.

"Better get moving before we're stuck facing too many," Ryan said.

Hisoki started to shake his head, lowering his hand and stepping back instead. "If you haven't joined me within ten minutes, I will return for you."

Emica didn't answer, only stepped towards the cages, both swords in her hands.

Mallory cast vanish I on her then put a lightning trap on the ground near the cages, grinning when one of them activated it. She cast poison dart next, waiting for her mana to regen so she'd be able to cast vanish I on Emica when she became visible. She tossed up using more of the crystals. When Jorgen came out of the shadows, wielding both stilettos and attacking the five enemies that were now trying to find Emica, Mallory drank the two mana potions in her satchel. She cast vanish I on him.

Ryan remained at her side. "If I attack with the hunting bow, they'll know where we're hiding."

"What are we going to do when it's time to retreat?" Mallory watched the enemies who randomly slashed out at the two attacking them. One of them dropped to the ground, but another three were running towards the fight. "We're not going to be able to escape." She tried not to think about what it felt like to die, but it was still too clear in her mind.

"There has to be something we can do to cause a distraction," Ryan said.

"I don't-" She broke off as an idea occurred to her. "Fire." She said the word at the same time as Ryan, returning his grin. "I'll set the large house on fire. No one is in it." She looked from where their enemies continued to fight and the large house. "I need to get closer."

"I'll come with you."

She shook her head, stepping away from Ryan. "It'll take too much mana to hide both of us."

He captured her hand, squeezing it lightly before letting go. "Don't try tanking things."

She smiled. "Don't you try tanking things either." She hurried towards the house with one more glance over her shoulder, unable to see Ryan in the shadows once she was a few metres from him. Reaching the building next to the large one, she tried the front door, surprised to find it was unlocked. Although she doubted any of the locals would go on a crime spree if they had to answer to Rass for their actions.

Leaving the door open, in case she needed to make a retreat inside, she cast flame at the large house. Jorgen and Emica were both visible, but seemed to be holding their own so she left them visible while she concentrated on trying to get the flames to take hold on the timber roof of the house.

A shout went up and she drew on the mana crystal, making Emica invisible, the crystal becoming dust. She needed to use another crystal so she could cast vanish I on Jorgen. When their enemies ran towards the large house, she stepped inside the building, closing the door in case they looked in her direction. Inside the building was filled with the scent of dried herbs.

She moved further into the shop. It was an apothecary? Hands outstretched, she tried to find the merchandise. Finding it, she winced when she knocked a vial off the shelf and it crashed onto the floor. She froze. What if it was something like poison mist? Did it have a smell? She checked her stats. They remained unchanged. She didn't even have enough light to find a night vision potion in her satchel so she could see what it was. When nothing happened, Mallory randomly grabbed a handful of potions off the shelves and shoved them in her satchel. Hopefully, there were some useful ones amongst them.

Peeking out the door, she saw a bucket brigade had formed for the house next door. She cast flame at it once more, wanting to keep them busy as long as possible. She'd been inside long enough she was able to use vanish I on herself. Slipping outside, trying not to open the door much, Mallory carefully closed it behind herself before heading towards the trees.

"Is that you, Mallory?" Emica asked from under the trees.

"Yeah. Where's the barn?"

"This way."

She followed the sound of Emica's voice, relieved when she was close enough to make out the shadowy figure of the kitsune. "Where is everyone else?"

"They went to make sure the wagon is ready to move. None of them wanted to leave. Do they think we can't take care of ourselves?" Emica demanded.

Mallory followed Emica across the open area behind the trees and a large building. She pressed herself against the side when she reached it. "They know we can take care of ourselves. At least Ryan does. He just doesn't like to desert me. He wants to fight at my side."

"It's not just him though. The five of you feel that way. Especially the four of you who are from that other world. Is that what they teach you there?" Emica paused at the corner of the building, peering around it.

Mallory shrugged, becoming visible again. "Not

exactly. In some ways, it's like here. People are all different from each other and want different things." She tried to see past Emica. "Should I make us invisible?"

"Not yet. Save it for an emergency." Emica darted across the open ground towards a small cluster of trees.

Mallory followed her from trees to buildings, heart racing each time she had to cross open ground. They avoided buildings that had fairly bright lights on inside, the soft glow of a lantern or flames they ignored.

Emica pressed herself against the side of a house, a large open area in front of her. "There's someone sitting outside that house over there to the left. See them?"

Mallory tried to see more than shadows. "No, I can't."

"Make yourself invisible. I can shapeshift. The barn is directly at the end of this road. We're nearly there and can get out of this place."

Chapter Thirty-Nine

Taking a deep breath, Mallory made herself invisible before she strode along the road. She wanted to be in cover before the spell wore off, but also didn't want to make noise and catch anyone's attention. She was nearly at the barn when the spell wore off. A glance in both directions showed nothing. She had no idea if she should cast the spell again or if it'd be a waste and she'd be desperate for the mana later. Before she could do little more than mentally debate the issue, she reached the barn. The door was slightly ajar.

Emica dashed past her and inside the barn, returning to her human form, but keeping her fox ears. "Are we going to be able to get a wagon out of here without anyone noticing?"

Hisoki swung the barn doors wide open. "You're late. I was coming to get you. The others said you were on your way. I expected you, not a message."

"I missed you." Emica opened her arms to hug her father.

Mallory grabbed her arm, tugging her back. "He's got broken ribs."

The wagon moved forward, drawn by both horses. Brodie, who was sitting on the wagon seat beside Danae, put out the lantern he carried.

Emica glared at her father, stepping back out of the way of the wagon. "Why didn't you tell me your ribs are broken?"

"We will discuss this later." Hisoki followed the wagon.

Mallory started after the wagon, freezing for a moment when she finally looked at it properly, She hurried after it, jumping up on the seat to sit beside her brother. "Where did everything come from?" From what she could see, which wasn't the best considering everything appeared to be shadows, they had furniture. "You've got chairs."

"There was a secondhand shop across from the barn," Brodie said. "I had to do something while I waited for you. We were told we could loot dark forces villages and towns."

Danae laughed softly. "You can raid dark forces places. And this is a dark forces village."

"Then what's the problem?" Brodie demanded.

Ryan, striding beside the wagon, chuckled. "I think your sister is commenting on your choice of items."

"I didn't know how much time I'd have," Brodie said. "I grabbed the first things I came to then went back for more when I was still stuck waiting around. It wasn't like I was gaining XP taking out the dark forces like you were."

"I don't know if they were with the dark forces. Other than Rass," Mallory said.

"Rass was there?" Brodie demanded.

Mallory nodded, telling him what had happened, including taking the map, letter and two copies of the one book. She frowned as she looked around. "Where are we going?"

"We had to find a path the wagon could take without going by road," Danae said. "I had a look around while we waited."

"Sounds like everyone has a story to share." Mallory glanced over her shoulder at the furniture blocking her view. It was typical of Brodie that he hadn't chosen less bulky items.

"Not as interesting as yours," Brodie muttered.

"Everyone made it to the wagon safely?" The furniture made it impossible for her to check. "And they found everyone they were looking for?"

"More than they were looking for," Danae said.

"There are a few people here from Velkden. We said you'd heal them a bit, feed them and take them at least as far as the intersection. We didn't know which direction we're going in next."

"Would you consider going to the capital?" Hisoki asked.

Mallory tried again to see past the items blocking her view of the rest of the wagon. "Were you wanting a lift home?"

"I would like you to escort Emica home," Hisoki said. "I can pay you for your services."

"Why?" Brodie demanded. "What? Not another quest. We didn't get any of the quests finished by going to Cutthroat Harbour. I thought that was meant to finish off some quests."

"We're not exactly away from Cutthroat Harbour yet," Danae said.

Mallory checked the journal notification while Danae and Brodie were talking. *Father's Request: Hisoki is willing to pay your party to escort his daughter to Shadhurst.* Wanting to check on everyone else, she hopped off the wagon and waited for it to move past her to clamber on the back of it. The wagon was more crowded than she'd expected. Along with Ryan, Callum, Emica, Jorgen, Welby, Roast, Hisoki and the traveller, there were five other people in the wagon.

With everything Brodie had put towards the front of the wagon, it didn't leave much space for passengers.

She sat near Hisoki. "Why did you want us to take Emica to Shadhurst? Why can't you take her?"

"I need to travel home as fast as possible to let the Duke know what the dark forces are trying to do," Hisoki said.

"You mean the an–"

Hisoki interrupted Mallory. "Are you interested in escorting my daughter to Shadhurst?"

"It's not just up to me." Mallory set his ribs and did rapid mend on them.

"You're an apothecary?" Hisoki asked.

"Yeah." Mallory turned to the woman sitting beside Roast, placing her hands on her. The woman wasn't anywhere near as bad as Hisoki and the traveller had been. She healed her twice, bringing her health close to full.

"I wanted to thank you for helping me rescue Merry," Roast said. "If there is ever anything I can do to help you, let me know.

"You have my thanks too," Welby said. "Without your help, I wouldn't have been able to free Barle. As Roast said, if there's anything I can ever do for you, just ask."

"You also have my thanks," Emica said.

"If you hadn't arrived when you did, I would have been sent to Shadhurst on behalf of the dark forces," Hisoki said. "You have my gratitude also. What can I do for all of you in exchange for all you've done?" He turned to Mallory. "Including for setting and doing rapid mend on my broken bones."

"Finally," Brodie exclaimed.

Mallory smiled when the journal icon appeared in the corner of her vision. "I'm glad we could help." She checked the new notifications. *Captured By Hellions: You helped the hunter and Arthur of Wildebay rescue their loved ones. Both have offered to repay your party with a future favour. You also earned ten experience points each. Dangerous Deeds: You helped Emica find Hisoki before he was forced to travel to Shadhurst on behalf of the dark forces. He has offered to repay your party for your help. You also earned ten experience points each.*

Smiling, she wondered if she should mention to Brodie that she'd gained another CAS point. Although she supposed he'd notice himself eventually. She now had fourteen experience points of the next one hundred and forty-nine that she needed to gain another CAS point and had two CAS points she hadn't used.

Danae had also gained a CAS point and now had five spare. She had four experience points of the next one hundred and twenty-three needed to gain her next CAS point and was halfway through character level two. Ryan had gained a CAS point and had twenty-three of the hundred and sixteen experience points he needed for his next CAS point. Considering they'd only earned twenty experience points from the two quests, she guessed he'd gained his CAS point when they'd reached Cutthroat Harbour. He only needed another two CAS points to reach character level two.

Her smile widened when she saw Brodie's stats. He also would have gained a CAS point when they reached Cutthroat Harbour since he now had twenty-one experience points of the hundred and fourteen needed for his next CAS point. And he wasn't that far behind Ryan, needing only two CAS points to catch up. Only Callum hadn't gained a CAS point. He had forty-one of the hundred and sixteen he needed for his next one.

"You've got to be kidding," Brodie exclaimed. "We got negative rep for Cutthroat Harbour."

Chapter Forty

Mallory checked her journal, finding they had negative fifteen reputation for the village. "I'm surprised it's not higher. We rescued seven people, burned the largest house in their village, raided an apothecary and secondhand shop and killed two of their important members. At least I assume they were important since they were both staying in the large house. I'm surprised the rep isn't worse."

Hisoki looked in the direction they'd come from, a faint lightening of the darkness hinting at the coming dawn. "Horse riders follow."

Ryan and Callum both jumped off the back of the wagon, Smudge in Callum's makeshift sling. Ryan readied his hunting bow. "We'll hold them off."

Mallory joined them. "Not just the two of you."

Emica and Jorgen jumped off the wagon, Emica ignoring her father's protests. Brodie and Fang joined them too. Brodie took out two throwing knives. "I didn't get the chance to take out any of the dark forces while we were in Cutthroat Harbour."

Emica laughed. "How thoughtful of them to chase after you so you could end their lives."

Ryan chuckled. "Isn't it."

Mallory waved Welby back when he would have joined them. "Someone needs to protect the wagon." She noticed Roast was trying to untangle his hand from Merry who argued with him in a whisper. "I need you to stay with the wagon too, Roast. We can't leave everyone unprotected."

"They're in sight." Callum drew back an arrow.

His words reminded Mallory that she had the spyglass. "I need to return the spyglass to you."

"When we've dealt with these." Callum let the string go.

Mallory hurriedly cast a fireball at the oncoming riders. There were eight of them. She grinned when she noticed her brother was attacking each of them, one after the other. "Worried you'll miss out on some XP, Brodie?"

Callum did the same. "You should be checking their health. You only need one hand to cast spells."

She hadn't thought of that. Before she could check, the riders were amongst them, horses rearing and causing the six of them to scatter. Mallory managed to cast poison dart at three of them in between avoiding being trampled. She was unable to take out the spyglass. She was kept too busy trying not to get trampled. They weren't going to last if they didn't start taking some of them out. "Focus on the one in the grey tunic." She threw two fireballs at him. Arrows thudded into his body, knocking him from the horse.

"One at the back of the group," Ryan said.

Their target tried to race out of the way. She only managed to turn the horse around before being taken down. The rest of them tried to escape.

"Don't let them get away," Emica said. "They'll bring more back to hunt us down."

Mallory took out the spyglass. "One second from the left, Ryan and Callum. One on the far right, everyone else." She grinned when the two were knocked from their horses, one of them vanishing. "We really need glasses like this. Attack the one on the right again." The enemy was knocked from the horse. She called them out, hurrying forward so their enemies couldn't get out of sight. Around her, those with her did the same.

"Hell yeah." Brodie victory punched the air when

the last enemy fell. "Finally got a tonne of XP. We should see if we can catch their horses."

Mallory checked over their new stats while she helped catch the horses. She'd gained twenty experience points while Ryan had only gained sixteen. Both Brodie and Callum had each gained thirty-two.

It was Callum who caught a horse, Brodie ending up scaring most of them away with his attempts. Callum held onto the reins, murmuring reassurances to the horse as he ran a hand across its neck. When the horse lowered its head to nuzzle at Callum and then Smudge who peeked over the edge of the makeshift sling, he patted the horse once more before swinging into the saddle.

"What about the rest of them?" Brodie looked in the direction of Cutthroat Harbour.

"They're long gone," Emica said. "We need to get back to the wagon and make sure no one else has been sent after us."

"We've got to check bodies for loot first." Brodie stopped by the nearest body.

Between all of them, they found two silver and twenty-one copper pieces that everyone said to add to the group funds, enough arrows to replace what they'd used and gain four spares, a short bow, a better condition stiletto sheath for Jorgen and another stiletto. He left the nearly broken sheath behind. Remembering the throwing knives she'd found in Cutthroat Harbour, Mallory handed them over to Brodie. He took the four iron throwing knives out of the slots in his vambraces and put them in his satchel, replacing them with steel ones. The other two steel ones went in his satchel too.

Finished, they strode after the wagon, Callum riding the horse. They hadn't gone far before Brodie exclaimed, "What? No!"

"What's wrong?" Mallory asked.

"We lost another two rep from that fight. At this rate we'll end up with a negative global rep," Brodie said.

"Not unless you end up with negative seventy from that village," Emica said.

Brodie stared at her. "It takes that much to gain global rep?"

"Less for a town or capital," Emica said.

"How much less?" Callum asked.

"Every fifty rep for a town is one global rep and every thirty-five rep for a capital is one global rep," Emica said.

Brodie sighed heavily. "It's going to take us forever to gain any global rep."

They caught up to the wagon as it approached the barn of the abandoned orchard. The morning was now bright enough Mallory could see what was on the back of the wagon. A timber table took up the full width of the wagon, a chest and a tall cane basket packed underneath, the basket barely fitting. Two bedrolls were also jammed on top of the chest. On the table was stacked a wooden packing crate and six chairs. She slowly shook her head. "Table and chairs?"

Brodie grinned. "We can sell them. Or you can find one of those shrinking spells and an unshrinking one. We can set up camp in style."

"What's in the crate, chest and basket?" Callum asked.

"I just shoved everything I could find in the chest and basket." Brodie's expression sobered. "The crate is filled with rag dolls. They're not poppets yet, but it's an awful lot of dolls to be turned into poppets. Must be over a hundred. Do people buy them as dolls or are they only used as poppets?"

Ninette, who was swinging the doors of the barn wide open, looked over at Brodie. "Children play with rag dolls so people buy them for reasons other than making poppets."

"I found two while I was searching for my clan," Jorgen said.

"Found two what?" Mallory hurried forward to help the injured off the wagon now it was stopped, removing her coat first since it had warmed up. She noticed the rest had removed their warmer gear.

"Poppets." Jorgen took two small, timber boxes out of his satchel, two rows of holes spaced evenly across the lid of each box. "They were in the guildhouse."

Mallory took them, peering inside. "That can't be good for the people the poppets were made for."

Danae came to peer inside the boxes. "The string tied around the chest will make it hard for that person to breathe, the sharp pins stabbed into the knees, elbows and backs will cause them sharp pains and the poppet that is torn and slashed is slowly dying. You can see how the threads are starting to break down."

Mallory handed the first box to Danae so she could take out her wand. "If I use mend on it, will that keep the person from dying?"

"It should do." Danae rested the box on the back of the wagon, untying the string from around the chest of the poppet.

Mallory focused on the worst of the tears first, waiting for her mana to regen to continue to repair the poppet.

Ninette joined her while she worked. "I made stew if you're hungry."

"We should set up the table and chairs so we can sit at them for breakfast," Brodie said.

"There are only six chairs," Ninette said. "We won't all fit."

"Some of us will," Brodie argued.

"Get the chairs down," Mallory said. "It'll make it easier for me to heal everyone if they're seated on a chair rather than the ground." She cast mend I on the poppet again, this time healing a slash near the throat. The poppet began to disintegrate. "Danni, what's happening?" Fear raced through her. Had she killed the person?

Danae returned to her side. "What did you do?"

"I mended a tear near the throat." Mallory pointed to the location.

"Make the same tear. They might have a spell or enchantment on them to counteract the poppet problem," Danae said.

Chapter Forty-One

Mallory took out her dagger, making the same damage as the one she'd mended. The poppet stopped disintegrating. She let out a long, slow breath. "I was killing them?"

Danae rested a hand on Mallory's shoulder for a moment. "It wasn't deliberate. Most times it isn't a problem repairing what has been done to a poppet. Sometimes though, people have paid mages or apothecaries to help them."

Mallory looked at the rest of the damage that she hadn't repaired yet. "Should I keep going?"

Danae nodded. "A little bit at a time, but be ready to replicate the damage if the poppet starts to disintegrate."

It took Mallory a few minutes before she could bring herself to repair more of the poppet. By the time she'd finished, none of the other repairs having caused it to disintegrate, her hands were shaking. "That was the worst. I seriously thought I was going to kill them." She clasped her hands together, trying to get them to stop shaking before she put the lid on the box.

"Who gets the money from the poppets?" Brodie asked.

"We can share it," Jorgen said. "I would offer all of it to you for what you've done to help me and Esben, but we need to save money to pay for ship fare to Eridell."

Mallory gave the two boxes to Ninette. "Can you put them somewhere safe?"

"There should be enough air in the top of the panniers that we can store them in there." Ninette took the two boxes and strode over to the panniers that were on the wagon belonging to the wagoner.

"Can you fully heal Merry now we're out of danger?" Roast asked.

Mallory started to point out that they were too close to Cutthroat Harbour to be considered out of danger. Changing her mind, she smiled, nodding to the chairs Brodie and Callum had set up around the table they'd taken off the back of the wagon.

Merry sat in one of the chairs, clutching hold of Mallory's hand. "Thank you so much for coming after us. You can't imagine how horrible it was. They took my cousin too. She jumped overboard trying to escape. They laughed when undines came after her. One of the other people they captured from Wildebay protested and they stabbed him and threw him overboard saying it was better the undines went after the two of them rather than the ship."

Mallory healed her three more times, bringing her health up to full. "I'm sorry about your cousin."

Merry's eyes watered. "Barle and I are the only ones who survived. There was another who made it to Cutthroat Harbour with us, but didn't last for long." She glanced up at Roast. "And I've lost my parents too."

Roast put his arm around Merry's shoulders. "We'll be able to go home soon."

Welby brought Barle over to be healed. "We're thinking of travelling back to Velkden with the three we set free from Cutthroat Harbour. We can rest up for a couple of days then head further north. Unless you're thinking of going that way yourself."

Mallory glanced around the barn. Her gaze rested on Emica for a moment. Even if they didn't escort Emica home, there was a harp they needed to track down. They might not have stolen it, but she felt partially responsible since they were the ones who'd taken Deneg to Kyla's farm. "I don't think so."

Emica inclined her head, smiling at her.

Mallory returned her attention to Barle, slowly healing him as her mana returned, also mending a couple of the worst tears in his clothes. "Only you and your brother are travelling back to Wildebay?"

When Welby nodded, Merry said, "I wish I could travel with you too. I just want to go home. But it's too far for me to walk."

The wagoner joined them. "I was able to buy plenty of essence crystals from Rodina. Once they'd made certain they had enough to pay all of you." He turned to Mallory. "I asked Kruth if he'd be interested in travelling to Buckneth with me, then escorting me to Surith. I know a wagoner up there who's looking for a permanent guard on his journeys between Surith and Lilica. Most of the time he travels between Ursen and Lilica, only going to Surith every couple of weeks."

Kruth came over to the table. "I wouldn't desert you like that. You've paid for my services in advance."

Mallory was tempted to sigh. She stepped back from Barle, who she'd finished healing. "We wouldn't expect you to stay with us instead of taking a job you're interested in. And that money wasn't in advance."

Ryan, who'd been sitting at the table eating a bowl of stew, set aside his empty bowl, getting to his feet. "Think of it as danger pay."

"You don't need me?" Kruth looked at each of them.

"We can see you when we take Danni to her dad's." Brodie grinned. "And you can teach me some more insults."

Mallory laughed. "Like you need to learn any more."

"You'd be happy for me to leave?" Kruth asked.

Ryan clapped Kruth on the shoulder. "Of course we won't be happy to see you go. We'll miss you. But we're happy you've got a job offer that won't have you stuck guarding a mine."

"Are you interested in the job?" Callum asked.

Kruth nodded. "It sounds good. I've liked travelling down here. I didn't think I'd enjoy this kind of work, but I do."

"There you go then." Ryan grinned at him. "It's settled. You and your danger pay can escort the wagoner home."

It took Mallory two hours to partially heal everyone, set bones and do rapid mend on the other two who needed it. Stepping back from her last patient, Esben, Mallory stretched. Even with her patients seated on chairs, she'd needed to do a lot of bending over them as she checked wounds that were slow to heal and set bones. She'd also used her two cure disease potions on Hisoki and Esben.

While she'd been healing everyone, the wagoner and Kruth had sorted the gear, transferring their chest and items to the new wagon. Welby had also left some of the venison with them so they wouldn't have to worry about hunting for meat for a couple of days. Brodie had talked the wagoner into trading a spare canvas he'd bought in Velkden, worried the canvas over the top wouldn't be enough to keep the rain off the chests if they should have heavy rain. Brodie had traded the crate of rag dolls, minus the crate, for the canvas. His estimation had been close and there had been a hundred dolls in the crate. The crate was filled with some of their gear that had been in the chests the wagoner had brought with him.

Danae looked over the horse Callum had caught. "It's only good for riding."

"What makes Bug and Augusta so different they can pull a cart?" Brodie asked.

"As well as they've been trained to pull one, their build," Danae said.

"It's going to be too expensive to buy another horse to pull the wagon," Brodie muttered.

"Might get lucky and be able to do a quest for one," Ryan said.

Brodie's expression brightened. "Hell yeah. That'd be the way to get one."

They traipsed outside to see everyone off. Mallory strode to the front of the wagon where the wagoner sat with Kruth. "Which direction are you taking?"

"The way we came," the wagoner said.

Mallory took the potion out of her satchel that they'd found at Cutthroat Harbour and held it out to Kruth. "Could you return this to the frog mage and let him know he can stop worrying about it?"

Nodding, Kruth took the potion. "Gladly. Is there anything else you'd like me to do for you?"

"Can you let my mother know I'm well and didn't lose any revives at Cutthroat Harbour?" Danae asked.

Kruth again nodded.

"And say hello to NFB for me and give him a pat," Brodie said.

"Who is NFB?" Kruth asked.

"Not For Bacon, Brodie's pet pig that Sarisa is taking care of," Callum said.

Ryan chuckled. "At this rate they'll be in Wayholt all day."

"They will not," Brodie muttered.

Ryan held out his hand, shaking the wagoner's. "We'll see you next time we're in Buckneth." He smiled. "We still have business there."

"I'll let the hunter know," the wagoner said.

Before anyone else could say anything, a black cat looked out from under the wagon seat and miaowed. Mallory laughed. "Isn't that the cat you fed at Velkden, Ryan?"

"Good thing they're going back there," Brodie said.

The cat leapt from the wagon, launching himself at Ryan who put out his hands to grab him. "I don't think he likes that idea."

One of the villagers they'd rescued from Velkden, looked out from around the edge of the canvas. "That's the apothecary's cat. The apothecary was one of the first who died when the invaders attacked."

"The cat has no owner?" Brodie asked.

The villager shook their head.

"No wonder it looks so hungry." Brodie took the cat from Ryan. "Better get you some of that stew." He headed inside the barn carrying the cat, glancing over his shoulder to say goodbye as he stepped through the doors, Fang at his side.

"Does it have a name?" Mallory asked.

The villager shrugged. "The apothecary called it cat or kitty."

"Kitty works," Ryan said.

Callum slowly shook his head. "You're terrible at naming animals."

Chapter Forty-Two

The rest of the goodbyes were soon said, Roast thanking them numerous times and reminding them they could stay with him if they were ever in the area. Mallory stood beside Ryan, her arm around his waist, his around her shoulders, waving as the wagon disappeared along the road. "I'm going to miss having all of them around."

Ryan's arm momentarily tightened around her. "We'll see them again."

"What about when we go to Eridell? We mightn't come back this way for years," Mallory said.

Danae stared along the empty road. "I don't think I'd like to wait years to visit my parents."

"There you go," Ryan said. "We'll be back." He turned to face the barn. "We need to make plans and decide where we're heading today. It's probably best not to stick around here too long. Who knows where Rass' revive will take him."

"I want to get a proper look at what I got from the secondhand shop," Brodie said. "I kept the lantern I used turned down low so I didn't get a good look at everything."

Callum helped Brodie take the chest and tall cane basket off the back of the wagon, bringing both over and setting them down beside the table, Smudge and Fang following the two of them around and getting in the way. Brodie took the lid off the cane basket first, taking items out and placing them on the table. There were four pieces of folded material, two black a dark brown and a pale blue.

Danae ran a hand over the pale blue material that was on the top of the pile. "There's enough in each piece to make a couple of garments."

"Look what else I got." Brodie placed four large essence crystals on the table. "I looked to see if they had any more in the shop, but there were none. They were behind the counter so I don't think they were meant to be for sale."

"They'll come in handy," Mallory said.

Brodie took out eight fleece lined jackets, placing them on one end of the table. "They had a heap of snow gear." He returned to the basket. "They also had matching ear flap hats to go with them." He put the eight fleece lined hats with the jackets.

"Ushanka," Callum said.

"U-what?"Brodie asked.

Callum laughed. "It's what the hats are called. Ushankas."

"Yeah well, I got some of them and matching boots too. And eight pairs of gloves." Brodie gestured towards the cane basket. "That's all that's left in there." He started to return the items to the basket.

Mallory placed her hand on the crystals when he went to move them. "They can go in the other chest with the crystals Rodina gave us."

"I can put them away." Ninette collected the crystals.

Mallory was tempted to again point out to Ninette that she didn't need to run around after them. But Danae spoke.

"Why did you take all the clothing and boots suited to snowy environments?"

Brodie shrugged. "Thought they'd be worth more than all the other types of clothes. They didn't have any trousers, but I suppose the boots go to your knees and the jacket almost to your knees so most of you should be rugged up." He put the jackets back in the basket. "They should fit us if we want to keep them and sell the extras. I tried to make sure I got the right sizes and a few extra sizes in case I didn't get the right ones. I don't know what the weather is like in Eridell and I bet stuff like this costs a fortune."

Ryan chuckled. "It wouldn't surprise me if it did."

Brodie put the lid back on the cane basket before opening the lid of the chest. He grinned as he held up two pieces of paper. "I found some of that demonic paper. The one you can write on and see the words on the other." He held a piece out to Danae. "For when you're at the academy and we're off adventuring."

Danae smiled, taking the piece of paper from Brodie. "Thank you." She folded the paper and put it in her satchel.

Brodie folded his and put it in his own satchel. "You can let us know when you're ready to join us again."

"I will," Danae said.

Callum strode over to the chest. "What else did you get? Anything else useful?"

Brodie took a large leather-bound notebook out. "It's got writing in the first twenty or so pages, but I thought Mallory could tear them out and use it to keep her daily notes in when she's used up the other ones."

Callum took it from him, frowning as he flicked through the pages. "This is information about shipping routes."

Hisoki joined them, taking the book from Callum. "Someone appears to be passing on information about shipping routes for the Thornlight Shipping Company. Their headquarters is in Mistview."

"Where is that?" Brodie asked.

"Didn't you read Legend Of The Ancestral King?" Callum asked.

"Yeah, of course I did." Brodie paused a moment. "Mostly."

Ryan grinned. "He probably skipped half of it so he could find out how it ends."

"I didn't skip half of it," Brodie muttered.

"It's the capital of Eridell," Hisoki said. "Each of these ships listed here travel to Ruby Isle, amongst other places. Sun Dancer, Spring Light, Bronze Dawn, Little Moon, Heart Song and Midnight Rose. This gives the shipping route for each of them during the next three months. As well as if they're stopping to pick up cargo, passengers or both."

"You've got to be kidding," Brodie exclaimed. "Not another quest. We just got rid of some."

Mallory checked the notification. *Trouble At Thornlight Shipping Company: Notify the company that someone is passing along information about their ships.* "How would we let them know about the problem?"

"They have holdings in Shadhurst." Hisoki looked at each of them. "If you do plan to let them know, I'll leave it for you to complete the quest." He glanced at Emica. "When you escort my daughter home."

"We haven't agreed to it yet," Ryan said.

With her journal still open, Mallory glanced over the rest of the quests. "Talking of quests, who would we notify in Shadhurst about a spy?"

Hisoki smiled. "That would be me. Where is the spy?"

Mallory placed her hand on Ninette's arm and added her to the party before she answered. "In the capital." She would have also added Emica, Jorgen and Esben if they'd been standing near her.

Hisoki stared at her for a moment. "The dark forces knew many details they shouldn't have, including which ship we'd take. I'll notify the Duke. Information like this is always rewarded. I'll see that you receive a reward when you come to Shadhurst."

"Hell yeah." Brodie victory punched the air. "A pity they aren't all this easy."

Reading over the quest details, Mallory was glad she'd added Ninette. *Spy In The Capital: An appropriate person has been notified about the spy. Your* party may collect a reward from the Duke when you are in Shadhurst. You also earned five experience points each. The warrior needed a lot more experience points if she was to catch up with them. She turned to Hisoki. "We still haven't agreed to escort Emica to Shadhurst. We actually have a few other things we need to do before we can go to the capital."

"That would work in well," Hisoki said. "I'd rather Emica wasn't in the capital for a few weeks while there's a spy watching our movements. And leaving her with people who have no actual connection to me makes a great deal of sense."

Ryan glanced at Emica. "You haven't asked your daughter what she wants."

Hisoki smiled. "Thank you. I was fairly certain you could be trusted, but comments like that reassure me." He glanced at Jorgen and Esben. "Although I'm not overly impressed that you have two crystalline wolves travelling with you. Do you realise it interferes with Emica's abilities?"

"She told us," Ryan said. "And you still haven't asked her."

Hisoki chuckled. "There's no need to ask Emica anything. My daughter is always very vocal when she isn't interested in doing something."

"You're happy to stay with us?" Ryan asked.

"I like the sound of your plans." Emica grinned, glancing at her father before returning her attention to Ryan. "Stealing eggs from a drake nest sounds like it could be interesting."

"Now wait a minute," Hisoki began.

Emica interrupted him. "Aren't you the one that tells me to always find out all the details?"

Hisoki sighed. "I've had a lot on my mind." He faced Ryan. "Are you going after drake eggs or is my daughter making fun of me?"

"We need to do other things first," Ryan said. "But we do plan to go after them." He grinned. "We've got some rogues with stealth and a mage who can make them invisible. It should be a breeze."

"Only the rogues will be getting close to the nest?" Hisoki asked.

Ryan shrugged. "We'll figure that out when we get to it. No point making plans when we don't know anything about the area."

Chapter Forty-Three

Mallory decided to take pity on Hisoki. "We need to track down a harp. The person with it was last headed to Delten."

"When you reach the intersection north east of here, head south towards Deadman Cove," Hisoki said. "You don't want to go into that village. It's another dark forces place, but there's a narrow track that'll take you around the village."

Ryan took out the map of Ruby Isle and put it on the table.

Hisoki ran his finger across the map. "You go from this road, cross over that one and then onto this one that will take you to South Point. The turnoff is on a bit of a rise where you'll catch your first glimpse of the sea."

Ryan folded up the map and returned it to his belt pouch. "Thanks."

"If you have a piece of paper, along with pen and ink, I can write a letter naming Emica as an emissary of the Duke. She can use it in villages and towns to gain free accommodation and food rather than be a burden on your resources," Hisoki offered.

Ryan shook his head. "Some of the places we've stayed in would find that a hardship."

Hisoki stared at him for a moment. "What are your plans for the future?"

"He wants to be a guardian," Emica said.

Hisoki slowly nodded. "It will suit you."

"Thanks," Ryan said.

"If you ever decide you'd be interested in something with a little more intrigue, come and see me."

Ryan didn't answer immediately. "Okay."

Hisoki glanced at his daughter before returning his attention to Ryan. "If I was to send a message to Emica, where would be the best place?"

Ryan shrugged. "I don't know. We'll be between a few places."

"Would you consider giving me one of the pieces of duplication paper you have?" Hisoki asked.

Danae turned to Brodie. "I won't need it until we travel to Merrow."

"What if he uses it all up?" Brodie asked.

"I will return it and a new pair," Hisoki offered.

Brodie held out his hand. "Deal."

Hisoki shook his hand, taking the piece of paper Danae handed him and slipping it in a pocket of his trousers. He took a step back. "I need to return to Shadhurst in case they have anything else planned." He took another step back towards the exit. "Is there anything I can do for you?"

"Can you find out information about someone for us?" Callum asked. "We've run into a hellion called Rass a few times."

"That's a good idea," Brodie said.

"Do you know where he lives? Or where he's from?" Hisoki asked.

"On the border of Cape Barren and Hellfire," Danae said. "We don't know much about him."

"I'll see what I can learn." He turned to Emica. "Walk me to the door." He started for the door, pausing to look over his shoulder. "I'll see all of you in Shadhurst when you arrive." He continued to the door, remaining there for a few minutes to talk quietly to Emica.

Mallory watched them, her mouth dropping open when Hisoki turned into a fox with three tails. He was out the door in a burst of speed and immediately out of sight.

Callum came to stand beside her. "That was pretty impressive."

Mallory nodded.

"Are we really going after Deneg?"

Mallory faced him. "We should." When he didn't say anything, she spoke again. "Does that bother you?"

"I thought he'd at least say goodbye when he left." Callum shrugged. "But I suppose when you need to leave in a hurry because you've stolen something valuable, there isn't time for goodbyes."

Mallory rested a hand on his arm. "I'm sorry."

"I barely knew him." Callum smiled wryly. "I guess I knew him even less than I thought."

Emica returned to where they stood around the table. "Are we going to find out the rest of what Brodie put in the chest?"

Brodie took out a cloth bag, grinning when he tipped the contents out onto the table. "Jewellery. Lots of jewellery we can sell."

Mallory laughed, the sound echoed by the rest of those standing by the table. "We shouldn't be surprised."

Brodie took two books out of the chest. "I also got these for Callum. One is about enchanting and the other is about weaver."

Callum took the books. "Cool." He flicked through them. "I can't wait until I get the full set."

"I hope that isn't until we have a base in Eridell," Ryan said.

Callum shrugged, answering with a smile.

Brodie started putting the jewellery back in the bag. "How do you tell if any of these have an enchantment on them?"

"Try them on. That way you can find any that will give you a buff," Danae said. "It won't tell you for certain if they don't have an enchantment though."

Jorgen helped Brodie put the jewellery in the bag. "What is our next plan?"

"We should travel to Delten," Ryan said.

Callum nodded. "Yeah. We need to get that harp back."

Ryan took out the map and placed it on the table. "We should figure out how far we can travel today."

"Did you want me to cut some saplings so we can create a shelter over the wagon?" Jorgen asked.

"That'd be good," Ryan said.

"I can help you," Ninette offered.

"I'll go with you too." Esben rose from the chair he'd been sitting on.

Mallory shook her head. "You're not doing anything with that broken arm. Sit down again and

I'll get the boneset salve." It wouldn't reduce the days it'd take for her to heal him, but hopefully it would reduce the pain if his injury was more healed.

"It feels a lot better," Esben protested.

Jorgen laughed. "My cousin practically had to be tied to his bed when he was younger and was injured enough to need bed rest."

"I was fine then too," Esben said.

Jorgen smiled. "Listen to the apothecary. She knows what she's talking about." He turned to Ninette. "I'd appreciate the help." He strode to the wagon, Ninette at his side.

"Being two years older than me doesn't make you the boss," Esben called out.

Jorgen kept walking. Grabbing the axe, he headed outside, Ninette remaining at his side.

Mallory collected the boneset salve from the chest she'd put it in and used it on Esben's arm before using spare shirts to create a makeshift sling. "Don't use it. I'll use rapid mend on you again this evening and continue to use it on you until you're healed. It'd be a lot quicker if we had more boneset salve."

"Thank you. It's a lot quicker than I could normally expect," Esben said.

By the time Jorgen and Ninette had returned with saplings and rigged a cover over the wagon with

Ryan's help, Callum had calculated how long it would take them to reach their next destination. Before he could tell them anything, the cat darted out from one of the corners of the barn and dropped a rat at Ryan's feet.

Callum laughed. "Looks like you've got a new friend."

"Are you going to make it your companion animal?" Brodie asked.

Mallory stared down at the skinny cat who looked up at Ryan as if waiting for a response. "It seems pretty smart. Look how it hid under the wagon seat so it could travel with us."

Ryan patted the cat on the head. "Thanks, but you have it. Looks like you need it more than I do." Straightening, he turned to Brodie. "Like Mallory said, it seems pretty smart. Who knows what it might end up like if it gains extra intelligence from becoming a companion animal."

The cat picked up the rat and sauntered over to the wagon to hide underneath it. Before Callum could do much more than make a sound, Smudge started to softly make his warning cry. Jorgen drew one of his stilettos. "Can you make me invisible?" He glanced at Mallory as he headed for the exit.

Chapter Forty-Four

Mallory cast the spell on Jorgen, hurrying towards the door and trying to remain out of sight as she peered outside. She could see nothing. But Smudge was never wrong. If he said there was something to be worried about, then there certainly was. A brush of air drew Mallory's attention. "Jorgen?" She kept her voice low.

"I recognise a couple of them from Cutthroat Harbour. There are six of them out there and they're closing in on the barn," Jorgen said, still invisible.

Emica drew her swords. "I say we take them out before they reach us. Mallory could make each of us invisible and we can hunt them down before they know we're coming."

"I don't have that much mana," Mallory protested. "And it doesn't regen that fast." Remembering Emica's comments about not being able to see her lightning trap, she added the rest of them to the party. "I don't want any of you being hurt if I put down lightning traps."

"There are nine of us. We should be able to take them down without a problem," Esben said.

Mallory pointed a finger at him. "You're not fighting anyone with that broken arm." She slowly shook her head. "What's with rogues who don't want to heal properly?" She cast two lightning traps in front of the door. "That should slow down any that try to enter."

"Why don't we stay in here and attack them from the cover of the barn?" Callum asked.

"Give me one of your stilettos, Jorgen. I don't want to be unarmed if they get inside." Esben held out his hand.

Brodie stared at Mallory's feet. "Why have you got streaks of purple on your boots?"

"Jorgen." Esben continued to hold out his hand.

Mallory looked at her boots. "I dropped a potion in the apothecary shop." She looked at Esben. "We have a spare stiletto you can borrow, but it doesn't have a sheath. We actually have two spare stilettos if you need two once your arm is healed. Neither have sheaths."

"I only need one. I'm not a high enough level to

wield two." Esben lowered his hand, glancing at her boots. "It was probably dye." When Mallory frowned, he gestured to her boots. "The potion you dropped. It was probably dye. Either permanent or temporary."

"I'll get the stiletto." Ninette hurried over to their gear that was mostly packed on the wagon or in the panniers sitting beside the wagon waiting to be carried by Bobbi.

"We can't stay in here. What if they set fire to the place?" Emica asked. "There's only one exit."

"Make two of us invisible," Jorgen said. "We can go out and start attacking the ones that are on their own as they try and surround the place."

"You better pick me," Brodie said. "I need the XP."

"That's why I won't be picking you." Mallory took out her wand. "Your stats are too low."

Ninette gave the stiletto to Esben, who thanked her.

Mallory turned to Danae. "Did you want to go out there?"

Danae smiled. "I'd love to, but it might be best to send someone who's noisier than me so Jorgen can keep track of where they are."

Callum stepped forward. "I'll go." He looked down at Smudge who ran over to him, placing a paw on his leg and holding the other one up. "You'll have to stay here."

"They should be close enough by now that he'll gain XP from anything you kill," Jorgen said.

Mallory cast vanish I on the two of them, listening to the soft footsteps as they walked across the dirt to the exit.

"I'm never going to level up," Brodie muttered.

Ryan chuckled. "Yeah, we know. It's so unfair." He drew his sword. "I'm going out there."

"Wait." Mallory drew mana from one of the small essence crystals. It crumbled to dust, leaving her with only one in her satchel. Her fingers brushed against a potion vial, reminding her that she still needed to check what she'd taken from the apothecary shop. "I'm going with you." She made him invisible. Her mana had regenerated enough that she was able to cast the spell on herself. Which also meant the other two would soon be visible. "Let's go." She strode towards the door, glancing at Smudge who peered around the edge of it. "Stay inside."

"This way."

Mallory headed left, in the direction Ryan's voice had come from. She drew her sword, wanting to let her mana regen enough that she could cast vanish I again if she needed to. She spotted the enemy she assumed Ryan was aiming for. Running lightly towards them, she attacked with her sword, dodging back when the warrior tried to strike her with his sword. Grinning, she slipped around behind him, attacking once more. This time when she tried to get out of the way, she ran into Ryan, stumbling back to avoid the warrior's sword.

The moment the two of them became visible, the warrior furiously attacked them. Mallory could barely manage to block. Worried he'd eventually get past them, she cast poison dart. He dropped to the ground three seconds later. She stood over his body, trying to catch her breath.

"He seemed determined to kill us," Ryan said.

Mallory scanned the area, trying to spot another one. "I wonder if he owned the shop Brodie raided."

Ryan chuckled. "Might explain it. Or it could have been owned by a friend or family member."

A shout went up near the entrance of the barn and the two of them broke into a run. Ryan reached the barn first, joining in the fight. Three rogues and an archer attacked, Mallory's lightning traps having been sprung. She cast a fireball at the archer since everyone else was focused on the ones near the doors.

When he aimed his arrow at her, Mallory stepped behind a tree, checking her mana. She had enough to cast vanish I, but wouldn't be able to do anything else for a moment. Taking out the spyglass she still hadn't returned to Callum, she peeked around the edge of the tree. The rogues had the least health. She cast a fireball at one with only six health, grinning when she took him out. Before she could attack one of the other two rogues, they were taken out.

Returning the spyglass to its holster, she cast poison dart at the archer, stepping back behind the tree when he fired at her. When she looked again, he was gone. She took a step forward. "Did he run or use a revive?"

"Revive." Brodie crouched to check over one of the bodies at his feet.

Mallory checked everyone's health, healing Ryan and Brodie as her mana regened. She touched Emica's hand as she walked past her, healing her twice. Ninette also needed to be healed twice. Jorgen and Esben were fine.

It didn't take them long to loot the bodies. As well as replacing their arrows they gained two spare, found a sheathed stiletto for Esben, twenty copper pieces, two steel throwing knives that were given to Brodie, a belt, a pair of navy trousers and a letter informing the receiver that they were on their last warning.

Brodie dropped the letter back on the body. "Good

thing he died now. I bet he wasn't in the sort of job where firing means letting you go to find another one."

Mallory returned the spyglass to Callum and removed the extras from their party. "Did you end up working out how long it would take us to get to South Point and then Delten?"

"It'll take us just under three hours to reach South Point and about two and a half hours from there to Delten." Callum put the spyglass and its holster back on his belt.

"Then let's get moving," Ryan said. "We can make it to South Point before dark. We'll see what the area is like before we figure out if we should risk travelling onto Delten in the dark. We need to keep moving or Deneg will get too far ahead of us."

"Do we get any of the coins that were on the bodies?" Esben asked.

"No," Jorgen stated.

"Why not?" Esben asked. "You helped kill them. How are we meant to afford to live?"

"They will see that we're fed for our help." Jorgen helped Ninette put out the fire and clean up the crockery.

Mallory sorted through the potions she'd grabbed, putting them in the chest Rodina had given them.

There were twenty potions. She had a ten minute water breathing potion, three mana potions containing ten mana, four health potions, two strong night vision potions, two cure corpse rot potions, two potions of swiftness, a fleeting years potion that added two years, four weapon poisons and the last one she held onto, staring at the label. Closing the lid of the chest, she jumped out of the wagon, holding up the potion.

Chapter Forty-Five

Mallory couldn't stop grinning. "We have a timeless potion. Four weeks. We can stop the ageing process for a short amount of time."

Brodie took the potion from her, examining the contents. "It kind of looks like weak pee."

Mallory took it back from her brother, making a face. "Did you have to mention that?"

Ryan chuckled. "Of course he did." He took the vial from Mallory, holding it up to the light coming in through the open door. "But he is right."

Callum took the vial. "The colour does look like it might be watered down urine."

Danae laughed softly. "That's the correct colour for that potion."

"Who gets it?" Brodie asked.

Callum returned it to Mallory. "No one yet. We should wait until we know we're going to be here for a bit." He turned to Danae. "That's if the potion can be split up that much."

Danae nodded. "It can."

"Are we going now?" Brodie demanded. "I want to get to South Point and earn some location XP. Do you think we can get close enough to Deadman Cove to get XP from there too?"

"No." Mallory put the potion in her satchel. "There's no way we're going close to a dark forces place when we have other things that need to be done." She glanced at the wagon. "Besides, if you raided another shop like you did in Cutthroat Harbour, there'd be no room for us."

"We're going now." Ryan started to stride towards the wagon.

"One moment." Jorgen took six beads out of his satchel. They matched the clan beads he wore in his plaits. Dark blue with swirls of silver running through them.

Esben shook his head. "No. They've done very little to deserve them. It takes more than saving the lives of two travellers. We can't give them to whoever we want."

"They've done more than that." Jorgen turned to Mallory, holding out a bead. "These are very rarely given to people outside our clan. You rescued me, treated me like I was one of your party and helped me rescue my cousin. You used your own resources and risked your lives to do so. Many people treat us with distrust and even outright hostility. None of you did that."

Mallory took the bead. "What does it do?"

"It tells people you're a friend of travellers and can be trusted." Esben turned to Jorgen. "This isn't the way we do things. Decisions aren't made by only one clan member."

Jorgen met his cousin's gaze, his words soft. "Sometimes they are." He turned to Mallory again. "I can put the bead in a single plait for you. Those not of the clan typically don't have eight plaits. Only the one to show they're friends."

Mallory smiled at him. "I'd like that."

Jorgen inclined his head before giving a bead to Ryan, Callum, Brodie and Danae.

Brodie stared at the bead. "Do I need to grow my hair?"

"You can wear a single plait if you wish," Jorgen said. "Or put it on an earing. Those who know will recognise the markings. Most others will think it only decorative."

Brodie slipped the bead into his belt pouch. "I was

thinking of growing my hair." He ran a hand over his head, his hair already longer than usual.

"Thanks for this." Ryan put the bead in his belt pouch. "We'd never turn our back on someone in need."

"I know." Jorgen took a step towards the wagon. "We can go now."

Mallory sat beside Jorgen in the back of the wagon, Ryan and Danae up the front where she was teaching him how to drive. Mallory waited until they were on the road before she spoke to Jorgen. "Where did you get the beads from?"

He didn't answer immediately. "Esben told me there were four others with him. He was the only one who survived. I couldn't leave the beads behind to be used by the dark forces. They were in the guildhouse."

Mallory rested her hand on his. "I'm sorry." She automatically checked his health, finding it was fine.

"There were two ships that captured people from our clan," Esben said. "They thought I was unconscious too, but I was only dazed. The Star Finder and The Nelly."

"The Nelly?" Brodie asked. "The dark forces have a ship called The Nelly?"

"They probably stole the ship," Esben said.

The Star Finder was the ship at Cutthroat Harbour," Callum said. "The one Ryan and I searched."

"Was there anyone on it?" Esben asked.

Callum shook his head. "Sorry. No."

"We need to find out where The Nelly went," Esben said.

"Great. Another one," Brodie muttered.

Laughing, Mallory checked her journal notification. *Hunt For The Nelly: Esben and Jorgen need to learn where the dark forces ship, The Nelly, sailed in order to learn what happened to other people from their clan.*

Esben looked from Brodie to Mallory. "I don't understand."

Callum laughed. "You will do eventually." He looked at Mallory. "When are we going home next."

"Never," Brodie muttered. "I'll probably spend my entire weekend in time out. How can it be time out when you have to share a room with someone else and they can come and go whenever they want? Our fake brother shouldn't be allowed in the room while I'm in timeout. At least then I could have a break from him."

"Can I return with you?" Jorgen asked. "There's so much more I want to learn about your world."

Esben straightened. "Another world? Can I go too?"

Ryan chuckled, looking over his shoulder, barely visible through the chairs stacked on top of the table. "I could do with some help getting the house cleaned and sorted out. You can keep your share of the money paid into the demonic bank account as payment for helping."

"I wish I could go too," Danae said.

"You probably could this time. Now we've got the house you can stay in," Ryan said. "The electricity isn't on, but that won't bother any of you. We can grab some candles and a portable gas cooker."

"I can go back with you?" Danae asked.

Ryan again glanced over his shoulder. "If Ninette is willing to stay behind and look after everything, including all the animals."

The cat was curled up on Ninette's lap, purring contentedly as she patted it. "I would have the animals all to myself while you were gone?"

Smudge scampered over to Ninette, chattering excitedly to her.

Ninette patted him on the head. "Sounds like he's happy with that too."

"When do we go?"

Mallory grinned at the amount of excitement she

could hear in the half-elf's voice. "When we're somewhere safe."

"I can't wait," Danae said.

Smiling, Mallory made her way to the chest she'd put her leather-bound notebook in. "I might make a start on writing about today's adventures. Who knows where we'll be tonight or what we'll be doing."

"It better involve some XP," Brodie muttered.

"You can gather resources once we put some distance between us and Cutthroat Harbour," Callum said.

Brodie's expression brightened. "Hell yeah. How far?"

Smiling, Mallory wrote in the notebook she'd taken from the chest, sitting in front of it as she did. Looking up from the page, she saw Jorgen watched her. She assumed the question in her mind about why he was looking in her direction was reflected in her expression since he smiled, inclined his head and looked out the back of the wagon. The view was partially blocked by Bobbi and the new riding horse that were tied to the back of the wagon, which was being pulled by Augusta and Bug.

Returning to writing in the notebook, she thought of all the things they still had to do. The many quests, the new books to read, the beads Jorgen had given them and the drake eggs they planned to take from a nest. No wonder Brodie didn't want to go home. She was tempted to stay a little longer this time. Dread filled her at the thought of going to her father's for the weekend. She wasn't looking forward to the arguments and her father's girlfriend's two annoying sons.

She pushed thoughts of the weekend aside, looking out the back of the wagon. She was on Inadon, a long way from parents, annoying fake siblings as Brodie called them and friends who assumed the worst. She glanced around at those seated with her. She had to agree with Brodie. She wasn't ready to go home. Not even close to being ready.

Final Stats

Character weight does not include any backpacks, satchels, their contents or items carried by livestock.

Mallory

Character Level: 5
Health: 42
Stamina: 70
Mana: 60
Weight: 5kg 280g/90kg

CAS XP: 54/149
Available CAS Points: 2
Available Class Points: 0
Level Progress: 5:1/10

Attributes

Strength: 9
Constitution: 14
Intelligence: 12
Wisdom: 12

Dexterity: 5
Charisma: 5
Luck: 6

Class

Mage: 2
Warrior: 3

Class Skills
None

Spells

Fireball: 0
Health I: 0
Poison Dart I: 0

(Expand For More Details)

Weapon and Armour Affinity

Wand: 1 (+1% damage)
Cloth Armour: 0
Short Sword: 0

(Expand For More Details)

Crafting

Alchemy: 1
Apothecary: 45
Wheelwright: 1

(Expand For More Details)

Reputation

Global: 0
Local Areas:
Ruby Isle
(Expand For More Details)

Buffs and Negative Stats

Necklace: doubles healing done
Silver bracelet: +1 mana every 15 secs

Available Revives 5

Mallory

Spells Expanded

*All attack spells have +37% damage to base attacks.

Level 0

Fireball: 0
Mana cost: 3
Cooldown: 2 seconds
Damage: low 3, normal 5, critical 7
Duration: Instant

Flame: 0
Mana cost: 5
Cooldown: 3 seconds
Damage: low 4, normal 6, critical 8
Damage Over Time: 4 every 2 seconds
Duration: Non-flammable materials 6 secs,
flammable materials until runs out of fuel

Lightning Strike: 0
Mana cost: 3
Cooldown: 2 seconds
Damage: low 3, normal 5, critical 7
Duration: Instant

Mend I: 0
Mana Cost: 17
Cooldown: 5 seconds
Area Of Effect: 1cm2
Duration: Instant

Level 1

Beacon: 0
Mana Cost: 15
Cooldown: 5 seconds
Area Of Effect: to be cast on a
solid surface
Duration: 10 mins

Poison Dart I: 0
Mana Cost: 6
Cooldown: 3 seconds
Damage: low 4, normal 6, crit 8
Damage Over Time: 5 every 3 seconds
Duration: 3 secs

Health I: 0
Restores health to target
Mana Cost: 6
Cooldown: 3 seconds
Area Of Effect: +1HP to target
within 2m
Duration: Instant

Level 2

Lightning Trap: 0
Mana Cost: 10
Cooldown: 5 seconds
Damage: 10
Duration: damage on contact

Vanish I: 0
Mana Cost: 25
Cooldown: 5 seconds
Area Of Effect: causes target, within
a 2m range, to vanish
Duration: 1 min

Mallory

Spells Expanded 2

Level 3

Magelight: 0
Mana Cost: 20
Cooldown: 10 seconds
Area Of Effect: creates a ball of light near caster
Duration: 15 mins

Weak Reanimate: 0
Mana Cost: 20
Cooldown: 5 seconds
Area Of Effect: reanimate one of the dead level 3
Range: 2m
Duration: 1 min

Weapon and Armour Affinity

Dagger (and enchanted): 1 (+1% damage)
Wand: 1 (+1% damage)
Cloth Armour: 0
Unarmed: 0

Chain Mail Armour: 0
Short Sword (and enchanted): 0
Shield (and enchanted): 0
Dual Swords: 0

Crafting Expanded

Alchemy: 1
Apothecary: 45
Bard: 0
Bartering: 0
Brewer: 0

Cooking: 0
Diplomacy: 0
Fishing: 0
Hunting: 0

Husbandry: 0
Languages: 0
Sailing: 0
Scribe: 0

Shipwright: 0
Thatcher: 0
Wheelwright: 1
Woodcutter: 0

Reputation Expanded

Ruby Isle:
Buckneth 22
Cutthroat Harbour -17

Mer Point 10
South Peak Mine 5
Surith 5

Velkden 42
Wayholt 10
Wildebay 10

Ryan

Character Level: 1
Health: 27
Stamina: 45
Mana: 20
Weight: 10kg 536g/90kg

CAS XP: 55/116
Available CAS Points: 10
Available Class Points: 0
Level Progress: 1:8/10

Attributes

Strength: 9
Constitution: 9
Intelligence: 5
Wisdom: 4

Dexterity: 5
Charisma: 5
Luck: 6

Class

Warrior: 1

Class Skills
None

Spells

None

Weapon and Armour Affinity

Chain Mail Armour: 0
Short Sword: 1 (+1% damage)
Shield: 1 (+1% damage)
(-1% damage taken)
Dual Swords: 0

Crafting

Hunting: 5
Wheelwright: 1

(Expand For More Details)

Reputation

Global: 0
Local Areas:
Ruby Isle
(Expand For More Details)

Buffs and Negative Stats

None

Available Revives 2

Ryan

Crafting Expanded

Alchemy: 0
Apothecary: 0
Bard: 0
Bartering: 0
Brewer: 0

Cooking: 0
Diplomacy: 0
Fishing: 0
Hunting: 5

Husbandry: 0
Languages: 0
Sailing: 0
Scribe: 0

Shipwright: 0
Thatcher: 0
Wheelwright: 1
Woodcutter: 0

Reputation Expanded

Ruby Isle:
Buckneth 22
Cutthroat Harbour -17

Mer Point 10
South Peak Mine 5
Surith 5

Velkden 42
Wayholt 10
Wildebay 10

Brodie

Character Level: 1
Health: 27
Stamina: 45
Mana: 25
Weight: 6kg 634g/50kg

CAS XP: 73/114
Available CAS Points: 4
Available Class Points: 0
Level Progress: 1:6/10

Attributes

Strength: 5
Constitution: 9
Intelligence: 4
Wisdom: 5

Dexterity: 8
Charisma: 7
Luck: 5

Class

Rogue: 1

Class Skills
Stealth: 0 (30 seconds,
1 hour cooldown)

Spells

None

Weapon and Armour Affinity

Stiletto: 1 (+1% damage)
Throwing Knives: 2
(+2% damage)
Leather Armour: 0

Crafting

Bartering: 1
Cooking: 7
Wheelwright: 1

(Expand For More Details)

Reputation

Global: 0
Local Areas:
Ruby Isle
(Expand For More Details)

Buffs and Negative Stats

None

Available Revives 1

Brodie

Crafting Expanded

Alchemy: 0
Apothecary: 0
Bard: 0
Bartering: 1
Brewer: 0

Cooking: 7
Diplomacy: 0
Fishing: 0
Hunting: 0

Husbandry: 0
Languages: 0
Sailing: 0
Scribe: 0

Shipwright: 0
Thatcher: 0
Wheelwright: 1
Woodcutter: 0

Reputation Expanded

Ruby Isle:
Bruckneth 22
Cutthroat Harbour -17

Mer Point 10
South Peak Mine 5
Surith 5

Velkden 42
Wayholt 10
Wildebay 10

Callum

Character Level: 1
Health: 21
Stamina: 35
Mana: 25
Weight: 7kg 616g/60kg

CAS XP: 88/116
Available CAS Points: 15
Available Class Points: 0
Level Progress: 1:8/10

Attributes

Strength: 6
Constitution: 7
Intelligence: 5
Wisdom: 5

Dexterity: 9
Charisma: 4
Luck: 7

Class

Archer: 1

Class Skills
None

Spells

None

Weapon and Armour Affinity

Short Bow (and enchanted): 1
(+1% damage)
Hunting Knife: 1 (+1% damage)
Studded Leather Armour: 0
Sling: 0
Slingshot

Crafting

Wheelwright: 1

(Expand For More Details)

Reputation

Global: 0
Local Areas:
Ruby Isle
(Expand For More Details)

Buffs and Negative Stats

Silver Ring: +2 damage to bow attacks

Available Revives 1

Callum

Crafting Expanded

Alchemy: 0
Apothecary: 0
Bard: 0
Bartering: 0
Brewer: 0

Cooking: 0
Diplomacy: 0
Fishing: 0
Hunting: 0

Husbandry: 0
Languages: 0
Sailing: 0
Scribe: 0

Shipwright: 0
Thatcher: 0
Wheelwright: 1
Woodcutter: 0

Reputation Expanded

Ruby Isle:
Buckneth 22
Cutthroat Harbour -17

Mer Point 10
South Peak Mine 5
Surith 5

Velkden 42
Wayholt 10
Wildebay 10

Danae

Character Level: 2
Health: 27
Stamina: 45
Mana: 25
Weight: 5kg 962g/60kg

CAS XP: 24/123
Available CAS Points: 5
Available Class Points: 0
Level Progress: 2:5/10

Attributes

Strength: 6
Constitution: 9
Intelligence: 5
Wisdom: 5

Dexterity: 11
Charisma: 4
Luck: 8

Class

Archer: 2

Class Skills
None

Spells

None

Weapon and Armour Affinity

Short Bow (and enchanted): 1
(+1% damage)
Hunting Knife: 1 (+1% damage)
Studded Leather Armour: 0

(Expand For More Details)

Crafting

Alchemy: 9
Bartering: 1
Cooking: 1
Glassblowing: 5

(Expand For More Details)

Reputation

Global: 0
Local Areas:
Ruby Isle
(Expand For More Details)

Buffs and Negative Stats

None

Racial Bonus

Archer +10% damage
Mage capable of using spells
one level above class level

Available Revives 2

Danae

Weapon and Armour Affinity Expanded

Short Bow (and enchanted): 1 (+1% damage)
Hunting Knife: 1 (+1% damage)
Studded Leather Armour: 0

Sling: 0
Slingshot
Enchanted Arrows
Unarmed: 1 (+1% damage)

Crafting Expanded

Alchemy: 9	Cooking: 1	Husbandry: 0	Shipwright: 0
Apothecary: 0	Diplomacy: 0	Languages: 0	Thatcher: 0
Bartering: 1	Fishing: 0	Sailing: 0	Wheelwright: 1
Brewer: 0	Glassblowing: 5	Scribe: 0	Woodcutter: 0
Clothier: 0			

Reputation Expanded

Ruby Isle:	Simria 22	Velkden 42
Buckneth 4	South Peak Mine 5	Wayholt 18
Cutthroat Harbour -17	Surith 5	Wildebay 10
Mer Point 10	Ursen 0	

COMPANION ANIMALS' FINAL STATS

Smudge 8HP (Callum)

1476XP/2000XP

Fang 6HP (Brodie)

1213XP/2000XP

Free Ebook

Subscribe to Avril's newsletter and receive a free ebook. This ebook is exclusive to those on her mailing list. To find out more about this offer visit:

www.avrilsabine.com/free-ebook

*

We value your privacy and will not sell, rent, exchange or loan your email address to third parties. Your information is confidential and you are under no obligation to remain on the mailing list and can unsubscribe at any time.

Acknowledgements

Thanks to all the usual crew and a special thanks to those of our readers who contacted us, begging for the next book in the series. Don't worry, there are more to come.

To The Reader

If you enjoyed this book, why not consider leaving a review to help other readers discover it too? Reader engagement is one of the few ways that lets an author know readers want more books in a particular series or genre. So leave a review and tell friends, not only about this book but also about other ones you've enjoyed, so you can continue to enjoy books by your favourite authors for years to come.

Dreams are meant to be lived,

Avril, Storm and Rhys.

About The Authors

Avril is an Australian author who lives with her family on acreage in South East Queensland. She writes mostly young adult and children's speculative fiction, but has been known to dabble in other genres. You can find more information about her at www.avrilsabine.com where you can also subscribe to her newsletter to be kept informed about new releases, current projects, blog posts and exclusive news.

Storm has a wide range of interests from gaming and blacksmithing to cooking and sewing. It's not unusual to find him cooking at any hour of the day or night, particularly after a long gaming session.

Rhys loves books and gaming and has thoroughly enjoyed combining two of his favourite things. He has been running tabletop gaming sessions for the past few years and enjoys creating characters and doing in depth worldbuilding.

Titles By Avril Sabine

Stories about strong characters and characters who discover their strengths.

SERIES

Assassins Of The Dead- Young Adult Fantasy/ Paranormal

Book 1: Dark Blade

Book 2: Dragon Touched

Book 3: Society Against Vampires

Book 4: King's Request

Dragon Blood- Young Adult Urban Fantasy (with elements of romance)

(5 book series)

Book 1: Pliethin

Book 2: Wyvern

Book 3: Surety

Book 4: Knight

Book 5: Mage

Dragon Mage- Young Adult Urban Fantasy (with elements of romance)

(Series two of Dragon Blood series)

Book 1: Promise

Dragon Blood Chronicles- Young Adult Urban Fantasy (with elements of romance)

(Companion stand alone series to Dragon Blood)

Book 1: Oath

Book 2: Betrayed

Guardians Of The Round Table- Young Adult Fantasy LitRPG

(Co-written with Storm and Rhys Petersen)

Book 1: Dexterity Fail

Book 2: Goblin Boots

Book 3: Singed Feathers

Book 4: Frog Mage

Book 5: Crystal Mine

Book 6: Cursed Harp

Rosie's Rangers- Young Adult Western Steampunk

(6 book series)

Book 1: Justice

Book 2: Vengeance

Book 3: Treachery

Book 4: Accused

Book 5: Wanted

Book 6: Corruption

Mark Of Kings- Children's Fantasy

(Upper middle grade/preteen)

(4 book series)

Book 1: The Arena

Book 2: The Island

Book 3: The Assassin

Book 4: The King

STAND ALONE SERIES

Demon Hunters- Young Adult Urban Fantasy/ Horror (with elements of romance)

Book 1: Blood Sacrifice

Book 2: Retribution

Book 3: Tainted

Book 4: Premonition

Book 5: Cursed

Book 6: Feud

Book 7: Extrication

Plea Of The Damned- Young Adult Urban Fantasy/Paranormal

(6 book series)

Book 1: Forgive Me Lucy

Book 2: Forgive Me Aiden

Book 3: Forgive Me Jena

Book 4: Forgive Me Kobe

Book 5: Forgive Me Marti

Book 6: Forgive Me Dawson

***Realms Of The Fae- Young Adult Urban Fantasy
(with elements of romance)***

The Sword (short story in Like A Girl Anthology)

Heart Of Stone

Book 1: A Debt Owed

Book 2: Marked By The Hunt

Book 3: The Magic Collector

Book 4: An Unexpected Betrayal

Book 5: Imprisoned By Iron

Fairytales Retold (Short Stories)

Snow-White And Rose-Red

The Twelve Brothers

The Light Princess

Beauty And The Beast

Sleeping Beauty

Aschenputtel

The Golden Bird

The Frog Prince

The Death Of Koshchei The Deathless

Myths And Legends Retold (Short Stories)

Ion, Son Of Apollo

Sir Gawain And The Maid With The Narrow Sleeves

Princess Ilse, The Giant's Daughter

YOUNG ADULT NOVELS

Young Adult Fantasy (with elements of romance)

Elf Sight

Earth Bound

Young Adult Urban Fantasy

Stone Warrior (with elements of romance)

The Jungle Inside

Young Adult Contemporary (with elements of romance)

Through Your Eyes

The Ugly Stepsister

Perfect Little Princess

Young Adult Contemporary/Paranormal

Whispers In The Dark (with elements of romance and same sex relationships)

Over Too Soon (with elements of romance)

Young Adult Sci-Fi

Experiment X-One-Six (Urban Sci-Fi/Superheroes)

An Endless Dawn (Post Apocalyptic Sci-Fi)

CHILDREN'S BOOKS

Dragon Lord (Preteen/early teens) (Fantasy)

The Irish Wizard (Upper middle grade) (Urban Fantasy)

SHORT STORIES

Urban Fantasy

Eternally Late

Dealings With Joe

Glimpses (short story in That Moment When Anthology)

Contemporary

The Brat Next Door

Fantasy LitRPG

(Set in the same world as Guardians Of The Round Table Series)

Tales Of Inadon 1: The Disc (Co-written with Storm and Rhys Petersen) (short story in Game On! Anthology)

Post Apocalyptic Sci-Fi

Compulsive Directive

NONFICTION

A Year Of Weekly Writing Exercises (Creative Writing)

Cooking For Families With Allergies (Cooking) (Co-written with Storm Petersen)

Tell Me A Story, Grandma (Memoir)

For the most up to date details on available titles visit:

www.avrilsabine.com/books/bibliography

Guardians Of The Round Table Series

To learn more about this series visit:

www.avrilsabine.com/series/gotrt

Find maps, more stats and details about the next book.

BOOKS AVAILABLE IN THE GUARDIANS OF THE ROUND TABLE SERIES

Book 1: Dexterity Fail

Book 2: Goblin Boots

Book 3: Singed Feathers

Book 4: Frog Mage

Book 5: Crystal Mine

Book 6: Cursed Harp

Book 7: Treasure Seeker

BOOKS SET IN THE SAME WORLD AS THE GUARDIANS OF THE ROUND TABLE SERIES

Adventurers Guild Handbook (Lore Book)

Legend Of The Ancestral King (Lore Book)

Lost And Powerful: Myths Of Misplaced Staves (Lore Book)

Disclaimer

This is a work of fiction. Names, characters, businesses, places, events and incidents are either the products of the author's imagination or used in a fictitious manner. Any resemblance to actual persons, living or dead, or actual events is purely coincidental. The opinions expressed or beliefs held are those of the characters and should not be assumed to be the opinions or beliefs of the author.